Meant to Be

Wesley Harper

Copyright © 2026 Wesley Harper

All rights reserved. No part of this book may be reproduced in any form or by any electronic or mechanical means, including information storage and retrieval systems, without written permission from the publisher, except for brief quotations used in reviews or critical articles.

This is a work of fiction. Names, characters, places, and incidents are products of the author's imagination or used fictitiously. Any resemblance to actual events, locales, or persons, living or dead, is entirely coincidental.

ISBN- 979-8-9943033-4-4 (paperback)

ISBN- 979-8-9943033-5-1 (e-book)

Cover design by: Juniper Hartmann of The Red Fox Creative
Photographer: A. McKay
Editor: Pace A.

For the Averys in my life, the ones who have been asking for her story since the beginning. Anything and everything, always.

Hello.

Hi. Look at us, back here again. Me, terrified, you, most likely impatient to just read the dang book. I really am sorry Avery's story took so long. I had some things to do, like look up how to be an author.

This was my first time sitting down to write a book. First time!

Backup. My first book, All In, I wrote on accident. Harper's story started as a rage journal in a locked note on my phone. Somehow, a small-town romance came out of it. I'm just as confused as you are. The second book? Well, Zoe was supposed to be a short story. Oops.

So, armed with research on How To Be An Author, I confidently sat down to write Avery's story.

I had a plan! I had an office, a plot outline, brand new colored pens with a cute matching notebook, and a timeline.

I was ready.

I was **not** ready. Writing a book is hard, y'all!

I threw it all away (okay not the pens or notebook, just the plan), plopped down on my couch with a foster puppy, and tried again.

It worked.

I mean, as you'll read in acknowledgements, it took a little more than the couch and puppy, but a book appeared on my screen.

I sat down to write a book and I wrote a book. So, here it is.

PROLOGUE
Avery
(eleven years ago)

"This has been the best week of my life," Coop says softly, pulling me into his broad chest.

"Mine, too." I blink away the tears that sting my eyes but there's no way to stop the dull ache in my heart. I tilt my chin up and he immediately presses his soft lips to mine. I have to turn around before the tears spill over.

One single week. That's all it's been. One perfect week in my favorite little beach town, my summer retreat. How does it feel like so much more?

I nestle my back into his chest as he wraps his arms around me, cocooning me in his clean scent, one I'd recognize anywhere. An unsteady sigh escapes me as he presses a gentle kiss to my cheek before resting his chin on my shoulder. I wish we could stay here forever.

"I'll never forget this view," he murmurs.

This view. My favorite view. Up here, surrounded by the tall Douglas firs with the tiny town of Three Rocks below and ocean waves as far as the eye can see, everything feels smaller. Quieter.

I've never shared this peaceful, hidden alcove with anyone, not even my best friend, Harper. Now it doesn't even feel like mine anymore, it feels like ours. Will I ever be able to come back up here and not think of him?

The sky is bursting with a kaleidoscope of color as the sun sets over the ocean. Brilliant shades of pink and red, inky swirls of purple, bright blue fading into turquoise, it's a perfect Oregon Coast sunset. Or it would be, if the sun wasn't sinking toward the horizon much too quickly, taunting me, reminding me just how little time Cooper and I have left together.

"Ave." Coop's whisper against my skin sends tingles down my spine. "That blue, it's the exact color of those little flecks in your eyes."

My breath catches. Has anyone noticed something so small, so specific, about me before? I've always been the quiet one, the introvert, the one that fades into the background.

"At first I thought your eyes were gray, like the fog that rolls in off the ocean every morning, but those little flecks," he continues, ignoring the fact that my heart might beat right out of my chest. "They're that exact blue."

"Cooper," I whisper thickly, fighting a losing battle against the emotions welling up inside me.

"My favorite blue," he adds.

"You can't say things like that," I force out, swallowing the lump in my throat.

"Why not?" He nuzzles into my neck, breathing me in, and my knees go weak. I'm unsure how I'm still standing. If it weren't for his arms, I'd be a puddle on the ground.

"Because you're making me fall for you." My voice cracks at the admission. Even though he can't see my face, I close my eyes.

I'm fifteen. I can't fall for a boy who lives thousands of miles away.

"I've already fallen, Ave." His words are just like him, sure and steady, no hitch to his voice, no hesitation.

I turn in his arms and peer up at him. His dark brown eyes lock on mine and a slight tremor runs through my body at the intensity of his gaze.

I can't hold my tears back any longer. "You mean it?"

"Of course I do, Ave. This," he stops and gestures between us. "This feels like more."

"We're just teenagers, Coop." I shake my head, unsure how we got here. How we fell so fast.

A flicker of hurt flashes in his eyes as he reaches a hand up to gently wipe the tears I feel tracking down my cheeks. "You don't feel it?"

I want to deny it. I want to close myself off, walk away from this week unscathed, my heart intact. One look at Cooper and I swallow the lie that was just on my lips. It's too late for that, anyway.

"I feel it." The truth comes out in a whisper. "It's just, we're basically kids, Cooper. People don't find this when they're our age, especially after one single week."

"Some do." He holds my gaze and I want so badly to believe him, but I can't see anything other than having to say goodbye to him tomorrow.

"Why couldn't we have met five years from now?" I might be the only teenager with a five-year plan, but I'm not going to push it aside for anyone or anything.

"What if we meet again five years from now," Coop says. A tiny spark of hope ignites at his words. It's not a question, it's a statement. A plan. He continues to swipe stray tears off my cheeks. "You'll be a best-selling author, living your dream, and I'll have to rescue you from some other douchebag."

I shake my head at the reminder of how we first met. "I didn't need to be rescued!" I say, trying to hide my laugh.

Cooper doesn't hide his. "I know you didn't."

"So we just go our separate ways and hope one day we meet again?" I ask. Could it really be as uncomplicated as that? So easy? So inevitable?

"Why not?"

I don't have an answer. Because he's right. Why not? No matter what, he's leaving tomorrow. No matter what, I'm going to be heartbroken. Why not at least hold on to the hope that someday we'll see each other again?

"So we're just going to leave it to fate?" I ask. I don't think I believe in fate. I don't even think things happen for a reason. But if anyone could convince me, it'd be Cooper.

"You can call it fate, but just know that I'll be finding my way back here."

Back here. With my eyes closed and his arms around me, I see it. Flashes of our week together blur in my mind, morphing into more. Into the future.

He takes his beanie off and tugs it onto my head. "We're meant to be, Ave, I know it," he whispers.

"Meant to be," I repeat, smiling up at him as the hope inside my chest burns brighter.

Chapter One
Cooper

Home. I am home. I take a deep breath, the first full breath I've taken in months, maybe years, as I turn off the highway into the tiny town of Three Rocks, Oregon.

"Nice to see it hasn't grown," Megan says wryly from the passenger seat.

I laugh. "You're not wrong," I tell my sister. If only she knew the small town phone tree I went through, pleading my case, practically begging to buy my little plot of land.

"Ooh!" Megan bounces a little in her seat and points toward the store on the left. "That looks new!"

"Definitely not new, don't you remember getting ice cream there?" The only time either of us has set foot in this town was for her high school graduation trip. Like a kid waiting for Christmas, I had counted down until my own graduation trip, but for our family, the two years between hadn't been easy and we pivoted to a weekend in the Ozarks.

"The Town Mercantile," she reads aloud. "The store was here, duh, but it looks way different!"

Again, she's not wrong. The building has a fresh coat of white paint, a new sign, even the deck out front looks new. Kent, the man at the end of the phone tree, mentioned an investor in town that was turning things around. I guess they started here.

"Want to check it out before we go to the rental?" Meg asks.

With a shrug, I pull into a parking spot and shut off the engine. This feels big. My first time in town as a resident. One of only a few dozen, according to Kent. Years of wishing, countless excuses, and I'm finally here.

"Come on!" Meg calls over her shoulder, already halfway across the small parking lot.

A trickle of hope makes its way into my veins the second I step out of the car. The cool, ocean air is both foreign and familiar, steadying me in a way I haven't felt in years. Eleven years, to be exact. This was the right move, I can feel it.

I jog to catch up to Meg and pull the door open, ushering her inside. I'm immediately hit with the only scent that's ever taken me to my knees, strawberry breeze lotion. The air whooshes out of my lungs in a single heartbeat. Is she actually here? She can't be.

"Megan?!"

My eyes fly to the woman behind the counter who somehow knows my sister.

It's not her.

I inhale the memory-laden air, searching the space for a glimpse of pale gray eyes, hoping against hope for an eyebrow raised in my direction or a crooked, flat grin.

"Harper? What are you doing here?" Megan is wide-eyed as she smiles at the woman with the bright pink hat.

Harper. Why is that familiar?

A grinning, gap-toothed student flits through my mind. Harper Cannon, sixth grade. That's the thing about teaching, every name sounds like I've heard it before.

"I live here now, what are *you* doing here?!" This Harper, the one standing at the coffee counter, eyes me. "Is this the lucky guy?"

"What? Oh, ew, no, this is my brother, Cooper. Coop, this is Harper, we met during my bachelorette in Austin," Megan replies. "Coop's under contract on some land here, I just came along to get away from the lucky guy...who is only lucky because I didn't murder him."

"I might still murder him," I mutter. It's on my to-do list. Probably not the best first impression to make on a new neighbor though, so I pull myself together and add, "Hi, nice to meet you."

"You, too," Harper replies with a wide smile, her hazel eyes dancing. "Welcome to The Merc."

Somehow, I know her. I can't tell if it's her infectious smile or just something about her, but I swear we've met. I glance between her and Megan again.

"Harper, I feel like I've met you before, but if you're from Texas, maybe not," I say, fishing for anything that would help me place her. I just keep seeing my blonde-haired, blue-eyed student instead. "If you live here now, I guess we will soon be neighbors."

"Moved here last spring from Austin, not long after meeting your sister," she says with another easy smile. "So no murders? I have a tarp and shovel out back if needed, plus my best friend is a lawyer."

Well, I might not know her, but I like her.

Megan snorts and holds up her bare left hand. "No murder, but also no husband. At least I got a fun bachelorette out of it though."

"That was fun, at least the part I crashed. Sorry about the asshole, though," Harper says, wincing and shaking her head. "I can't believe you're here. Don't you live in Missouri?"

"Kansas. It's a long story," Meg says, sounding a little defeated, which has been her baseline lately. "We're checking into a rental, a cute little garden house. Maybe we can hang out this weekend?"

My stomach growls and I wander toward a large refrigerator full of premade meals as they continue to chat. Three days of driving a U-haul, one morning spent unloading the U-haul into a storage unit, and zero good meals since leaving Kansas has left me suddenly starving.

After grabbing a sandwich for myself and a salad for Meg, I eye the pastries under the coffee counter. Giant cinnamon rolls, fluffy croissants, and muffins of all imaginable flavors fill the glass case, making my mouth water. I know exactly where I'll be getting breakfast tomorrow morning.

Like the exterior, the inside of the store looks completely new. Eleven years ago it was a vaguely beach-themed convenience store, now it's like a coffee shop, Etsy, and an organic neighborhood market had a baby.

Besides the ready-made options, there's a few aisles of pantry staples, just enough to get by for a meal or two. A large selection of beer fills the cooler along the back wall and the variety of hard cider is even more impressive. I don't even know what a marionberry is, let alone what it's doing in a cider.

The driftwood table spanning the center of the store holds everything from delicate necklaces to brightly colored sand buckets filled with plastic spades and toys. To the left of the door, there's an entire section of branded apparel. Hats, hoodies, even sandals, all with The Town Mercantile logo. The renovation is impressive. Maybe this investor can turn me around as well.

"That sounds fun. Coop, you can meet some more of your neighbors then," Megan says as I walk back over. I freeze, realizing I have no idea what she's talking about.

Harper nods toward a heavily tattooed man that just walked in. "I need to talk to him, but Katie will get you at the register when you're ready. I'm excited to catch up tonight!" She squeezes Meg's arm as she steps around us.

"If she lives here, you'll be just fine," Megan tells me, adding a green beanie to my stack of purchases.

I close my eyes and see a different green beanie, gray eyes blinking up at me from under it. I glance around. "What smells like strawberries in here?" I ask Meg, trying to find the source of my emotional turmoil.

"Oh my god, you and the strawberry lotion, did that start here, too?" Megan laughs and plucks a small tube of lotion from a display of candles, natural sponges, and lip balms in the middle of the rough driftwood table. She uncaps it and waves it under my nose.

Memories flood all of my senses. I have to blink away the visions of her running along the beach, long legs racing up the sand, easily outpacing me. I flex my hand and feel her skin under my fingertips, warm from the summer sun. I close my eyes once more, trying to shut it all out, trying to shut her out, but I can taste her on my lips. Strawberries. Fucking strawberries. When I open my eyes, Meg is capping the lotion. She tugs the beanie out of my hand and heads for the register.

"I'll get these, you get lunch!" she calls back over her shoulder.

I was wrong. I think this move was a bad idea.

***

"Oh. My. God." Megan stares slack-jawed at my piece of land and the endless view that stretches as far as the eye can see. "I thought you were crazy for doing this but it might be your best idea ever."

The town of Three Rocks sits below, the narrow roads breaking the picturesque village into tidy sections. A creek meanders along the eastern edge, parallel to the highway, before taking a sharp turn under the bridge and dumping into the Pacific Ocean at the base of Rejection Rock, the biggest of the three basalt sea stacks that give the town its name. The beach stretches as far as the eye can see in either direction, smaller rocks and outcroppings visible in the distance, and a low cloud cover hangs over the horizon, blurring the line between ocean and sky.

"Not bad, right?" I ask with a small smile at Meg's reaction.

"Was this road here before?" she asks, not taking her eyes off the panorama before us.

"Nope, used to just be an old, overgrown tsunami evacuation trail," I reply, once again having to blink away the memories.

"Of course you found some random trail and decided you needed to build a freaking house there a decade later," Meg says, laughing and shaking her head at me.

I don't reply. I still haven't told her the truth, the real reason I'm here.

I chance a glance past Megan but the spot that's seared into my mind is no longer a hidden alcove among the trees, it's buried beneath the deck of the only house up here. There's a truck parked in the driveway and I catch a glimpse of a man in the window.

"So, this is it," I say, suddenly unable to be here a second longer. "How about dinner?"

"Does the brewery that was listed in the rental welcome page sound okay? Then we can bring beers back for the community bonfire?" Meg asks hopefully.

"Definitely," I agree. Anything to get off this hill. The hill I spent years longing for. The hill that no longer feels like ours, thanks to a man and a truck.

I climb back in my car, claiming I need to look up directions, and drum the steering wheel as Megan takes pictures to send to our parents. I knew a house had already been built up here, that's why there's a road. This isn't a surprise, so why do I suddenly feel sick to my stomach?

"Maybe these will help them understand," Meg says, sliding into her seat. "That view, Cooper. Damn."

"Please don't use that," I moan as Megan puts a tiny dollop of strawberry lotion on her palm as soon as she buckles her seatbelt.

"Okay, Cooper. Spill. What is going on with you? You've been on edge since we walked into the store earlier. You've dreamed of this day for years, why all this?" She waves in my direction.

I start down the winding road and somehow, probably since I'm driving and unable to look my sister in the eye, I'm able to tell her a brief version of the truth. A quasi-truth. Just enough to confirm that I'm an idiot.

***

"You're an idiot," Meg says after we've been seated at the beachfront brewery one town north of Three Rocks.

"I know." I scrub a hand down my face. Time to face the music, or at least my sister.

"An idiot who definitely needs a beer," she continues.

"You're in luck, we have great beer!" Our waiter shows up right in time to hear Meg's comment.

"He needs *at least* one," Meg tells the waiter.

"How about our original taster flight? See what we have to offer?" Dave, as his name tag claims, suggests.

"Sold," I tell him.

"Yes, please!" Megan says.

"Anything else right now?" Dave asks.

We shake our heads and Megan picks up her menu. Dave gives Megan a lingering look before walking away, which she ignores. I smirk and she just rolls her eyes.

"Sorry I'm an asshole, Meggy," I tell her, needing to get it off my chest before we fall back into our usual sibling banter.

"You're not an asshole," Meg says. "I mean, you did break my friend's heart just a little, but something tells me she'll be just fine."

I nod silently. Brooke will be fine. She's probably already fine. Our lives were entwined to the point of our families spending holidays together so it was easy to fall into a relationship with my sister's best friend and even easier to stay.

Brooke was there through so much, it might have even been guilt that made her stay well past what should have been the end. When I woke up one morning to her sitting cross-legged on our bed, staring out the window with silent tears, I knew it was time. She wouldn't end it, I needed to.

Dave returns with our flights, interrupting my thoughts. It appears he did not lead us astray with his recommendation. He carefully sets the circular tray between us but it's no ordinary tasting flight, it's a carousel of color. A carved pelican sits atop the totem in the middle, a list of the beers running down the side. From bright golden ales to rich copper reds, all the way to a dark, creamy stout, I can already tell it's going to be difficult to choose a favorite.

"To you, my favorite brother, for finally living out your dream!" Meg selects the lightest beer, a blonde ale, after we've agreed to Dave's other recommendation, fish and chips, and raises the small glass in a toast.

"Only brother," I mutter, choosing my own glass. "To you, for not murdering He-Who-Must-Not-Be-Named!" I tip my Irish-style red ale toward hers.

"Ah yes, to me, for being a cuckold," Megan says, lifting her glass higher.

"Megan! No one even knows what that means!" I laugh.

"They do if they watch The Office." Megan shrugs, refusing to tap her glass to mine.

I bring my glass down and narrow my eyes. "Which episode?"

"When Michael is with Donna. Andy might even quote Shakespeare," she quickly replies. I shouldn't have questioned her Office knowledge, she's the reason we always won trivia night at Wingers, our favorite neighborhood bar near our parents' house.

"Damnit, you're right. But isn't it only if you're married? And male?" I question. "Either way, no, this isn't what we're toasting!"

"Yes, it is." Megan's still holding out her miniature taster glass, the beer coming precariously close to spilling as she continues to laugh. "To being a cuckold!"

I shake my head and tap my glass to hers, knowing a lost argument when I see one, and take a tentative sip of my amber ale. The beer is crisp and smooth, perfect for a late summer afternoon.

"I have so many questions," the man at the table behind us says, turning around. He's in a Three Rocks Fire Department tee shirt and Megan takes a quick inhale when he smiles at her.

"I have very few answers," she replies, giving him the first smile I've seen her give any man since Tyler, the emotional affair asshole, walked out of her life.

"Fair," the man says. "But consider this round on us."

The second man at the table, an older man in a matching Three Rocks Fire Department tee shirt, stands. He has a wide smile and his eyes twinkle at Meg as he holds his hand out.

"Brian," he says. "Three Rocks resident and fire chief."

"I'm Megan, and this is my brother Cooper, Three Rocks' newest resident," she says, shaking Brian's hand.

"Thought I recognized you from The Merc parking lot earlier. Welcome to town, Cooper," Brian tells me. I stand to shake his hand and he introduces us to the first man, Nate.

"You already have a place to live?" Nate asks.

"I bought Kent's lot up the old tsunami trail, still need to find a rental until I can get my house built." Something tells me the residents of Three Rocks are all on first-name basis with each other.

"Ah, finally got Kent to sell," Brian says, confirming my suspicion. "I wasn't too sure when they turned that trail into a road, us old-timers don't like change."

"You'll have a great neighbor," Nate says, making me wonder if the truck-driving man in the window works at the fire station along with them.

"Town hero," Brian adds, confirming my suspicions a second time.

"You guys coming to the community bonfire tonight?" Nate asks. He turns his gaze to my sister. "Should be a good time."

"We'll be there," I reply, watching Meg take a large gulp of her beer as Nate smiles at her.

"We better go help set up," Brian says. "Labor Day weekend means it's going to be a busy one."

"Nice to meet you," Megan says, her cheeks flushed.

Brian tips an imaginary hat in Megan's direction and then the two firefighters weave their way through the tables toward the door, stopping to speak to the bartender on their way out.

"So," I say teasingly, taking my seat once again. "Nate seems nice."

Meg huffs a laugh but her eyes remain on the younger firefighter as he makes his way out the door.

"Is she here?" she asks as soon as she turns back to me, her cheeks red.

"Who?" I ask, like I don't know exactly who she means.

"Come on, Coop. You can't tell me you moved here because of a girl and you don't know if she's here."

"No, I know." I scrub my hand down my face. "She's not here."

"She's not?" Meg's glass hits the table loudly. "You didn't think to include that earlier?"

I wince. "Well, at least I don't think she is."

"This is why you're an idiot. You moved here without knowing? Have you never heard of phones? Social media?" Megan eyes my phone on the table like it might hold answers.

"It wasn't like that." Even though we agreed that we'd go our separate ways until we found our way back, I did try to look her up, more than once. That's why I know she's not here.

Megan frowns in confusion. "What was it like then?"

"It was more, Meg. So much more." I sigh. There's no way to explain this. I mean, a summer fling when you're sixteen isn't a move-across-the-country situation to most.

"It was *more*, but not more enough to keep in touch, yet it was also somehow *more* enough to move across the country?" Megan shakes her head.

No, it was so much more that we *couldn't* keep in touch. Reality kept us thousands of miles apart but it wasn't just the distance between us, it was the dreams, the plans. Mainly hers, if I'm being honest. At that point football was a give or take for me. But it was knowing that I'd miss my life just to answer her call. That I'd change my life, just for her, and I wouldn't risk that she'd do the same. We were too young. We needed time. I just didn't realize it would end up being this much time.

Too much time.

But that sounds crazy. So, I don't say any of that.

"Yeah, that sums it up." I shrug. "I don't know. I just... even if she's not here, I need to be here. Maybe it wasn't her. Maybe it was this place."

Meg nudges my beer toward me. "It's a pretty great place."

I look out the window toward the rugged cape in the distance and nod. It *is* a pretty great place. And maybe it really was this place that changed me that summer, not her. Maybe it was the memory of this place that held me together for so many years, not her.

And maybe pigs fly.

"I'm sorry I'm abandoning you," I say quietly, sipping the darkest beer, a heavy stout. With its rich aroma and dark chocolate flavor, I can see why there's an option to add ice cream and make it a dessert.

"I think I abandoned you first, little brother," Megan says. "We're even."

"College doesn't count as abandonment," I tell her.

"Yeah, but that timing sure was shit, huh?" She looks at me with watery eyes and gives a small smile and shrug.

I think of all the years I thought I'd be here. Instead it was head down, eyes forward, going through the motions. Weight room, practice, hospital, back to practice. Off season weights. Doctor. Track sprints. Hospital. Make dinner. Online classes. Anything to help my mom, to reassure Dad, to keep Meg at college.

"It worked out, Meg. He's okay. We're all where we are supposed to be." I'm just a little later than I thought. Too late.

"It wasn't fair to you," she insists.

"Life isn't fair," I tell her patiently. "But I'd make the same decision every time, Meg. Family first."

"You were just so careful with your decisions for so long. You had to be. But you used to take risks, before." She pauses, probably trying to remember what *before* really was. A past life. One that no longer exists. "It's good to see you doing that again. Taking chances. Risking your heart for once."

I open my mouth to argue, after all, I dated her best friend for two years, but she holds her hand up.

"I'm your sister. She's my best friend. I always knew, Coop. She was the careful decision. And you were her safe choice after that asshole she dated in college. And I get it, I mean, look what happened when I risked my own heart," Meg continues. "I guess I'm just trying to say I'm happy for you."

I'm saved from replying by Dave, who sets two large plates of fish and chips in front of us. Megan orders a beer, choosing the first ale she sampled, and we both dig in. We eat in silence, both lost in thought.

My mind rolls Meg's words over and over. As smart as my sister is, she's wrong. The problem isn't that I haven't risked my heart; the problem is that I gave my heart to someone when I was sixteen years old and never got it back.

Chapter Two
Avery

Blink, blink, blink. Even my cursor is taunting me. The words that were tumbling through my brain disappear, just as they have every single time I've tried to write over the last six and a half years. Every. Single. Time. Why I thought this time would be different, I don't know.

I take a deep breath and then another. Breathe in for four, hold for four, out for four. Tex's breathing trick does nothing. I lay my head on my desk and let the weight of my own expectations press me further into this mood that I can't seem to shake off.

I have no right to mope. None. I'm living my dream. No, I'm living well beyond my childhood hopes and dreams. I'm a published author three times over, my best-selling trilogy bringing my anonymous pen name fame and my real name fortune, living in my custom-built cabin perched atop the newly paved tsunami trail above my favorite place in the entire world: Three Rocks, Oregon. My happy place, the only place I've ever wanted to live.

"Pull it together," I whisper. Because talking to yourself is definitely the definition of pulling it together.

I sit up and switch from Failing Author A. Marino to Avery Moore, Attorney at Law. If you would have asked me during my first years at college, back when I was still Successful Author A. Marino, if I'd not only follow in my father's footsteps to law school but also work with him, I would have laughed hysterically until I cried. Or banged my head against a wall. But when my words disappeared, I needed a new path. Law school seemed doable. Dad's disappointment slowly dissipated the closer I got to graduation, and, despite the job not being anything close to environmental law like I thought I'd go into, I took the chance on working with him late this last spring.

As a real estate attorney, Dad did well for himself. As a real estate investor, he's done even better. My own investments here in Three Rocks, The Town Mercantile and the short-term rentals I own, are thanks to him in a way. He might not have been thrilled with my teenage novels, but he was more than happy to help me learn how to manage the royalties they produced.

Now, we're working together in a new way. The property we are currently looking at boasts fifty acres on the edge of my hometown, Monitor Mills, which is just two stop signs along a country road. Monitor Mills is about seventy-five miles inland from the coast with hay fields, orchards, and nurseries spreading in every direction.

The one we're eyeing? Evanston Orchards. Something doesn't line up with this sale, but I can't put my finger on it. Crop yields, tree health, property lines, building plans, equipment inspections, taxes, the information in front of me is meticulously prepared, yet it doesn't add up. Dad is pushing it hard and I honestly don't know why I'm pushing back, something is just telling me to look harder.

Now I'm staring at a different blinking cursor.

Luckily, the silence is broken by a buzz from the living room. I jump to my feet. My best friend, Harper, AKA Tex, AKA the manager of my businesses, AKA my co-host for the community bonfire tonight, has been throwing up nearly nonstop since getting pregnant and I'm always worried I'm going to miss an SOS from her.

Tex:
Lots of people'ing to do later. Go for your run!

I snort. She knows me too well. Every single time we've hosted a community event over the last few months, I've gone for a run beforehand. It's my way of recharging, mentally preparing myself before I have to spend hours "people'ing." Her word, not mine.

I honestly don't know how I thought I could do all of this without her. I didn't even realize how overwhelmed I was until she burst into town last spring and took over my entire life. There was about a week where I was worried, I mean, she had fled her life in Texas and showed up on my doorstep with two days' warning, but that worry quickly disappeared as she found her footing here in my favorite place.

I might have rebuilt the store from the inside out, but Tex is the reason The Town Mercantile has become one of the busiest stops along our section of the Oregon coastline. Well, her and every single one of my employees. What they've done with my short-term rentals is even more impressive. We are booked through Thanksgiving with new requests coming in daily.

Tex's most impressive feat and my personal fave? Team Merc, whose name, like Tex's nickname, started as a joke, brought back the community events from my childhood. With the help of the few other businesses in our tiny town, Kelsey, the college-bound beam of energy, Tex, and I reintroduced rotating block parties, the Fourth Festival, and community bonfires to Three Rocks. I might need a run before joining the fun, but they have been some of my favorite times this summer.

Tex:
Run. Now.

Aves:
Going. I'll swing by!

Guilt flickers as I return to my office and take one last look at Evanston Orchards. I still haven't managed to tell my best friend about what I've been doing in the free time she's created in my schedule. I'm pretty sure she thinks I'm writing. To say she's not my dad's biggest fan would be putting it lightly. Before I get pulled back into the numbers on my screen, I close my laptop.

Tex is right. Run. Now. I've sought solace through running nearly as long as she's been my best friend. In fact, I think she's the one that convinced me to join the running club in elementary school. Running quickly escalated from racing laps around the track with classmates to miles and miles logged through the farmland and orchards surrounding my childhood home, training for longer races each year. Now it feels like it's ingrained in my soul–I'm lost without it.

Just lacing up my shoes and tying my hair back loosens the knot of tension in my chest. By the time I'm running the narrow streets of Three Rocks, it's like the disastrous writing attempt and mini meltdown didn't happen. I wave to Brian as he steps out of Nate's truck in the fire station parking lot, laughing when he waves a white envelope in the air then shakes his fist at me.

"How'd you get in my truck?" Nate calls across the lot.

"I'll never tell!" I wave again and continue past, knowing if I stop to chat, my inability to lie will lose Team Merc this round of the battle.

Kelsey. It was Kelsey. I chose not to ask any follow up questions when she gleefully volunteered to take the latest thank you card by the station.

What I didn't necessarily expect, but always hoped, when Tex floated the idea of bringing back the summer events, was that Three Rocks would regain its sense of community. It was a slow change, but each time I ran through town, I noticed more people stopping to chat, more greetings called, more impromptu gatherings. Now, for the first time in years, our town is flourishing. Brian, with all of his help during the Fourth Festival, probably deserves credit for the assist, or perhaps yet another thank you card.

This town was so much more than just my summer stomping grounds. It was biking the narrow roads, fishing in the creek, and climbing the rock at low tide with the rest of the kids I'd see for only a few short weeks each year, learning to navigate part-time friendships that spanned over a decade. It was peace amidst the nonstop tension that seemed like a living, breathing part of our family, the crashing of the waves drowning out my parents' arguments. It was the place I knew with great clarity by the ripe old age of thirteen, I wanted to live when I was an adult. By fourteen, I thought I had it all figured out, including how to drink alcohol. Two sips of warm beer at a bonfire with Tex proved otherwise. The next summer, I wrote the majority of my first book laying on my oversized towel on the beach. I even had my first kiss on the old tsunami trail, where my house now sits.

My first kiss. Who, at twenty-six years old, still thinks of their first kiss? Maybe everyone, at least from time to time. But who builds their house there? I'd bet no one.

I lengthen my stride and quicken my pace, pushing my lungs toward their limit, trying to break my train of thought. It works, as running always does. I wind my way through the streets, relishing the burn in my muscles, the quiet in my mind.

"Aves!" Tex's voice startles me.

I look up to realize I'm running past The Town Mercantile, AKA The Merc, AKA my pride and joy. I stop my watch and jog through the parking lot, laughing when I see her holding out an unopened envelope.

"He already got us?" I ask, hands on my knees. "I just saw him!"

"This is getting out of hand but I *refuse* to give in. How many does this make?" Tex flips the envelope and I see "Team Merc" written in thick block letters.

"A freaking lot!" I can't help but laugh. Who would have thought that I'd have a stack of thank you cards piling up on my kitchen counter, for no reason other than pure stubbornness on the part of, well, all of us, I guess.

"I think I saw one in your stack of mail earlier, too," Tex says. "I sent it up with West after he stopped by The Merc."

"Oh, yeah, I heard him in the kitchen while I was on a call." I totally forgot that he came by earlier. Luckily, after building my deck and my custom bookshelves, he's used to letting himself in and out of my house if I don't answer the door.

"Hey, you're still good to hang out with Liam tonight, right?" The abrupt subject change from our ongoing thank you card war with the firefighters to her boyfriend's newly sober best friend tells me she's on edge.

I straighten out of my stretch to look at her more closely. "Of course, is he doing okay?"

She tilts her head back and forth, contemplating my question. "I think so, he and West finished packing Kelsey for college earlier. Tonight just feels like it could be a recipe for disaster, you know?"

I nod, even though I don't know. I've never been in Liam's position before. He's spent weeks working to earn the opportunity to see his young son, Colt, again, and tonight's the night. While I know nothing about parenting, I do know about fighting for a relationship with my dad. I think about using this as a segway into telling Tex about going into business with Dad and decide that it's time. She might not like him, but she loves me. She'll support me no matter what. She always has.

What comes out of my mouth is not that.

"It's going to be so quiet without Kelsey around here."

What the actual hell was that? That was not what I meant to say. I duck down into a hamstring stretch, avoiding eye contact.

Tex sits down on the steps and I can see her smile out of the corner of my eye. "We definitely couldn't have pulled this all off without her. Remember the paintbrush throwing?"

"I thought for sure you were going to drop that." I laugh at the memory of Tex and Kelsey standing on kitchen counters, tossing paintbrushes back and forth during a rental remodel. "I had this vision of pink paint everywhere."

"I bet even if we did, she would have come up with a way to turn it into marketing gold," Tex muses.

"It's like the two of you were determined to push me right to my breaking point," I say, still laughing. I move to stand on the step next to her and drop one heel down, stretching my tight left calf.

"Oh, come on, you might have needed some convincing, but you always had fun!" Tex protests.

"The Emmy hangover wasn't fun," I remind her. I haven't had tequila since Tex's best friend from Austin came for a visit and it might be a long while before I do again.

"But the dancing was!"

"The dancing was," I admit, switching to stretch my right calf. Most of the things that Tex has convinced me to do over our twenty years of friendship have been fun.

"What a freaking summer," Tex says.

"Amen," I answer with a small shake of my head. What a freaking summer is right.

We drop into silence, Tex enjoying the afternoon sun, me wincing as my hip flexor protests the stretch as I pull my ankle toward my glute. I breathe through the pain, watching as Tex absentmindedly puts her left hand on her stomach, her thumb pressing on the scar inside her ring finger. My jaw clenches. All the summer fun in the world will never erase the memory of the night she got that scar. To this day, I still catch myself glancing over my shoulder, looking, searching.

"It wasn't just West, you know," she says. I tilt my head, confused. She holds up her hand and taps the scar, or maybe the small wave tattoo over it. I still only see the scar. "The peace I feel now…I mean yeah, he's obviously a big part of it, he helps calm my anxiety in a lot of ways, but it's more than that. It's this place. It's my wild dog running on the beach, it's the sunsets over the waves, it's the wind through the trees at the North House. It's this town, the people. It's all of it. And I'm here because of you. Because you've caught me every time I've needed you. Especially recently. So, it's also just you."

Her words make tears unexpectedly spring to my eyes. I blink them back. "I'm so happy you ended up here," I tell her, swallowing down the lump in my throat. I'm glad I didn't ruin this moment with my secret. I sit down next to her and nudge her shoulder. "Even though you made me two-step at a bar that you somehow turned into a dang honky-tonk for a night, this summer has been amazing."

Tex has brought so much more than her unique brand of chaotic organization to my life over the last few months. I don't think I realized how lonely I had let my life become until she barged back in, wild Doberman in tow. I still love my quiet nights tucked in my cozy cabin, I *need* that alone time, but I also love our dinners together, which thankfully I usually cook. I love our morning walks on the beach, Zero racing circles around us as fast as her paws will take her, the thick gray fog rolling off the ocean, cocooning us in our own world. I love our Friday meetings and even the times when she barges in my office, demanding a dance party break. I just love having her here.

"Pulling you out of your shell since elementary school," Tex says.

"I'm glad you're the extrovert that adopted me," I reply, laughing.

"I don't think I'm a *real* extrovert. We both were too shy to talk to anyone else back then, remember?" she counters.

"Well, whatever you are, you're better at pretending to be an extrovert."

"I didn't have a dad that tried to mold m-" Tex stops mid-sentence. "Sorry."

"Mold me into a quiet, emotionless robot to do his bidding?" I ask, raising an eyebrow.

"I was drunk when I said that!" she protests. "Drunk Tex is a whole different person."

"Drunk Tex drew a freaking graph!" She really did. Stanford has a world-renowned creative writing program and she was in drunken tears that night over my decision to switch from English to an undergraduate degree in History with my sights set on law school.

"I used it in my psych class later that week!" she brags. "Got an A!"

"You used the graph you drew while we were FaceTiming, and, I should add, you were drunk, in an actual college class?" I ask in disbelief, shaking my head. Only her. "How does this not surprise me? And how did I not know this until right now?"

"Nature versus nurture: are you a real introvert or is your dad just a real asshole?" Tex quips.

I wince. I hate to think what her professor had to say about that. "He's trying now. I know you haven't seen him since you've been back, but he's trying."

"I'm glad he's trying," Tex says after a beat. I know she has more to say, but I think we both know that we will never see eye to eye on this.

We fall back into silence, me trying to convince myself to tell her the truth, and her rubbing her scar. It's not until I start the trek back up the hill that it hits me. Elementary school. Introverts. Extroverts. Evanston Orchards. Lila Evanston. The most extroverted of extroverts. I know how to find what I've been missing.

Chapter Three
Avery
(before)

"*Avery!*"

I startle at the voice calling my name and quickly shove my notebook under the corner of my towel, making sure it's out of sight.

"Hey," Kev says, dropping down beside me. He shoots me a confident, toothy smile and leans toward me. His cologne is overwhelming, which is quite the feat since there's a breeze blowing in off the ocean and the lingering scent of sunscreen clings to my skin.

"Hi." I shift on my towel, unsure what to say or do, suddenly very aware of the fact I'm in my bikini. I try not to squirm as Kevin's eyes peruse my body, taking me in head to toe.

I've known Kev forever, our families have been friends for decades, since before I was born. Our grandfathers went to college together and now my dad is their attorney. We've seen each other every summer since before we could walk, but right now, I wish I could melt into the sand.

"I thought we could hang out," Kevin says, reaching a hand toward my knee.

I pull back, an automatic response, but his hand still lands on my bare skin. My stomach turns. My dad will kill me if I ruin his business relationship with Kevin's parents. My mind trips over reasons to leave, excuses to use, but before I can use a single one, we're interrupted.

"Hey!" A guy I don't recognize jogs toward us. "Sorry I'm late, my sister and her friend took forever."

He must be one of Kevin's friends. He's tall, broad, muscular, and has that cocky, overconfident look that half the boys my age seem to have. Everything about him, from his aviator sunglasses to his backward hat, makes me think he's Kevin's double.

Great, there's two of them. At least Kev might leave me alone now.

"Sup, man?" Kevin gives the guy a chin jut but doesn't get up.

The new guy pulls his sunglasses off, tucking them into the neckline of his tee shirt, and smiles directly at me. My breath catches in my throat as his dark eyes settle on mine.

Without acknowledging Kevin, he says, "Sorry again, Megan takes forever."

My confusion must show because he tilts his head toward two girls further down the beach. I drag my eyes from his and one of the girls waves. I lift my hand, even more puzzled. I don't know those girls. When I look back, he's still watching me. He tips his head ever so slightly toward Kevin and raises an eyebrow.

"Hi?" As hard as I try, I can't help my voice from rising into a question. Is he doing what I think he's doing?

"Hey, I'm Cooper," he says, finally moving his attention to Kevin.

"Kevin," Kev says flatly, his eyes narrowing. He looks between the new guy, Cooper, I guess, and I. "How do you know Avery? Haven't seen you around."

"Oh, we met yesterday," Cooper says vaguely, smiling like he's completely unbothered by Kevin's hostile tone. He pulls his hat off and runs his hand through his messy hair, which makes his bicep flex, straining against his tee shirt. He grins as he tugs his hat back in place and I know I've been caught staring. "Avery said she'd show me around town today since I've never been here. No worries if you two are busy though."

Kevin's hand tightens on my knee and the decision is made for me.

"Sorry, Kev, I did promise," I tell him. I'm not sorry. Not sorry at all.

I quickly stand, dislodging his hand from my knee, and pull my tee shirt on over my head. As soon as Kevin stands, I grab my towel, carefully keeping my notebook hidden. The last thing I need is for it to get back to my dad that I've been writing.

"Nice to meet you," Cooper tells Kevin. "Maybe I'll see you around."

I snort quietly when I see the murderous glare Kevin gives him. Without a backward glance, I grab my flip flops from the sand and start up the path. With each step, I wonder what I've gotten myself into. I know nothing about this guy. Just because he has the kind of eyes I could get lost in and a perfect smile doesn't mean he's any different than the other boys my age.

"I didn't need to be rescued," I tell Cooper when he catches up to me.

"You don't seem like the type to need rescuing," he immediately replies. "I just couldn't resist the opportunity."

"Opportunity? To play the hero?" I ask, giving him a sidelong glance. I guess he is another Kevin. I resist the urge to roll my eyes.

"To meet you," he says quietly.

I trip over my own feet at what sounds like a rehearsed line and his hand shoots out to cup my elbow. I startle at his touch, nearly tripping again. He pulls his hand away and shoves it in his pocket. Heat floods my cheeks as we reach the street. Awkward Avery, as usual.

I drop my flip flops on the asphalt, set my towel on top, notebook still hidden, and turn to face him, ready to make a quick excuse. But instead of the cocky grin I'm expecting, Cooper's looking at me with a quiet intensity. He shifts his weight and I wonder if I've misjudged him.

"Do you really want a tour?" I ask uncertainly. "The town has like five streets, it'd be pretty hard to get lost." I gesture toward the narrow road, which parallels the beach and runs less than a mile north until it circles back along the creek.

He glances down the street then back to me. "I want a tour from you, Avery," he says, his cheeks tinged with pink.

My stomach swoops. "Okay," I say, biting the inside of my cheek to hide my smile.

"Yeah?" Cooper's eyes light up and a smile overtakes his face.

"Yeah." I can't help but grin back.

Chapter Four
Cooper

Rejection Rock is merely a dark silhouette as we walk down the beach toward the community bonfire, the setting sun casting the entire tree-covered face of the rock into darkness. We were too busy unpacking for the week and reorganizing my classroom supplies to make it down here when it was still light, and I suddenly wonder if the trail to the top still exists or if time has crumbled the footholds.

"Damn, Harper knows how to throw a party! I didn't know this town had this many people," Meg says in surprise as we get closer.

The sun might be dipping into the ocean, but the party appears to be in full swing with no signs of stopping. A volleyball is being bounced around near the water's edge and there's a glowing frisbee flying overhead. Laughter and raucous cheers coming from the cornhole game fill the lulls between the rhythmic waves.

Friendly smiles and head nods greet us as we weave through small groups gathered together. I nudge Megan and jut my chin in the direction of the bonfire. Harper is fast asleep in a chair. She stirs when a little girl races past, and blinks awake slowly as we approach.

"Harper, why are you sleeping in a chair by the fire?" Megan asks. She holds out a beer for Harper, one of the light ales we sampled with dinner.

"Oh, hey guys," Harper says after yawning. She nods to the two empty chairs beside her. "Have a seat!"

"Hi, Harper," I say, smiling and taking one of the camp chairs. I still can't figure out why she seems so familiar.

Megan sinks into the empty chair between us and offers Harper a beer again now that she's not rubbing sleep out of her eyes.

"So, funny story," Harper says, shaking her head at Meg's offer. "I'm kinda knocked up."

"Sorry, I swear I just heard you say you're pregnant," Megan says. Her voice rises just enough that I notice, but Harper doesn't seem to.

"That's awesome, congrats!" I tell Harper. I look at Meg out of the corner of my eye and catch her wince. Fucking Tyler. I should have taken Harper up on the tarp and shovel.

"Yeah, long story short, we met in…March? Right? So, in May I dumped my live-in boyfriend, left Austin that night, and drove here. My best friend owns The Town Mercantile and offered me a job. She's a badass, you'll meet her in a few minutes, I'm sure. But short story even shorter, a hot lumberjack slash tattoo artist swept me off my feet and knocked me up."

I blink at Harper's short story. That's a lot to take in. But also, she moved here on a whim and looks happy as hell. That's reassuring.

"Wow, okay, well, congrats!" Megan says, her eyes a little wide. No tears though, just a big gulp of beer.

"So, how'd you guys end up here?" Harper asks curiously, her head tilted as she studies me.

"I took a job, very last minute I should add, at Rock Beach Middle School," I tell her, glad to have the attention on me and not Megan and her reaction to Harper's news. "I teach science."

"But why this town if you're from Kansas?" Harper's brow furrows and she glances between Meg and I.

"We came here the summer after I graduated high school, spent like a week here with our family, drove down 101, spent a week in San Francisco," Megan explains quickly. "My brother really loved it and randomly decided to find a way to move here."

"I mean, same," Harper tells me, laughing. "I understand that, one hundred percent."

"Just fell in love, couldn't stay away," I say, basically handing Megan the ammunition I know she wants. Anything to distract her from Tyler and the future she thought they'd share. "Someone showed me the old tsunami trail that summer, we hiked to the top, and I've wanted to build a house there ever since."

"*Someone* showed you, huh?" Megan asks with a smirk. I knew she wouldn't be able to resist. At least she's smiling again.

"The old tsunami trail, you mean the one across the highway that's now a road?" Harper asks, giving me an indecipherable look.

"Yeah, best view ever," I say quietly as strawberry-scented memories of whispered promises wash over me once more.

"It's amazing," Harper agrees. There's a far-off look in her eye and I can tell she feels that same pull to this town, this place, that I do. She brings her attention back to me. "So you're building up there? Where are you staying in the meantime?"

"Working on figuring that out, might have to be Rock Beach but I'd love something here in Three Rocks," I tell her. I lean back in my chair and link my hands behind my head, still stiff from driving the U-haul across the country.

Harper nods slowly. "Our short-term rentals are slowing down for the season," she says. She gives me another look that I can't quite figure out, like I'm missing something. "Maybe I can talk to Avery about something long term for the winter."

Avery.

Avery, whose intense gray eyes, those little flecks of blue shining through, take your breath away with just one glance.

Avery, who makes mochas with whipped cream and sprinkles, best enjoyed on early morning beach walks.

Avery, with her wide, flat smile, barely turned up at the corners of her strawberry lips.

Avery, whose hand flies across the page as she writes, pouring her soul into the words.

Avery, who has legs for days, outpacing me on every run I foolishly agreed to.

Avery, whose laugh I can still hear when I close my eyes.

Avery, my dream girl, the one who got away.

Avery, the reason I'm here.

Avery, who is standing across the fire, a very familiar green beanie on her head.

Avery is here.

Our eyes lock and the beach goes silent for a split second before a weird buzzing sound fills the night air. I feel it vibrating in my chest, squeezing my lungs. I have to fight for air, inhaling like it might be my last breath.

"Avery," I breathe. "Hi."

"Cooper," Avery gasps, the bags of marshmallows falling from her arms to the sand below.

"Hi." Did I already say that? I think I already said that. "You're here," I add dumbly.

I can see Meg and Harper out of the corner of my eye, they might even be saying something, but I can't tear my eyes away from Avery. She's everything I remember, only more.

She's taller; her long, lean, muscular legs immediately take me back to the days spent chasing her down the beach before we'd sprawl on an oversized towel, me gasping for air, her laughing. Her clear, gray eyes don't have a single hint of blue and I wonder if that was all my imagination, a trick of my mind, or if it's just the fading light and the shadows cast by the bonfire flames. Her cheeks are tinged with red, the same way they used to when she'd catch me looking at her.

Avery recovers first and her lips tug upward in a small smile as she looks me up and down. "I live here," she replies, raising an eyebrow at me. "What are you doing here?"

"I, uh," I stammer. What am I doing here?

"He's your new neighbor," Harper helpfully chimes in, gathering the dropped bags at Avery's feet. "Bought Kent's lot next door."

Neighbor. The house over our spot. My heart sinks. The house over our spot with a man in the window.

"Let me help you," Meg says loudly, grabbing a bag from Harper's arms like a few ounces of marshmallows is really something that needs a team effort.

"We need to take these way over there," Harper says, nodding across the fire to the tables set in the sand.

"Subtle, yes?" Avery asks as Megan and Harper scurry around the bonfire, leaving us staring at each other.

I manage a laugh that sounds almost normal as she sits in the chair Harper just vacated, leaving an empty seat between us. There's a beat of silence as we study each other. Avery bites the inside of her cheek and that familiar nervous habit sends my emotions into a free fall.

I want to pull her into the chair with me, breathe in her strawberry scent as she tucks her head under my chin, and feel her melt into me.

I want to ask her why she never found me; I made sure it was easy enough.

I want to tell her I love her books, that I devoured each one like a man obsessed, hoping she was writing our story.

I want to tell her that she ruined me, that I've never found anyone or anything close to what we had.

I want to tug my beanie down tighter around her ears and watch her cheeks turn pink.

I want to ask how she can live in our spot with the wrong man.

"So, want a tour?" Avery finally asks when the silence stretches too long.

My heartbeat thunders through my veins at the question. At the memory. At *all* the memories. They flip through my mind, one after another, blurring together, stealing the air from my lungs once more.

"It hasn't changed much," she adds, visibly uncomfortable, shifting in her chair and glancing around the fire when I remain silent.

I clear my throat, fighting to find both air and words. "I don't know about that. The store looks amazing, like it's brand new. Harper claims her best friend owns it." I raise an eyebrow in her direction and smile when her cheeks flush once again.

"Thanks. This place has meant a lot to me for a lot of years, it felt like giving back, you know?" She shrugs, smiling when I nod at her words.

"Cooper! You made it!" Brian booms as he places a hand on the back of Avery's chair, making her jump, and reaches the other out to me.

I stand to shake Brian's hand. "Yes, sir, I did. Happy to be here."

"And it looks like you met Avery," he says, smiling fondly at her.

"We've met," she says dryly. She bites her lip but is unable to hide her small smile.

"Well, it's about that time," he says, holding a hand out to Avery.

"Brian," she groans. "Really?"

"Come on, you knew this was coming!" he says cheerfully, pulling her up from her chair.

"Sorry," she whispers as he tugs her past me. There's a hint of strawberries left in their wake.

I can't breathe.

Avery shoots a look over her shoulder before the crowd closes around her. I sit back down and drop my face into my hands. Holy shit, she's actually here.

"Hey, let's go!" Harper is back, grabbing my hand before I can argue.

Curious, I stand and let her tug me along. When she drops my hand and squeezes her way through two guys in familiar Three Rocks Fire Department shirts, I realize the crowd has gathered into a loose circle.

"Hey man," Nate says as soon as he recognizes me, shaking my hand.

"Thanks for the beer earlier," I tell him, clapping him on the shoulder.

"Seemed like the right thing to do," he says with a shrug. "This is Mike, a volunteer at the station. He lives up the highway with his wife and kid."

I shake hands with the other firefighter, a man with an impressive moustache, and then Megan appears.

"Hey," she says, smiling and tipping her bottle at Nate. She lowers her voice and leans toward me. "Holy shit, she's here!"

"Okay, everyone!" Brian calls from the center of the circle, saving me from having to reply to my sister. "Thank you all for coming tonight to the last Three Rocks community bonfire of the season, and thanks for sticking around to hear this old man talk."

He pauses, waiting for the chatter to die down. Avery, Harper, and a younger woman stand in the circle with him. Harper nudges Avery and sends me a very obvious wink. Avery rolls her eyes at her friend but then her eyes dart my way, a cautious smile playing on her lips.

"I've lived here a lot of years," Brian starts, raising his beer bottle and laughing when someone asks just how old that makes him. "And I've met a lot of people in those years. Tourists, summer residents, year-rounders, hikers and bikers, summer vacationers and winter king tide watchers. I've seen our town in good times and bad. It's no secret that the last handful of years haven't been the best here in Three Rocks. Understandable, but still hard to see. Right now though, we're on the upswing, and as a town, as a community, we'd like to say thank you to Team Merc here, for their rather large part in that."

"Hear hear!" A man with a bandana sticking out from his back pocket calls, raising his beer.

Avery shifts uncomfortably and Harper immediately wraps her arm around her waist and whispers something that makes her laugh.

"So, from the entire town of Three Rocks, thank you," Brian continues. "Bringing back the bonfires and the Fourth Festival was no small task and not only did you pull it off, but you brought our community back together with a little extra Team Merc flair. I'd also like to personally thank you for all of those cinnamon roll deliveries to the fire station." He pats his stomach and grimaces.

"Oh, stop," the third of the trio swats Brian's hand and rolls her eyes.

"To Team Merc!" Brian calls, lifting his beer in toast.

"To Team Merc!" I lift my beer with the rest of the crowd.

Harper gives an overexaggerated curtsy and the younger woman takes a bow, playing to the crowd. Avery smiles before reaching over and squeezing Brian's bicep affectionately.

"Well, on behalf of the three of us, thank you," Harper says, after glancing at Avery who gives a slight shake of her head, declining to speak. "Thank you, thank you, thank you. I think you've all realized that Kelsey and I are the chaos of Team Merc, the faces of it all, but it was Avery that set us loose. It was Avery that quietly started this mission to bring Three Rocks back from those hard years. I'm so grateful she trusted me with this job, which, by the way, she tricked me into, and I'm so thankful to have met all y'all." Harper raises her can of sparkling water and looks around the circle at her rapt audience. "To many more summers of fun, friends, and fireworks, but mostly, to Avery!"

"To Avery!" Bandana Guy yells.

"To Avery!" I tip my beer in toast, watching as Avery accepts hugs from two older women, one of which I'm assuming is Brian's wife, based on the kiss he plants on her lips and the ring on her finger.

The pieces have all clicked into place. Avery is the investor Kurt told me about. Team Merc, which seems to be this trio of women, run The Town Mercantile as well as the short-term rentals like the one I'm staying in, and community events, including this bonfire. It's all Avery. It all started with her.

I smile and shake my head. I knew she'd go on to do amazing things, I just didn't realize how much that meant.

"Oh, you're fucked," Nate says suddenly. Megan laughs.

"What?" I ask in confusion, turning my attention to the grinning firefighter and my sister.

He motions toward the three women that are still accepting hugs. "Well, Kelsey is eighteen, so that's a bad idea, and then we've got the one with the boyfriend the size of a goddamn mountain-"

"What?" I ask, cutting him off, my eyes returning to the trio of women accepting compliments. Kelsey is obviously the younger one, so that leaves Avery and Harper.

"He's seriously bigger than a bear," Nate replies.

"Not helpful." But it is. The man in the window was definitely a big man, I wouldn't want to line up across the ball from him. I glance around the crowd but don't see him anywhere. Strange. You'd think Avery's boyfriend would be here, celebrating her and all of her accomplishments.

"And-" Nate is cut off by Harper, who grabs his hand and Meg's, pulling them toward the cornhole game.

"Sorry!" Harper calls over her shoulder. "I need a teammate and I know your sister is stupid competitive. And Nate sucks, so he's on Kelsey's team!"

Megan holds up her empty beer bottle and taps it, a silent plea for another. I nod, dutiful brother that I am, and turn to fetch her a new one from the cooler. Instead, my eyes catch on Avery. She turns, a wide smile on her face, and I wish I could turn away, not because of the threat of a mountain of a boyfriend, but because it's eleven years later and I'm still not over her. Not only that, but I doubt I ever will be.

This move was a very bad idea.

Chapter Five
Avery

Despite the crowd between us, Cooper's dark eyes hold mine captive, drawing me in, just like they did back then. Except unlike before, there's a cautious edge to his gaze, a wariness, maybe. Or like he moved halfway across the country only to be surprised by his past.

In all fairness, it went both ways. I'm lucky I only dropped marshmallows. Of all the things that could happen tonight, in no world did I think this was one of them. Colt and Liam's reunion going well? Of course I hoped for that. Nate to flirt with Tex just to see West simmer with rage? Guaranteed. Running out of marshmallows? Unfortunate but easily remedied.

But Cooper? Nothing could have prepared me for him. It took everything in me to sit down next to him, to pretend everything was fine, that every emotion I've ever felt in my entire life wasn't building up behind my eyes, threatening to spill over. Thank god for all the years of being an emotionless robot and for Brian, who showed up at the exact moment I needed him.

"Proud of you, Avery," Brian says as he pulls me into a bear hug, breaking both my thoughts and the staring contest between Cooper and I. Rescued again.

"Does this mean you'll call truce on the thank you cards?" I raise my eyebrow and he laughs. Over Brian's shoulder, I see Cooper disappear into the crowd. I swallow down my disappointment.

"I make no promises," Brian says solemnly. There's a twinkle in his eye as his gaze darts to Kelsey, who is trying to escape her mom's embrace just behind me. Kelsey, who has a white envelope sticking out of her pocket. Kelsey, who did *not* have a white envelope sticking out of her pocket two minutes ago.

I snag the envelope from her pocket before she darts toward the cornhole game and sure enough, "Team Merc" is written on the front. Damn, he's good.

"Really? Already?" I ask, laughing. I tuck it in my pocket with a smile.

"Go have fun with your friends, we'll take it from here," Brian says. He nods toward Mike, a volunteer firefighter I've met a handful of times.

"We got it, Avery," Mike says.

I stand frozen, undecided, even as they both nod reassuringly. Team Merc is the official host tonight, as well as the organizer of every single event this summer, but I could really use a minute or two or twenty-seven to process this entire night.

"Go, enjoy," Brian says, this time more firmly.

"If you're sure?" I ask.

Brian deserves much more than a thank you card for all he's done this summer. If anyone should be enjoying the evening, it's him.

"Absolutely. After all, this is my crowd now." He motions toward the crowd that's slowly drifting back toward the fire.

A quick glance confirms that Brian's right. Rachel, his wife, is sitting with Kelsey's mom, AKA Mrs. G. She pats the open chair next to her, for him or for me, I'm not sure. Brian hands me a fresh beer and practically pushes me away, taking the seat next to his wife.

Now I stand frozen, undecided, for a new reason. To my right I can hear Tex and Kelsey and the thunk of beanbags hitting boards. To my left, the path that leads me home. I'm not ready for either of those. Instead, I walk toward the creek that skirts around Rejection Rock before slipping into the Pacific. The sounds of the crowd follow me, but soon the waves crashing against the rock all but drown them out.

If only they could drown out my thoughts. My single thought.

Cooper.

Cooper is here.

As ridiculous as it sounds, he's the one guy I measure every man against. One week. We had one single week when we were teenagers. That's it. Yet no one measures up. No one ever has.

No one has slipped past my walls so easily, accepted me for who I am without question. And now he's here. He's different though. He's still tall, duh, if the long legs stretched toward the fire earlier are any indication, but he's no longer a lanky, lean teenager. He's filled out, his shoulders and chest stretch his shirt and hint at hours spent in the gym. I wonder if he still runs.

Movement along the creek makes me pause. A lone figure sits, and even from here, even in the dark, even after only seeing him briefly, I know it's him. I *feel* it's him. Just like back then, my heart pulls me in his direction, and just like before, I follow it.

I walk slowly across the dry sand, wondering just what I'm doing. What should I say? Do I dive right in with the past? Do I ask if I'm the only one with regrets? If I'm the only one that's thought "what if" more days than not? Do I ask if he's here because of us? Because of me?

"Great idea, Ave," I mutter to myself, because once again, talking to myself seems to be my thing. "Lead with that. It's not like you're a successful business owner and attorney. Lead with the fact you've never gotten over him. No. Absolutely not. It was eleven freaking years ago. Pull yourself together."

I should have walked the other way.

"What was that?" Cooper asks, looking up as I approach. Of course he heard me talking to myself. Great.

"I asked if this seat's taken?" I stop next to him and hope he buys my lie.

"Nope," Cooper replies, giving me the same smile he's given all night. The one that's almost right, but not quite. It still makes my heart stutter though. "All yours."

I drop down next to him and watch the water ebb and flow as waves make their way around Rejection Rock and up the creek to where we sit. I still don't know what to say.

"Hi-ey."

I want to bury my face in my hands. That's what I went with? Really? I guess it was the initial shock of seeing him that had me holding it together earlier, but this proves I'm still Awkward Avery around him. A simple 'hi' or 'hey' would have been fine, but that? Ugh. I take a large gulp of my beer, wishing it was one of the ales from my favorite brewery, not one of Brian's IPAs.

"Hi," Cooper says. His eyes remain on the creek flowing past.

"Hi," I repeat. I watch the water as well, half wishing a sneaker wave would rush up and wash me out to sea, saving me from myself.

Silence stretches between us, so tangible it might actually be sitting here, too. I can feel the heat radiating off him and I'm immediately taken back to a similar night, our bodies pressed closely together and my head on his shoulder. The silence back then was comfortable. I don't think I can say the same right now.

"The store really does look incredible," Cooper finally says.

"Thank you." I glance at him out of the corner of my eye.

He pulls his hat off and runs his fingers through his hair, the motion so familiar I could cry. When he turns it backward, tears really do fill my eyes. I blink rapidly. What is wrong with me?

"Kent went on and on about how the town was coming back, a silent investor that was turning the whole place around. What you've done, it's amazing, Avery." His voice is deeper, a little less playful than it used to be, reminding me again of how long it's actually been.

I shake my head and will my voice to be steady. "Kent. I can't believe you got him to sell, I've been trying for years." And years and years. At this moment I can't decide if I want to curse or kiss the cranky old man for finally selling.

"I had to write an essay," Cooper deadpans.

I nearly snort beer out my nose. "An essay?" I ask in disbelief.

"That was *after* a seven-person phone tree."

I glance over and the tug at the corner of his lips tells me he's at least a little amused by Kent's quirkiness. He turns his head and his dark eyes land on mine like a grenade. I was not prepared for this. He's leaning closer, or maybe I am, because his elbow jostles mine. My breath catches. He immediately pulls away.

I swallow down the emotions his tiny, probably unintentional rejection sets loose and clear my throat. "Was one of those seven named Betty, by chance?"

Betty is legendary. Her favorite pastimes are propositioning Lucas and telling wild stories about Tex.

"Ah, yes, the one who wanted a headshot." Cooper shakes his head in amusement.

I can't help but laugh. That's actually tamer than I thought. "Well, congrats on passing the test."

"Does that mean you failed the test? I can't see you failing at anything." He turns his gaze past Rejection Rock to the ocean, barely visible under the dark night sky.

"Kent shut me down the second I tried. I couldn't even *start* the test. Said the land wasn't calling for me." I keep my tone light, although I really do wish I would have gotten both lots…I think.

"Huh." He gives me a sidelong glance. "I'm sorry if I took it away from you."

"If you made it past Betty, you won fair and square."

"I think it's the profession. She said she was a teacher and you're looking at Rock Beach Middle School's newest teacher."

"Teacher?" I tilt my head. I can easily imagine the boy I once knew becoming a teacher. I bet his students adore him. I cannot imagine ornery Betty teaching children though, that thought makes me shudder.

"Seventh grade science," Cooper confirms.

"Not my favorite age." Understatement of the century. Middle school sucked. The only good thing to come out of it was finding the cross country team.

"So what did you do after you got your books published?" he asks, changing the subject before I can ask any follow up questions, like why, out of all the schools in the country, did he choose a middle school in Rock Beach, Oregon?

"How did you know?" The question is automatic.

There are, of course, whispers of who A. Marino really is, and I've recently realized half my town knows, but thanks to my dad, ever since that very first manuscript was sent out, my identity has been a closely guarded secret. He thought he was protecting me, and when my books turned into a best-selling trilogy, he was right. *By the Three Moons* fans are rabid with curiosity about me, I can't imagine what my life would be like if my identity was known.

"How wouldn't I know?" he counters, raising an eyebrow at me.

"I just thought..." I trail off as the memory hits.

"I'll search every bookstore until I have every single one of your books."

He found them. Of course he did. He would have known as soon as he saw the cover.

"Of course I've read them," he says softly. "Which is why I was so shocked when you walked up. What happened to North Carolina?"

My heart drops. My author bio. He thought I was on the other coast, three thousand miles away. Is that why he finally came? Because he thought I was gone?

I might have finished writing the trilogy well before I turned twenty, but the most recent special edition box set was released after I had turned my sights to law school and for some reason, probably to push the mystery of who A. Marino really is, and therefore sales, I was asked to update my bio.

"Didn't pan out." I don't elaborate. There's no way I'm admitting our week together is even a fraction of the reason I changed my mind. The second I started to pack the first box, I knew. Wrong coast, wrong person, wrong everything.

"Ave?" The tone of his voice has me turning toward him. The look in his dark eyes is so familiar, it takes my breath away.

"Yeah?"

"I didn't mean it like that," he says gently. "I was shocked, obviously, but I'm glad you're here."

"Me, too," I whisper. "I mean, I'm glad *you're* here. But that I'm here, too. That, I mean. No. Oh my god, stop talking."

"I didn't say anything," he says, his eyes shining with laughter.

"You make me an awkward teenager all over again," I groan. "I was talking to myself. Apparently it's my thing now."

Cooper laughs and I bury my face in my hands. Why am I like this?

"Ave?" He gently tugs my wrist so I drop my hands to my lap and face him. Face my embarrassment.

But I'm not facing my embarrassment, I'm facing Cooper. The one who has always seen me. We stare at each other in the dark and the world narrows. I only see him. I see him now, the man he's become. His dark eyes, though still playful in the moonlight, show a hint of turmoil. His jaw clenches and I notice the dark stubble, a hint of five o'clock shadow, and I suddenly want to feel it under my fingertips, or dragging gently along my own jaw, down my neck. My pulse races as his eyes drop to my lips for a fraction of a second.

"Coop?" I whisper.

There's a shout from the crowd at the bonfire behind us and the moment breaks. We both blink, like we're coming out of a trance.

Cooper clears his throat. "Want to head back?" he asks, looking over his shoulder.

"I should probably check in with the girls," I lie quickly. I mean, I should, but I can clearly hear Tex's laughter from here. She's more than fine and Kelsey is always fine.

Cooper pushes to his feet and offers me his hand, easily pulling me to my feet. I don't let myself think about how his hand feels wrapped around mine, how I wish we could erase the last nearly dozen years and stay hand-in-hand. Instead, I quickly retrieve my beer from the sand and turn back toward the crowd, determined to leave Awkward Avery here by the creek.

Of course that's not what happens. Instead, I find myself running directly into Cooper's chest.

The difference between sixteen-year-old Cooper and adult Cooper is about three inches and thirty pounds. A shiver races down my spine, confirming once again that while he might have changed, my reaction to him has not. Not. At. All.

For one lingering second, our eyes meet. Then, with a single tic of his jaw, he starts back toward the fire. When I stay rooted in place, he turns.

I force my emotions down. He only came after he thought I was gone, I remind myself. Stop making this a bigger thing than it is.

"Sorry," I mumble, hurrying to catch up.

"I really did read your books," Cooper says quietly when we're nearly back to the crowd. "They got me through some hard times and I've always wanted to say thank you. So, thank you, Ave."

My mask slips again and I blink quickly. As an anonymous writer, I don't hear from my readers. Sure, I get fan mail forwarded twice a year from my publisher and I can read reviews, a dark rabbit hole I went down once and vowed never to again, but I've never had anyone tell me in person that my books *helped* them. For it to be him?

"I-" I have to ask if he knows.

"Cooper!" Megan cuts me off, bouncing nervously in front of us. "Ready?"

"Well..." He looks at his sister and then back at me.

"Please?" Megan looks behind her.

Cooper focuses on his sister, suddenly looking concerned. "Are you okay?"

I glance around, bewildered, and see Tex doubled over with laughter as Nate rubs the back of his neck, looking sheepish. I shake my head, unsurprised that Tex has something to do with whatever just happened.

"Yep, just, you know, ready to go." Megan's cheeks flame red. "Good to see you again Avery, I'm sure we'll see you around town!" She practically drags Cooper away before I can respond.

"Hey, Ave?" Cooper calls from the top of the path.

"Yeah?" I can just make out his silhouette, as well as Megan behind him.

"Nice beanie!" With that, he's gone.

I raise my hand and tug my beanie off. It's the one he pulled off his own head and put on mine all those years ago.

The one I wear nearly daily.

Chapter Six
Cooper
(before)

"No way," I tell Avery flatly.

We've spent nearly every waking minute together from the time I didn't rescue her from Kevin yesterday afternoon until right now. I've learned that she's a year younger than me, she's been coming here every summer since she was born, and she's an only child. She speaks fluent sarcasm, her eyes are gray but I swear sometimes they look a little blue, and she's in all AP and advanced classes at her small-town high school. She runs more miles in a week than I have in my entire life, her hand flies across the page when she writes in that mysterious tattered notebook, and she's as quietly funny as she is smart. She's the girl of my dreams.

Also, she's crazy hot.

"It's only four miles, quarterback," she says.

Oh, did I mention that she's thoroughly unimpressed with both my sport and my position? A little shocking and very refreshing. Is football not a big thing in Oregon?

"You said four miles one way," I say, throwing my hands up, hoping to make her laugh. "That means eight miles, Avery. Eight, not four."

"Okay, well, I guess we can catch up later?" She raises a single eyebrow at me, tilting her head, probably knowing exactly what that will do to me.

I can't run eight miles. I don't think I can run four miles. Football is basically the opposite of distance running. But thinking about not spending...however long it takes to run eight miles...with her? Not an option. If I only have a week with her, I'm not missing a single second. Or, a single mile. Fuck. I hate running.

"Fine," I say. "But when I can't walk tomorrow, that's on you."

Four painful miles later, I'm watching a seal pup wiggle its way back into the ocean as waves crash against the bottom of yet another one of the weird, giant rocks that dot the beach here.

This is nothing like the Gulf Shores, Alabama, the only beach I've ever been to. Instead of white sand, oil rigs, and warm waters, it's rocky and rugged and the water is freezing cold, way too cold to swim.

"You might have to carry me back, but this is really cool," I admit.

"Not as many people come all the way up to this part of the beach, so usually there's more wildlife," Avery says, smiling as the pup disappears into the surf. "Race you to the top!"

"The top of what?" I yell after her retreating back.

The next thing I know, she's timed the retreating waves and is racing to the base of the giant, fifty foot rock. I shake my head. I really cannot keep up with her. At least this one isn't nearly as tall as Rejection Rock, the one four miles behind us back in town.

I make my bid as the next wave retreats and gingerly climb up after her, quickly figuring out how to maneuver around the barnacles to find footholds. The steep section gives way to a gentle slope that leads to one large, natural step up to the top.

Luckily, the top of the rock is completely flat, with grass growing over an area that's about the size of a soccer goal. Avery is laying on her back, legs hung over the far edge of the rock, which is a sheer drop to the beach below. I avoid thinking about how high we are and only focus on Avery.

Not hard to do.

"The eagles nest up there," Avery says when I lay down next to her, pointing to the cliff that rises above us over the coastline.

"This place is amazing." I wasn't sure why Meg had decided on the west coast as her graduation trip, but now I get it. This entire coastline is almost as breathtaking as the girl laying next to me.

"It's my favorite place in the whole world," Avery declares. "I'm going to live here someday."

"You already know where you want to live?" I ask, turning my head her way. I don't even know where I want to go to college. Or if I want to go to college.

"Yep," she says. She turns her head toward me. "You don't?"

I'm distracted by how close she is. Our shoulders are nearly touching and her lips are only inches away. Her serious, gray eyes are on mine and as the sun hits them, I notice little blue flecks along the outside. She blinks before I can memorize the color.

"I guess I haven't really thought about it," I finally say.

"I think I've always known," Avery tells me seriously. "This just feels like it to me, you know?"

Uh, yeah, it does. I swallow down that thought. I've only known her for twenty-four hours, I need to rein it in.

I clear my throat. "You ready to carry me back?" I ask as I carefully push to my feet, still very aware of how close we are to the edge.

Avery rolls her eyes. "I think you're going to be just fine, quarterback."

I offer her my hand and she lets me pull her to her feet. She wobbles slightly and I tighten my grip. Her eyes shoot to mine but I can't read her expression, so I reluctantly let go and pick my way down the rock, trying not to slip and make a fool of myself or, you know, fall and die before I get the chance to marry her. Or at least kiss her.

Chapter Seven
Cooper

It's barely light when my shoes hit the sand and a light breeze blows in from the ocean, sending waves of mist and fog over the beach and into the dunes. I head north, needing the miles ahead to clear my mind after last night. I find my rhythm over the packed sand that the tide has left behind and let my mind wander.

Avery is here. I hadn't even dared hope she'd be here, I couldn't allow myself the possibility. That last author bio had hit me like a punch to the gut. At the same time, it was what I had always hoped, that she'd chase her dreams until the physical proof was sitting on my bookshelf.

Despite what we promised, as soon as I saw *By the Three Moons* at the pop-up bookstore in the hospital lobby, I tried to find her. It felt like a sign. Her name might not have been on the cover, but that compass in the corner, true north pointing toward a crescent moon, told me it was her.

With every word, I could hear her voice and see her handwriting scrawled across a wind-torn page. She was there, sitting in that sterile hospital room with me, her words wrapping around me, steadying every shaky breath I took, muting the constant beeping of machines that was the soundtrack of my life.

My search failed. She didn't exist. No social media. None. A message to an author account didn't get a response. An email to the publisher gave me a generic "thanks for reaching out!" reply. I forced myself to move on. I had promised her we'd live our own lives and it was time for me to uphold that promise, not only for her, but for my family, which was barely holding on. I buckled down on schoolwork and football, learned to cook, and memorized the hospital hallways.

Then the second book came out. This time it was even worse. Those characters? They felt entirely too familiar. Oregon called but I needed to be closer to home. Not just needed, but I wanted to be close, just in case. The previous months weighed heavily on me, like each pound Dad lost, I carried with me. I spoke with every coach within a half day's drive of Kansas City, finally settling on K-State.

Despite in-state tuition for Megan and an athletic scholarship for me, Dad's medical bills meant my senior trip was canceled. No beach, no surprising Avery. Just a weekend in a cabin, the four of us, happy to be together outside the confines of a hospital room.

After that, it was back to the football field, this time as a Wildcat. It was everything college football was supposed to be: hard work, grit, brothers found in my teammates. It was also my assistant coach sitting at the hospital with me, going over plays in the hallway. It was my teammates coming home with me in the off season, mowing the lawn, fixing the fence, and painting the porch railing. Nash, my go-to wide receiver and best friend on the team, even built new planter boxes under the kitchen window, just because my mom mentioned it over dinner one night.

It was also girls, parties, repeat. After freshman year, for the first time in two long years, I didn't have the everyday worry of Dad's health. He was not only in remission, but thriving. I took it a little far. Girls, parties, repeat. Girls, parties, repeat.

The third book, released the week we found out Dad's cancer had recurred, changed everything. Guy finally gets the girl. I mean, the girl does save herself, the boy, and the whole world, but I focused on the ending that I wanted. I wanted to get the girl. Not the girls at the parties, the ones that only saw me as the quarterback, but *the* girl. My dream girl. Dream Girl, capitalized.

I still lived my life, worked my ass off on the field and in the classroom, and maybe went to a party or two, but my priorities were different. I wanted what my parents had, what I watched them fight so hard for every single day. A love that endures. A love straight from a book. A very specific book, written by a specific anonymous author.

Weights, study, practice, hospital, repeat.

Then, the last special edition box set was released. Finally, a new author bio. An update on her life, her accomplishments. But it wasn't the one I wanted. It was the opposite of that. We weren't meant to be. I couldn't believe I held on to that foolish fantasy for so long. No one finds their soulmate in some sleepy little town when they're a teenager. That's not the way the real world works.

But she *is* here. So now fucking what? Now I just have to watch her live her *meant to be* with someone else?

In the distance, I can just make out the vague outline of a rocky outcropping jutting into the ocean. I can't resist. I lengthen my stride, hoping the fire in my lungs and the burn in my muscles will push aside the painful sting of the memories.

When I reach the base of the rock, I start my scramble to the top. I'm too distracted and my foot slips, making my heart race even faster than my run did. I try to see the footholds but I can't focus on anything other than the last time I was here. It's ridiculous that I'm this out of sorts over a woman I spent a single week with over a decade ago. But she's more than that, she always has been. She's-

"Good morning." Avery's voice startles me.

She's here.

Avery is sitting at the edge of the rock, her legs dangling over the sheer drop off the back, looking over her shoulder at me, just the ghost of a smile on her lips. Her cheeks are flushed and her hair is pulled up high on top of her head. The light gray long sleeve shirt she's wearing is the exact color of her eyes and her leggings are a very familiar shade of sage green. If that wasn't enough, her watchband peeking through a sleeve is sunset blue.

The memories I had been running from two minutes ago come crashing back.

"Not surprising that you're still a runner," I tell her without moving. Am I frozen in place because of that cautious smile she's giving me or because we're fifty feet in the air?

"Surprising that you are a runner," she replies, arching an eyebrow at me.

"Been a runner ever since, but a very mediocre one, just to be clear." I hold my watch up as evidence.

She laughs as I carefully edge toward her. "Well, you're four miles from home, so that means you're willingly running eight miles at 6 a.m. on a Saturday, so that's a little more than mediocre."

"When I set out, it was only for a few miles, but it turns out, I couldn't resist the pull," I admit, sitting down beside her. "Now I realize I have four more miles to run and then at least twelve hours of moving into a classroom, but you did just say 'home' so that helps. I am home. Finally."

Avery shifts next to me and when I glance over, she's laying on her back, just like she did back then. She shrugs her shoulder and gazes up at the cliffs. I lay back beside her despite the voice shouting in my head that she has a live-in boyfriend. I ignored the voice last night by the creek, I might as well keep it up.

"There," she says, pointing.

Sure enough, an eagle soars from the cliff, lazily circling overhead before flying off through the fog.

There aren't words for this moment, so we both stay silent. It's the good kind of quiet, the same comfortable silence that was between us before, that I didn't know I'd needed back then. That I might need now more than ever.

The last decade has been noisy. *So* incredibly noisy. It started with hospital machines beeping, crowded cafeterias, buzzing overhead lights, and murmured voices in every hallway. It moved to tiny shared dorm rooms, parties playing music with too much bass, and coaches yelling, weights clanging. The noise has since morphed into general classroom chaos, something that college professors can't properly prepare you for. Even my runs have been filled with the sound of my own breathing and the doubts that filled my mind.

But right now? Only the rhythmic waves break the silence between us. It's calm. Quiet. I can breathe.

"Hey Coop?" Avery says softly.

I turn my gaze from the cliffs to her. She's so close, I can see every shade of gray in her eyes as they reflect the fog that's rolling in off the ocean, surrounding us in a disorienting haze. Her pale lips tip up into a smile, the kind of smile that she used to give, right before she would challenge me to something ridiculous. I narrow my eyes.

"Race you back?" she asks, sitting up and grinning down at me.

I don't know if there's a single thing she could have said better than that. It takes me right back to our week together, the hikes and runs, the card games and late night dares, and one very cold ocean swim.

"Loser buys coffee?" she adds when I don't immediately respond.

I mentally shake myself out of my memories and sit up, leaning back on my hands so I don't have to look over the edge. "So, to be clear, when I win, you have to buy me a coffee from your own store?" I ask. I shift further back from the edge and stand up slowly.

"No, when I win, you'll have to buy me a mocha from my store," she says, standing up and watching me shuffle toward the middle of the rock. "Uh, Cooper, are you afraid of heights?"

"Yes," I reluctantly admit, carefully stepping down off the small grassy ledge onto the slippery, exposed rock below. "Always have been."

"Then why are you up here?" she questions.

"Well, the first time, I was trying to impress a cute girl. This time, well-" My words are cut off when my foot slips. "Shit. I hate this. So much."

"Here, step where I step," Avery says, touching my shoulder as she hops down beside me. I can still feel the brush of her fingertips as I descend slowly and methodically, making sure to place my feet exactly where she puts hers.

Once we're on solid ground, or, well, shifting sand, there's a beat where we just stare at each other. To avoid doing something stupid like reaching for her, I glance down at my watch. With a quick grin, I push the 'start' button and take off in a near-sprint toward Three Rocks. Even with the head start, I know I have no chance of beating her.

Sure enough, Avery catches me quickly. I can't help but smile. She matches my pace and halfway home, when I start to falter, she slows down and stays beside me.

"Thanks," I say without turning my head in her direction.

"Don't worry, I still plan on winning." And with half a mile left, she lets her legs fly. I'm a dozen steps behind her when she flings her arms out, crossing an invisible finish line.

It's the same thing she'd do as a teenager and I'd laugh if I had any extra oxygen. "I can't believe this is my life," I pant instead, hands on my knees. "This is where I live. I can run on the beach whenever I want."

"Welcome home to Three Rocks, Coop," Avery says.

Home. I am home.

***

"Good run?" Meg asks when I walk back inside, still smiling.

"I just ran eight miles in the sand; I'm pretty sure my hamstrings are going to shrivel up and die," I say, handing her the mocha I ordered for her.

"That sounds really conducive to moving a classroom," Meg says. She takes a tentative sip of her mocha and her eyes widen. "Oh, that's really fucking good. Did a certain store owner make it, by chance?"

"Perhaps. I might have seen a firefighter or two on my way back," I reply, meeting her gaze with a knowing smirk. She refused to tell me why we had to leave the bonfire so quickly but I'm sure it has to do with Nate.

"You're an idiot," Meg tells me, rolling her eyes.

"Well this idiot is going to shower, then want to take a walk on the beach?" I ask. "Leslie said she'd be there a little later to get me started since I missed last week."

This job is so last minute that classes start on Tuesday and I haven't even been inside the building. Leslie Giddings, the principal, said we'd be able to make it work even though I wasn't able to make it to the teacher service days. The school is small enough that I'm the only science teacher for seventh grade, but the sixth and eighth grade teachers have definitely stepped up to help, meeting with me over Zoom the last two weeks to share curriculums and advice. My biggest takeaway? The Long brothers, all five of them, are the kids to watch out for.

"Bribing me with coffee and a beach walk? Is this any indication of how much work is ahead of us?" Megan gives me a smile so I know she's still happy to be here.

"I mean, it's definitely going to be a lot of work, but at least there's a beach?"

Meg just shoos me away, her eyes back on her laptop, a smile hidden behind her hand. Maybe she should move here, too.

When I return to the kitchen, I'm a little concerned that she did move here. There are papers everywhere. I have no idea where they came from. They definitely were not there ten minutes ago.

"Uh, Meg, what's going on here?"

"That fucking asshole…" She reaches for a pen and spills her mocha all over the table. Instead of swearing or jumping up to find a towel, she just lays her forehead down.

"Meg?" I crouch down next to her.

"He's trying to take the house," she whispers. The house is actually *her* house, which then became *their* house.

"Oh, Meg," I say, rubbing her back. "What can I do?"

She lifts her head to look at me. Her eyes are red, but she refuses to let the tears spill over. "I don't know," she whispers. "I finally felt like me again for like five whole seconds, now this."

Megan lays her head back down. At least this time she puts her arms on the table to use as a pillow. Face-to-table was concerning. Either way, this is not like my sister. I honestly don't know what to do. The only thing I do know is that this is a rental house, apparently Avery's rental house, so I need to clean up the spilled mocha. Meg doesn't move a muscle as I mop up the mess around her. As I shuffle things around on the table, I find a folder with "Voldemort" written on the front, so at least I know where the sopping wet papers came from.

"Okay, Meggy, new plan. We're going for a goddamn walk on the goddamn beach. Right now. After that, you're going to shower while I research how murder-for-hire actually works."

That gets me a small snort. It also gets Meg out of her chair. I hope Harper still has that tarp and shovel.

***

"You're back," the older woman says when I walk up to the coffee counter for the second time this morning.

I glance around the store, hoping to see Avery. Is this my future? Looking for Avery every time I leave my house? The house I need to build. Which will be right next to hers. And her boyfriend's. I really need to figure this out, because that just sounds super stalker-y.

No Avery here now though and I have Meg to think about, not my teenage dream girl that I'm accidentally stalking. In a cute, made-for-TV-Hallmark-movie way, not a serial killer way.

"There was a mocha incident," I tell her. "I think if it's not replaced, there will be more than one murder." I should stop thinking about murders and serial killers and stalking. Not a good look for the new guy in town.

"Oh, good, we decided on murder?" Harper appears next to me, leaning on the counter. "My offer stands."

"Somehow, I knew I could count on you," I joke, picturing the imaginary headline.

Local Woman Duped into Murder Scheme by Stalker Disguised as Middle School Science Teacher.

Not just any woman, but Avery's best friend, the friend that, according to the fire chief, is beloved by this town. Probably shouldn't lure her into my murder scheme, no matter how tempting.

"Can I just make the mocha and stay out of any murder plots?" The woman behind the counter shakes her head with a small smile.

"Marabelle, I've seen you wield a knife many times. I know there's a little murdery part somewhere inside, just waiting to come out," Harper says, winking at me as she places a hand over her abdomen.

"You have an unborn child to think about, I shouldn't pull you into my murder plot," I tell Harper, made-up headline still in my head. I edit it slightly.

Local <u>Pregnant</u> Woman Duped into Murder Scheme by Stalker Disguised as Middle School Science Teacher.

That's definitely worse.

"True," she says with a thoughtful nod. "I appreciate that."

"Murder?" Avery's voice floats across the store.

She's freshly showered, her hair wet around her shoulders, the seafoam green fleece making her eyes appear more blue than gray as she smiles at me. The man next to her? The one from the window? Not smiling at me.

"If anyone is doing any murders, it's me," I tell them, trying not to let my heart sink at the sight of the man from the window. This town, or at least one citizen, is sending me on a roller coaster of emotions and I haven't even been here one full day. "But first, I need to get this mocha to Megan, otherwise *I* will be the one getting murdered."

"Who are we murdering?" The bouncy college student, Kelsey, breezes into the store. Maybe she just seems bouncy because I'm usually surrounded by middle schoolers who have perfected the art of dragging their feet. "Nate? The guy with your sister last night? Was he being Nate-ish again?"

Avery and Harper laugh, even Marabelle smiles as she hands me the replacement mocha.

"I don't know what that means, but no, *we* are not murdering anyone," I say, gesturing at the group with the coffee cup. "This is a solo murder."

Kelsey washes her hands and starts packaging up cinnamon rolls. My mouth waters at the sight of them. I wonder if there will be any left after she fills the box.

"Didn't you say you were a teacher?" Harper asks, tilting her head. "I feel like murder is frowned upon in your profession."

"To be clear, murder is frowned upon in all professions," Avery cuts in. "Legally and morally."

"Not always," the man still towering over her says. His voice matches both his stature at his beard. He steps toward me and offers me his hand. "West."

"Cooper." I shake his calloused, tattooed hand. Then I watch in shock as he leans down and kisses the woman next to me.

Harper melts into him, winding her hands around his massive frame and tucking herself under his arm.

Relief, or maybe hope, washes over me. West and Harper. **Not** West and Avery. That was him in the window though, right?

"Nate-ish just means, well, I don't know, I was going to say pushy, but he's not pushy, I think he's just a flirt. Am I the asshole? Using the term Nate-ish?" Kelsey ponders, oblivious to the internal meltdown I'm having. She tapes an envelope inside the lid of the pastry box and carefully closes it. "Damnit, I think he's actually a nice guy, he just tries not to let it show. Ugh. Don't ever tell him I said that." With a shake of her head, she bounces back out of the store.

West leans down and whispers something in Harper's ear and her eyes dart toward me. I take that as my cue.

"Okay, so, again, to recap, this is a solo murder mission, please do not murder anyone, including Nate," I say. I hold up Meg's mocha after dropping cash on the counter. "Thank you, Marabelle, for this, and again, no murders please."

I back away slowly, my eyes drawn to Avery. She gives me a small smile and I remember what nice guy Nate said last night when he caught me staring at her during Brian's speech.

"Oh, you're fucked."

Yes, yes I am.

Chapter Eight
Avery

I can't tear my eyes away from Cooper as he walks out of my store. Why he still has this effect on me over a decade later is a mystery. I've had other relationships since our summer fling, do I think about them? No. Although maybe that's part of the problem. Every relationship I've had, especially the ones that lasted longer than a few months, have ended in total disappointment.

High school boyfriend, Jordan: a misguided attempt to get over Cooper. A sweet boy who got me through the darkest night of my life only to scoff when I told him I had written a novel.

College boyfriend, Evan: happy to have my study help, yet got irrationally angry when I outscored him on every exam. I started hiding test scores, lying about grades. Needless to say, I was an idiot.

Other College boyfriend, Zack: spent months convincing me that North Carolina was our future. It was his, not mine. See author bio.

Law school boyfriend, Blake: unsure he's even worth mentioning.

I guess that's the thing about a week-long relationship, there's no time for it to become anything other than perfect. No wonder why I feel so flustered, I've built him and our week together up so high, he's lounging on a pedestal in my mind, long runner legs stretched out in front of him, muscular arms crossed over his wide chest, giving me that cocky smile of his, not knowing what it does to me.

Tex catches me staring after Cooper and grins. "Well, aren't you just glowing this morning," she says. "I wonder who, I mean what, that could be about."

"Isn't that what I'm supposed to say to you, my pregnant friend?" I raise my eyebrow. She's not glowing though, she's nauseas, I can tell with just a quick glance at her. "Here, let me do that."

I have never seen anyone throw up as much as Tex has with this pregnancy. I've also never seen anyone come into their own like she has with this pregnancy. She's gone from scared and throwing up to determined and throwing up to happy (and still determined) and throwing up. Well, also a little miserable, because, well, the throwing up part.

"Where'd West go?" I ask, realizing he's not hovering over her, overprotective bear of a man that he is.

"Meeting Jessie out front to take Colt." Tex slides to the ground. "Can't you just distract me with the tales of your teenage love that's soon to be rekindled?" She leans back against the cupboard, closes her eyes, and takes a few deep breaths.

"Pretty bad this morning?" I ignore her question as I busy myself getting our Team Merc mugs ready.

I hate that I can't make this better for her. She's been my person for nearly two decades. From skinned knees at recess to that one awful night in the woods above a river, teary midnight calls to panicked early morning FaceTimes, I've always been the one to catch her, even when we've been separated by thousands of miles.

"So we're going with the avoidance route?" Tex asks without opening her eyes. "Next up, denial? Spiral?"

I snort, knowing where she's going with this. "No."

"Oooh, jumping right in with all three? The Triple Threat Trio?"

Yep, she named my emotional management technique years ago. She's pale, her eyes are closed, but she still manages to give me a hard time.

"You know me too well," I say, trying not to laugh.

"It's okay to have feelings about this, Aves. About him," she says quietly from her spot on the floor. "Just the fact you barely said a word about that week, that says everything."

I sigh. She's right. I didn't tell her *anything* about him back then. We were fifteen. It felt too raw, too big, too far-fetched if I said it out loud. When I was finally ready to talk, everything had changed.

"I just…." I trail off.

Wait. Is that part of it? That summer with Cooper was the last summer before my world tilted. Before my books took over my life, before the night that changed both Harper and I. Before she moved. My parents' divorce. Is that why nothing, no one, has compared?

"It's okay," Tex repeats, finally opening her eyes to look up at me. She gives me a small smile. "I get it. Thanks to West, I get it."

"Bad morning?" Jessie asks as she walks in. West must have given her a heads up.

"She's a little under the weather," I immediately reply, thankful for the escape from this conversation. Tex might call me out on many things, but never in front of anyone else.

"Three seconds ago I was fine!" Tex groans, letting me off the hook like I knew she would. "Now I just want to throw up but I also want to eat ice cream! Real ice cream, not stupid dairy-free, fake ice cream!"

"West said these help," Jessie says quietly, holding out a ginger candy as she steps behind the counter to join us.

"They're actually from Liam," Tex says, unwrapping the chew and popping it in her mouth.

Jessie gives a tiny hint of a smile. "I heard."

"You okay?" I ask her.

While Liam and Colt's reunion went well last night, it's still a dumb question. She's not okay.

Jessie hands me the sprinkles for my mocha, a tradition Tex and I started as teenagers and I refuse to give up, and one of the tea bags that we hide from Tex so she won't throw them away. Yes, despite the fact the tea helps, she will throw them away.

"Sometimes things are just a lot, you know?" Jessie says with a shrug.

"Amen to that," Tex says from her spot on the floor.

Sometimes things are just a lot. A-freaking-men indeed.

"Pretend sisters!" The front door flies open and Kelsey bursts back in the store after running a fresh batch of cinnamon rolls to the fire station, a thank you card taped to the inside lid of the box. "This meeting had better be a party!"

Tex miraculously pops up from the floor. "Of course it is! College day!" She lays a hand over her stomach and I silently push her toward the door. Fresh air.

I follow her out, tea in hand, and set her pink Yeti mug in front of her.

"Don't think our conversation is over," Tex says.

I just shake my head. Time for the Triple Threat Trio to commence. Avoid, deny, spiral. Well, after this team meeting.

***

I watch my blinking cursor and chew on my lip. I really thought I had something. Some little inkling of an idea, an inspiration. I was wrong. I've stared at this cursor more this weekend than I have in years. On the deck in my favorite chair with a blanket wrapped around my shoulders, standing at the kitchen island with the window open to let in the sound of rain, sitting at my desk with noise canceling headphones playing classical music. Still nothing.

I think back to what Helen, my writing coach, told me when I first struggled with writer's block. *"Write Avery, not A.Marino."*

But Avery, the real me, hasn't been inspired, either. The last few years have just been law school, The Merc, and work.

But I felt it again, I know I did, the flutter of an idea floating past as I sat around the table the other morning with my friends. Our team meeting rapidly turned into shared tubs of dairy-free ice cream passed between us as we reminisced on all the changes in our lives.

I felt the twitch in my fingers, the burning need to write, when Zoe, social media star, ran up the steps (and into our meeting) and declared her love for Lucas, one of my Merc employees. I don't know if it was the lovestruck look in her eyes or how she bravely wears her heart on her sleeve, but something made me offer her a job, and now she's the newest member of Team Merc.

I felt it watching Kelsey's excitement as she counted down the hours until she escaped this tiny town that's been her only home, so completely ready to spread her wings.

I felt it when Tex talked about the opposite-escaping *to* this tiny town, planting her roots here, her left hand on her belly, right hand digging into the dairy-free ice cream.

I felt it when Jessie shared her relief at finding sanctuary here in Three Rocks, not just a home but a community to lean on as she and Colt find their footing.

Is that the inspiration? This town? That's definitely very Avery and not at all A.Marino. I tap my keyboard. Close. I'm so close.

I think about another piece of advice from Helen. *"Stuck? Start small. Google a prompt. Then just type."*

The first writing prompt that Google suggests makes me sigh.

"The lives of two people are forever changed when they engage in a weekend-long affair."

It wasn't an affair that forever changed me, it was a week-long summer fling. A perfect week. And I absolutely don't need to put it on paper, it's been burned in my mind ever since.

"Not cool, Google. Not. Cool," I mutter.

I'm two-thirds into my Triple Threat Trio, I don't need to be pushed over the edge.

Avoidance: locking myself in my cabin, staring at this screen.

Denial: the "just busy!" text I sent Tex yesterday morning.

Spiral: what will happen if I attempt this writing prompt.

I lean back, roll my neck in a few slow circles, then stretch my arms overhead. I glance at the time. I've missed nearly the entire weekend. It's Labor Day, AKA the unofficial end to summer, and I haven't even set foot in town since ice cream breakfast. Avoidance level: advanced.

My Garmin watch buzzes on my wrist, another "move!" reminder. I glance out my window and then back to the blinking cursor. Today isn't the day to spiral. I'll save that for tomorrow.

Seven minutes later, I'm running across the bridge to the beach access path closest to The Merc. I breathe in the salty sea air and let everything else go. The failed writing attempt. The memories. I let go in the way that only running allows me. My legs and lungs take over, my mind quiets, and I just run.

It's the run every runner hopes for but only gets every once in a blue moon. My mind is clear and I float over the sand, my strides as rhythmic and unhurried as the waves. The sun sinks lazily toward the horizon, lighting the few clouds in the sky with beams of color. I don't even have to look at my watch to know this is the best run I've had all summer. All year. When I turn around at the end of the North Road houses, I fly back to town.

The one bad thing about living at the top of the old tsunami trail, besides the memories that taunt me, is that every run ends uphill. Some days it makes a good cool down walk, others it's the struggle I need. This evening, I sprint up the hill, embracing the burning in my lungs, the heaviness of my legs, already looking forward to watching the sunset from my deck with a glass of white wine. I fling my arms out over the imaginary finish line I picture, then drop my hands to my knees, gulping in the cool, salty ocean air.

"Did you win?" Cooper's voice carries across the narrow road, humor laced in his tone.

"Holy shit!" I gasp. "You scared me!" I look up and see him smiling broadly at me from his new lot, the for sale sign still staked in the ground.

"Sorry, I didn't mean to scare you but it felt weirder to stand here quietly. I could tell you were in your own world in that race up the hill." He continues to smile at me as I continue to wish there was more oxygen in the air.

"It was that run, you know? The one you always want to have," I tell him between breaths. "God, it felt so fucking good."

That makes his smile grow even wider. His deep brown eyes crinkle the tiniest bit in the corners. Each grin inches closer to the smile he used to toss my way with abandon.

"So fucking good, huh?" he teases. "Guess you learned how to swear in the last decade."

"That last part was supposed to be in my head," I mumble. I collapse onto my driveway, starfishing on the asphalt and closing my eyes as my run catches up to me. It's definitely the run that has my heart racing, not Cooper's smile, or his teasing, or the light stubble on his jaw, or his dark brown eyes, or-

"You okay?" Cooper sounds concerned.

I can only give a thumbs up. Endorphins, this is endorphins making me feel this way. My skin prickles in awareness, telling me he's close. I open my eyes and he's sitting next to me.

"Hi." Cooper grins down at me. "Are you sure you're okay?"

"Never better. Not a bad view, right?" I ask, gesturing lamely toward the sky, still too tired to sit up and enjoy the sunset.

"Been waiting on it for a long time." He moves his eyes back out over the trees to the sun sinking toward the water.

I push up to sit, lean back on my hands, and join him in staring at the horizon. Sunsets like this make the long, rainy, dark winter months worth it.

"This is my favorite part of living up here," I tell him. "When the sunset burns orange, the clouds turn pink, and everything is still. Peaceful."

"That's why I came up here, to see the sunset from my favorite place. Meg went to the beach with, well, I'm guessing everyone in town, but I needed this. The quiet."

His favorite place. My heart takes off again at his declaration, pounding so hard against my ribcage I'm sure Cooper can hear it. So much for the quiet.

There's a thousand things I want to ask him but I'm too scared. Avoidance level: expert.

So we sit in silence, like we aren't twenty yards from the place we whispered promises of a future together, and watch the sun sink into the ocean.

Chapter Nine
Avery
(before)

"What are three things no one knows about you?" Cooper asks suddenly, rolling over on our shared, oversized towel to face me.

I set my book down slowly and narrow my eyes. "I'm just supposed to tell you three things no one knows? Like three secrets?" I'm not really the secret-sharing type.

Coop smiles. "Yep."

*I get butterflies every time you smile at me. I absolutely melt when you do that thing where you run your hand through your hair and turn your hat backwards. I feel like I could drown in the depths of your dark eyes. I love the way you make anything and everything fun. I wish you lived in the same state as me, the same town. I want your hand that's half an inch away to grab mine. I like you. I **like** you like you. A lot.*

I don't say any of those. I clear my throat and stare at the ocean. Am I supposed to say something funny? Do I say something real? Am I making this more complicated than it should be?

"I'll go first," Cooper announces. He sits up so we're side by side, both of us leaning back against the rocks. "One, I'm terrified of spiders. Every time my sister makes me kill one, I shake in fear."

I laugh. I can't help it. Just this morning I caught a spider in the bathtub and moved it outside for Grandma. At his playful glare, I purse my lips to hide my smile.

"Two..." He trails off and rubs the back of his neck. His eyes follow two boys playing catch along the shoreline. "I don't think I want to play football anymore. I know I'm good, I'll probably get college offers, I just...I don't know. Am I doing it for my dad or for me? It was our thing when I was little, and now, he wouldn't be mad or anything, I just don't want to disappoint him."

I wonder what that's like, having a dad that cares so much about something you do. Having a dad who you have "a thing" with. Like, an actual thing. Anything. Mine has never been interested in what I do. He's never watched a race and I'm not sure if he even knows that I won districts last year. He sure as hell isn't supportive of my writing.

I don't know what to say so I just bump my shoulder against his. "I'm glad you told me."

He nods, seemingly lost in thought. One of the boys whoops excitedly as his friend catches the football and a small smile flashes across Cooper's face. It disappears so quickly I wonder if it was ever there. I haven't seen him this way. I tentatively slide my hand toward him. When my fingers brush over his, he flips his palm up and laces our fingers together.

"Three," he says quietly, turning to look at me. "I've wanted to hold your hand ever since I didn't save you from Kevin."

My cheeks flush as his dark eyes hold mine captive. I swallow hard and squeeze his hand. "I've wanted you to do this since you didn't save me from Kevin."

"I knew we had so much in common," he says with a small, teasing smile.

We have nothing in common. He's the quarterback of the football team; I run cross country. I take as many advanced classes as my small school has to offer; he's happy to skate by with Bs and Cs. He has so many friends I can't keep their names straight; I have Harper and my study group. I have a five-year plan; he might have the next five minutes planned. He would eat a cheeseburger for every meal if he could; I've been a vegetarian since I was ten years old.

"Your turn," Cooper says.

I want another smile so I go for shock and awe. "I stole a pen from my teacher in first grade."

"Wow, Ave, the criminal!" Cooper laughs.

"I still have guilt!" I add. I seriously do. I should take her a pen to replace the stolen one. She doesn't teach anymore but thanks to small town life, I know which house is hers.

"As you should," Cooper says seriously. He shakes his head. "Thief."

An easy silence falls between us as I try to think of something else to tell him. Cooper waits patiently, watching the football fly back and forth. A third kid, a little girl, has joined the game. Based on the matching blonde curls, I'm assuming she's the sister of the boy in blue. I always wanted a sibling, preferably a sister, but a big brother would be nice.

I smile as I watch as the boy helps his younger sister, showing her how to throw the ball that's far too big for her small hands. He's so patient with her.

Honestly, I should be relieved I don't have siblings. No one else should have to listen to the arguments, witness the tears. It's bad enough that Harper gets caught at my house at times.

"Two, I wish my parents would just get a divorce already," I say quietly. I've never said that out loud. I've thought it nearly daily, but I've never said it.

Cooper squeezes my hand gently. "Want to talk about it?"

"Not really." It does feel good to say it out loud though.

"I'm glad you told me," he says. He shifts so our shoulders are touching.

We sit in comfortable silence as his thumb traces circles over my knuckles. I lean my head on his shoulder and watch as the little girl throws the football. Her dad jumps from his chair and cheers. Cooper sighs and I know my third secret.

"Three, I've always wanted to learn to throw a football," I say. I turn to look at him and cock my brow.

A slow smile spreads across his face. He turns his hat backward, jumps to his feet, and offers me his hand. "Well, what are we waiting for?"

Chapter Ten
Cooper

Teaching is exhausting. Teaching at a new middle school is even more exhausting. Their mood swings alone might kill me. But I love it. I love the awkwardness of this age, those times when I can get the kids excited about learning, and seeing my students grow and challenge themselves within the classroom. Did I mention it's exhausting though?

I reach for my coffee as my students file in, shaking my head when I see Megan stuck a Town Mercantile sticker on my travel mug. Like the annoying sister she is, she's managed to slip a reminder of Avery into my day all week. I probably shouldn't have told her about our sunset Monday, because, for someone very anti-love at this point in her life, she's gone a little overboard.

I haven't seen Avery since that sunset, so while I won't admit it to Meg, these little reminders are getting me through the stress of the first week of school. Megan has also managed to find me a small, minimalist cottage to rent (owned by Avery), making it worth my while to put up with her teasing. Although, according to Harper, it's only available until Memorial Day. I have nine months to figure my life out. I take another drink of coffee. Nine months. Totally doable.

By third period, my confidence in nearly everything is waning.

"Bruh," Micah Long, the middle sibling of the five brothers I've been warned about, says. "Homework the first week?"

The kid has yet to call me Mr. Miller. He also has yet to sit still.

"Micah, if you're not going to call me Mr. Miller, or even Mr. Cooper, can we at least go with something that acknowledges my authority, like Brofessor?" I toss him a stress ball, hoping that will give him something to do besides drum a pen on his desk.

"Mr. Miller?" Sadie Howell, a dark-haired girl that I can already tell is going to be one of the brightest students I've ever taught, raises her hand as she speaks. "Do you want it double-spaced? Is there a page limit? Should it be in essay format?"

"All I ask is that you tell me three things about yourself, two things you think I should try here in my new town, and one thing you like about school," I tick off, using my fingers to count down like I'm a kindergarten teacher. "I've lived here just over a week, I need all the help I can get, you guys. Best beaches, hikes, places to eat, cool shops. I need it all. You can write a list on a sticky note and put it on the board for everyone to see, write an entire essay and turn it in on Google Classroom, draw a comic strip, however you want to communicate those things to me. Be as creative as you want."

Sadie nods eagerly, taking notes on her laptop as her ponytail swings. Micah twirls his makeshift drumstick between his fingers, stress ball already forgotten, and immediately drops the pen on the floor. The rest of the class either sighs heavily or contemplates the assignment. Tough crowd. I think they're as tired by this first week of school as I am.

The rest of the day goes about the same. Names and faces blur together as they have all week and I cannot for the life of me figure out this small-town hierarchy between the kids. I spend my lunch period working through training modules, which is probably how my weekend will be spent as well, assuming I make it through tomorrow.

I'm questioning a lot of my life choices as I trudge through the parking lot toward my car. The elementary school across the street is letting out and when I see fire truck backpacks and Barbie lunch boxes, I briefly wonder why I didn't choose elementary education. I could be handing out stickers instead of trying to decipher whatever foreign language this new middle school slang is.

"Hey, Brofessor!"

I can't hold in my laugh. Of course, just when I'm having a pity party, Micah shows up. I can hear his footsteps thundering behind me.

"What can I help you with, Micah?" I ask, turning to face him.

"I finished my homework early," he says breathlessly, reaching out and placing a sticky note on the strap of my backpack. Without another word, he spins around and jogs back across the parking lot.

The kid goes from complaining about having homework to finishing it early? I pluck the sticky note from my chest.

1. I have too many brothers, I'm not allowed to play football, I think science is dumb
2. Rage room, then the rage room again
3. Sadie

I can't help but laugh. This is the exact kind of list I would have made at his age. Today, if asked what I like about my new town, there'd definitely be a name in that last slot.

***

"Miss Avery!" Colt races into The Town Mercantile as soon as I open the door. "I started kindergarten!"

I keep the door propped open with my foot as I attempt to loop Zero's leash around the railing outside while she glares at me, miffed I won't let her into the store that very clearly has a "no dogs" sign on the door.

"I know! What a big week for you! How was it?" I hear Avery enthusiastically ask Colt.

"Kinda boring, but my new friend Theo likes rocks, too," he tells her. "We finded some at recess."

"Who are you here with today? Wait! Let me guess. Almost Auntie Tex after your sleepover?"

"She's barfing," he says and I laugh to myself. It was the first thing he said when he opened the door for me at Harper and West's house. Not quite what I expected, especially since I was pretty sure they didn't have a kid.

"So probably not Uncle West either," Avery says. "Mrs. G?"

"Nope!" he cries, gleeful that she hasn't guessed correctly yet.

"The Easter Bunny?"

"Mr. Cooper!" Colt says, fist pumping as I enter the store, Zero finally secured outside.

"Good morning," I tell Avery, drinking in the sight of her.

She's in jeans that hug her long legs, hiking boots, a gray fleece with the store logo, the color nearly perfectly matching her eyes, and a beanie. Not mine though.

"How'd you get so lucky to hang out with Colt today?" she asks, a slight flush creeping up her neck when she catches me staring at her.

"I've come to realize that the 'Team Merc' girl gang that runs this town isn't to be messed with," I reply with a wry grin.

As soon as Megan connected with Harper, it was all over. While I've been slogging through lesson plans every night since the bonfire, Meg's been all over town. She befriended Jessie, who is Colt's mom and West's sister, as well as Zoe, some YouTube yoga girl I vaguely recognize from Meg and Brooke's living room yoga sessions.

"In a good way or a bad way?" Avery raises an eyebrow and tilts her head, just like she did as a teenager. I wish, for the twenty-seventh time this week, that we could go back to that week.

"Well, you heard the whole murder-for-hire issue from last weekend that I really hope did not pan out while I was busy dealing with middle schoolers this week, then my sister met Zoe and Jessie, and now instead of driving Meg to the airport, I get to hang out with Colt."

"And Zero!" Colt chimes in, skipping off to the counter.

"And Zero," I confirm. "Zoe and her boyfriend, Lucas? Right? They took Meg to the airport since they were headed into Portland anyway, then when I went to get the key to my new rental from Harper, Colt said she was a little under the weather."

"So now you have a kindergartener and a dog?" Avery asks.

"I was promised hot chocolate out of this excursion. He even brought his own money. I'd be a fool to turn that down," I tell her seriously, watching her lip twitch as she tries not to smile. She fails. She's probably smiling at Colt, who is discussing sprinkles with the employee behind the counter, but I hope she's smiling because of me.

"It's the same hot chocolate Tex and I used to make as kids," she tells me, turning her gaze to mine.

"So is that what I should take back for her?" I ask. Avery immediately wrinkles her nose. "No?"

"No," she confirms. "She can't have dairy anymore. And if she's been throwing up, she'll need tea. She says it's gross but I know it makes her feel at least slightly better."

"And for her mountain of a boyfriend?" My guess is black coffee. I couldn't get a read on the man that handed his nephew over to my care, but something tells me I'm not far off the mark.

"Black coffee for West." Bingo.

"I better go place that order. Do I need to get anything for Zero? She looked at me like an abused puppy when I tethered her outside." I could almost hear the sad music playing in the background when she laid down and tucked her nose under her paw.

"She can be dramatic like that," Avery says with a laugh. "We keep free dog treats next to the register. I'm sure Colt is already getting one for her."

Sure enough, Colt has a cup of what looks like whipped cream and sprinkles in one hand and a dog biscuit in the other. The apron-wearing employee holds up a few dollars, I'm assuming his change. Colt looks between his full hands and the money, unsure what to do.

"Hey, Colt, why don't you and Mr. Cooper take Zero her treat while I help Miss Katie make Almost Auntie Tex some tea to make her feel better?" Avery suggests.

Colt looks at the money again. The girl, Katie, laughs and reaches across the counter to tuck it into the pocket on his shirt.

"Come on, Mr. Cooper!" Colt calls, licking the whipped cream mustache that adorns his lip.

I hold the door open and sit down next to Colt on the steps even though there are perfectly good tables lining the store's front porch. Colt launches into a running commentary about kindergarten, leaving no room for any interjections from me. I'm listening to an extensive list of Mrs. Bailey's class rules when a cup appears in my peripheral vision. I turn to see Avery holding it out with a smile.

"Miss Avery!" Colt jumps up and wraps a sticky hand around her leg.

"How's that hot chocolate?" she asks with a smile.

"Mmm!" he hums as he takes a comically large, overexaggerated gulp.

"I made a slight alteration to your special hot chocolate, I hope you don't mind," she says. "Don't worry, it still has sprinkles."

I stand and take the cup, my fingers lightly brushing hers. I take a sip and break into a smile. It's a mocha.

"Perfect," I tell her. "Thank you."

She gets that slightly flushed look again and bites her lip, drawing my eyes to her mouth. I blink and make myself focus back on her eyes. And then on her hand, which is holding a drink carrier with three cups. I reach forward to take it from her, wondering why there are three drinks. Colt has his in hand, I have mine, it's only Harper and West at their house.

"Would you like some company on your walk?" she asks, her eyes darting to the ground. "I was a pretty bad friend this week, I'd like to check on Tex, see if she needs anything else."

"Is this your way of offering a tour?" I grin as her cheeks turn even more red.

I don't know if I've just been busy this week or if she's been avoiding me, but even if I just get a ten-minute walk with her, my weekend will be complete, and it's only Saturday morning.

"There's like five streets," she deadpans.

I laugh. "Colt? Zero? What do you guys think? Should Miss Avery walk with us?"

"Yes!" Colt cheers while Zero jumps around him, tangling them in her leash.

Avery makes quick work of saving Colt from tripping and then tugs one of the cups from the carrier in my hand. She tips it toward me in a silent toast as we start down the road, Colt and Zero just ahead of us as he carefully holds his special hot chocolate in one hand and the leash in the other.

"So, how was your first week of being a Three Rocks resident?" Avery asks, just as her phone buzzes. She reaches into her pocket and I see the name "Edward" on the screen. She frowns and pockets it before looking at me expectantly.

"Overwhelming and exhausting," I admit. "But in a really good way. It already feels like home. It's going to be weird without Megan here though. Thank you, by the way, for helping her out with Tyler."

"He never had a chance in hell of getting the house but it was quite satisfying to draft that for her." She shoots me a quick smile before taking a sip from her to-go cup.

"Still, thank you. I know it took a weight off her shoulders." I'm not quite sure how Avery heard about the Tyler/house issue, I'm assuming from the unstoppable Team Merc, but when I hugged Meg goodbye this morning, she was happier than I've seen her in months.

"Glad to be able to help." She shrugs and takes another sip. "And how's school?"

"I'm going to need another week or two to really get the hang of each class's dynamic, but we're off to a good start," I tell her. It's true, I'm exhausted, but I already love my new school. "My colleagues are amazing, passionate educators, all the admins are helpful, and I have a couple students who have already wormed their way in."

"I bet you're a great teacher," she says, looking at me out of the corner of her eye.

I wonder what she's thinking, what memory has her biting the inside of her cheek.

"The bestest teacher!" Colt adds, having stopped to untangle the leash once again. "Can I be in your class next year?"

"I think you have a couple years, bud," Avery tells him with a laugh. She takes his empty cup and he takes off in a sprint up the narrow, empty street, Zero loping alongside him at an easy pace.

Silence falls between us as we watch the two of them. It's not exactly awkward, but it's not *not* awkward, walking next to each other, taking small, oddly timed sips out of matching cups, pretending we aren't watching each other. As my dad always says, sometimes the only way through, is through.

"So, bad friend this week?" I ask, my voice sounding oddly loud. "Just because she's been sick?"

"No, I got busy with work and just, yeah, bad friend," she replies. There's a flicker of guilt in her eyes that I don't quite understand.

"You've been best friends for like twenty years, right? There's going to be weeks where things are busy. That's life."

"It's complicated," she replies as she watches Colt and Zero, wincing when Colt nearly trips over the leash.

Instead of taking the hint that she doesn't want to talk about Harper, I barge ahead. The only way through, is through, right? "I've been meaning to ask about her nickname, it seems like no one in town actually calls her by her real name? Is there more to the story than just where she lived?"

Ever since Megan showed me the different Instagram accounts for the store and Avery's multiple short-term rentals, I've been curious about the nickname. Harper and Kelsey are in most of them, along with Zero, and they're all hilarious. They're also the only time I've heard Harper's southern drawl; in person, there's barely a hint of a twang.

There's an immediate shift in Avery's body language. I know without a word that I've made a mistake.

"I gave it to her a long time ago, and after that night, I just…" She trails off, glances over her shoulder, then glues her eyes to the ground.

"Ave, you don't have to answer." I wish I could take the question back, that we could go back to the weird silence.

She's silent for a few steps and then takes a deep, steadying breath. "It was a dumb nickname fueled by teenage drinking and the fact she was moving away, but something happened that night, something bad," she says in a measured tone that betrays more than she probably thinks. "So after that, for a long time, I just…I couldn't say her name."

"I'm sorry," I say quietly. I don't know what else to say. All I know is that I'm not going to use Tex's real name anymore, especially in front of Avery.

"Then when she showed up here, I said it more as a joke because she was in total Texas clothes, flip flops and bright sunglasses even though it was cold and misty, but it caught on. Now only West calls her by her real name, and sometimes me, usually when I'm annoyed," she continues, cracking a small smile. "So now she's Tex. And Kelsey took that and ran with it on all the social media marketing."

"Meg showed me. They're funny together, although Zero is the real star." What Tex said at the bonfire is true, she and Kelsey are the chaos of Team Merc, at least on Instagram.

Avery smiles briefly. "I've never told anyone, not even Harper, why I used that dumb nickname for so long," she says quietly, her eyes still on the ground.

"I'm glad you told me." I gently knock my shoulder against hers, hoping she remembers that day so long ago.

When she swings her gaze to meet mine, I know she does. She smiles softly and I see a flash of blue in her eyes. My steps falter. She slows beside me.

"Cooper," Avery says, pausing to lick her lips. "Why-"

"What are you waiting for?" Colt yells, interrupting her.

"One sec!" Avery calls back.

"Kid stole my line," I mutter, which makes Avery laugh. "But what were you going to ask?"

She just shakes her head. "Nothing."

Bullshit. I can see her chewing on the corner of her lip. But I've already asked the wrong questions this morning, so instead, I turn my attention to Colt and Zero and ask the question I already know the answer to.

"Wanna race?" I call.

"Yes!" He fist pumps and takes off down the street with no warning. Cheater.

I hand Avery the drink carrier and reach up, turning my hat backward. I give her a wink, grinning when her cheeks flush again, then chase Colt down one of the five streets of my new town.

Chapter Eleven
Avery

"I can't believe you have seven houses," Cooper says, shaking his head with a wry grin. "I have zero."

When I walked down to The Merc this morning, I thought I was going to be spending a few hours catching up with my best friend, maybe even doing something besides holding her hair while she puked. Instead, I found her at home in bed looking miserable and she asked me to move the last boxes out of her cottage so Cooper could move in.

There were two boxes. Two. It took me thirty seconds to carry them out to my car. Now I'm helping Cooper move in, which I'm sure was Tex's real plan. I'm honestly surprised the boxes weren't empty.

"Well, I couldn't write, my heart was never set on the whole lawyer thing, so I just…" I trail off, watching his biceps flex as he carries a heavy box across the living room. I've already stumbled through Tex's nickname, am I really about to share how my best friend had to save me from failing my entire town? What is it about him that makes me spill my secrets?

"Just bought a bunch of houses?" Cooper supplies, setting the box on the floor next to the bookshelf.

I laugh. "Well, yes. The most expensive, ridiculous distraction from my failures."

"Ah, yes, graduating law school, passing the bar, buying a business. Such failures," he teases. He motions to the box. "I saw you eyeing this, want to see what's inside?"

"Is it books?"

The box is clearly labeled "books" so he doesn't answer.

The promise of a peek inside his bookshelf has me eagerly crossing the small living room. I drop to the floor as he deftly cuts through the packing tape. When I reach to open the box, his warm hand covers mine. My heart stutters with the contact. There's a beat of silence where we just stare at each other. An uneasy look flits across his face for a fraction of a second. Before I can contemplate why, his eyes drop to the box and he takes his hand from mine. I open the box slowly, like whatever books are inside might bite.

It feels like they do. He has every edition of all three of my books. Paperbacks, hardcovers, special edition cover art, box set. All of them.

"Coop." I can't find any words, which feels fitting as I stare at my books that contain thousands of them.

"I'll search every bookstore until I have every single one of your books."

I have to blink back tears. He didn't just read my books like he said, he searched them out, he found every single one. The words that got me through the years after him, he read them all. I take an unsteady breath.

"Stalker or sweet?" he asks with a grimace. "Because as soon as I lifted my hand, I realized this could go either way."

"I..." I huff a laugh. I'm sure some would say stalker, but this feels like fulfilling a promise. "You told me you'd buy them all."

"I knew you'd do it." Cooper shrugs, like there was never any doubt. "I was ready to buy a lot more."

"I thought I was ready to write a lot more," I say. I look down at the box again. "But I guess I wasn't."

"I didn't mean it that way. I meant I was always rooting for you." He takes the top book, a very worn paperback edition of my debut novel, my pen name in tiny script below the title, and holds it up. "And hoping that someday I'd get this signed by the author."

To have the only person I ever let read the very first rough draft of my book sitting in front of me, that very book in his hand, is completely surreal on so many levels. The first time I held it in my own hands, staring at it in wonder, my finger tracing the small compass in the corner in disbelief, I wondered if he'd ever stumble upon it. If he'd remember, if he'd know it was me.

"Cooper," I breathe.

"I-" He's cut off by the buzz of his phone. I barely have time to register the change in his demeanor before he's answering. "Dad? Everything okay?" Tension fills his voice and rolls off him in waves.

I scoot back, wanting to give him space for whatever this is, but before I can stand, Cooper's hand finds my arm. He shakes his head, silently asking me to stay. I nod, busying myself with taking the books from the box and carefully lining them up on the small bookshelf next to the fireplace.

"I wouldn't have changed anything, you know that," Cooper says quietly into the phone.

I sneak a glance out of the corner of my eye and breathe a sigh of relief when I see him leaning back against the couch, all signs of tension and fear gone. He smiles when he catches me watching and I feel my cheeks flush. I return to my task, shelving books one by one.

When I find Throne of Glass, one of my own favorite books, I pause. This is not what I'd expect a twenty-seven year old man to read.

"Reminded me of your books," Cooper says, nudging my thigh with his foot.

He's no longer on the phone but he stays leaning back against the couch. He gives me a small smile but his eyes drop back to his phone. He tugs his hat down low, shielding his eyes from my stare, so I return to my task once more.

Cooper clears his throat. "Thanks," he says, his voice rough, making me glance back over at him. "For…this." He juts his chin toward the shelf.

"Everything okay?" I ask.

He nods. "Habit, I think."

I frown, confused.

"My reaction, when he calls. He…he went through a lot, he was sick for a long time, and it just feels weird to be here. Not there."

I can picture his dad, his easy smile mirroring Cooper's as I held out my shaky hand the first time I met him. "Sorry, I'm a hugger," he'd said before he pulled me in for a hug as Cooper groaned.

A small pang strikes my ribs at the memory. In the few days I knew Cooper's dad, he hugged me more than my own father did that entire year.

"Is he okay?" I ask hesitantly. There's a pit in my stomach as I wait for his answer.

"Other than telling me I haven't lived my life and that he will show up on my doorstep if I mess it up anymore, he's fine," Cooper replies wryly.

"Is that what moving here is? Living your life? Or is it messing it up?" I try to act like it's a casual question. But the real question is why? Why did he move here? And why is my heart beating out of my chest as I wait for his answer?

Cooper laughs. "Both? I don't know. I've spent my entire adult life making my decisions based on what's best for him, for my mom, for Meg. Making sure they were okay, always putting them first. I'd do it again and again, family first, right? But when that's all you know, it's like I don't even know *how* to live life for myself," he says. His gaze finds mine, heavy and intense. "The life I thought...it's like it doesn't exist."

The life he thought. The life *we* thought.

"What if we meet again five years from now?"

How foolish were we? Thinking it'd be so easy.

I clear my throat but realize I don't have any words. What am I supposed to say? That I wish he would have chosen me over his family? No. I don't wish that, not even for one second. I see the toll the last eleven years have taken. It's the hurt in his eyes, the smile that's not quite his, not the one that's lived in my memory. He's lived an entire lifetime since then. I'm more heartbroken for him, for his family, than for what we thought would be.

"But I wish it did," he adds.

I can't breathe. What does he mean?

"So, can we consider this meeting again?" he asks quietly.

"I'm pretty sure that's what this is." I don't know how I get the words out, my heart is firmly planted in my throat.

"Well," he says, tugging the book from my hand. "In that case, hi, I'm Cooper. Any chance you can give me a tour of town?"

"There's like five streets," I deadpan and his real smile, the one I saw eleven years ago, makes its first appearance.

His warm brown eyes light up as the grin overtakes his entire face. "So?" he asks, standing and holding his hand out for me. "What are we waiting for?"

"Really? A tour?" I ask, letting him pull me up from the floor.

"I want a tour from you, Avery." His voice dips playfully, teasingly. He takes his hat off and runs his hands through his hair before replacing it. Backwards.

My stomach swoops. "Okay," I say, biting the inside of my cheek to hide my smile.

"Yeah?" Cooper's smile somehow gets even wider.

"Yeah." I can't help but grin back.

***

"No, you distract Nate and I'll sneak in," Cooper argues, holding the thank you note above his head.

"Breaking and entering is in no way part of the tour," I protest, laughing. I don't even know how we ended up here. Here being hiding behind a dumpster in the fire station parking lot. But also, here being together, eleven years later.

"Did you or did you not say that they got you last?" he asks. "Is it your turn or not?"

"Fine," I say with a sigh. "How am I even supposed to distract him?"

Cooper raises an eyebrow before looking me slowly up and down, head to toe and back again. "You're distracting as is."

Heat floods my cheeks. How does he do this, fluster me so easily? The last six hours have been the most fun I've had since Emmy's tequila-fueled visit that ended in two-step lessons. What started as a five-street tour (there's actually more than five streets), complete with stops at the golf course for three holes of frisbee golf, pointing out which houses are my rentals, a quick climb of Rejection Rock, and a behind-the-scenes tour of The Merc has now escalated into breaking and entering.

Before I can reply, he shoves the card at me. "On second thought, no. I'll go talk to him while you sneak the card inside through the back door."

"What? Why? I can do it," I argue. I'm not sure that I can, Nate's probably going to see right through me.

Cooper holds his hands up and refuses to take the card back. "Nope, you're the criminal now!"

I shake my head as he strides across the lot toward the station entrance, his long legs eating up the ground. While he has spent a lot of our time today flustering me, the time he's spent smiling and laughing is what stands out the most. He's not the same easygoing, slightly cocky guy he once was, but no one is the same as they were a decade ago, especially if they've been through what he has. He's only shared small pieces over the course of the tour, but it's been enough to paint a clear picture of what his life has been like.

Dedicating himself to football for his dad, staying close to home to help his mom, shouldering more responsibility to shield his sister, all completely unsurprising. He might have come off as an overconfident football player back then, but it didn't take long for me to see how much more he was. Sensitive, funny, kind, smart.

"God, he's so dreamy," a voice whispers in my ear just as Cooper steps into the station.

I shriek and spin around. Nate ducks just in time.

"Nate!" I unfist my hand and put it over my racing heart.

"Damn, Avery!" Nate says, laughing. "You nearly got me. Where'd you learn to throw a punch?"

"It's a good thing you're a freaking medic, you about gave me a heart attack," I tell him, ignoring the question. When your world changes in a single night, you learn self defense. You look over your shoulder. Also, you don't really talk about it.

"I thought you heard me, I wasn't exactly quiet," he replies, rubbing the back of his neck guiltily. Then he grins and cuts a glance toward the station. "Little distracted?"

I don't reply. Yes, I am a little distracted but I'm not about to admit it. Nate just grins wider at my silence. I glare back.

"So, I believe that's for me?" He nods to the thank you card I hold in a death grip in my left hand. At least I didn't try to punch him with it.

"Ugh," I groan. "Failed."

"I won't tell," he says, plucking it from my fingers.

"That might even be worse," I mutter. Without Kelsey, our sneak-attacks have been lacking.

The radio clipped to Nate's shoulder buzzes with static then Brian's voice comes through. "Water rescue, Rejection Rock. Two on."

Nate shakes his head. "High tide, gets 'em every time."

Another voice comes over the radio, using codes and beach path entry numbers, and Nate turns without another word as he listens intently.

"Stay safe!" I call after him as he jogs back toward the station.

He holds up the white envelope in response.

The big garage doors open and barely fifteen seconds later, two off-road trucks pull out, lights flashing.

"Well, that didn't go as planned," Cooper says, walking back across the lot. "And weren't we just up the rock? How did the tide come in so fast?"

I shrug. "It didn't, sometimes people just get surprised when they come back down and see the waves coming up the creek. Also, we were there like three hours ago."

Cooper looks at his watch. "I didn't realize what time it was. Does this mean we have to break for dinner?"

I can't help but laugh. My mom's beach house rules included always being back for dinner. I could spend all day with the summer kids, those of us whose families spent more time than not in Three Rocks every summer, but I had to come back to the house for dinner. I never minded the rule, in fact, many (most) afternoons I would have already separated myself from the group, but that week with Cooper, I hated it. I also hate the idea today.

"I think we can skip that rule today," I say, starting to walk across the large lot. "But I am hungry. Ready for the last stop on the tour?" I motion toward the cafe, which shares a parking lot with The Merc.

Cooper winces and my heart falls. Was he trying to insinuate he wanted to go our separate ways? Have I been the only one feeling whatever this is between us? I suddenly feel like Awkward Avery again, fumbling and inexperienced, never sure how to read the situation.

"Or we can conclude the tour early?" I ask, my steps faltering.

"Ave," Cooper says, stopping and waiting until I turn and look at him. "I was just disappointed that it was the last stop. I'd love to have dinner with you."

A warm flush spreads through my veins and I'm sure directly to my cheeks. I bite the corner of my lip to stop from smiling too hard. I really am my teenage self around him.

"So, if that rule doesn't exist anymore," Cooper says as we start walking again. "How about the phone one?"

The. Phone. One.

AKA one of my biggest regrets.

That first day, the day he didn't save me from Kevin, Cooper asked for my phone number. I told him that it wasn't really a thing here in Three Rocks, at least for us summer kids. It was more a "meet you back here in the morning!" sort of place, leftover from childhood's past. I wasn't a huge texter anyway, other than with Harper, and that first day I was still convinced he was just being a nice guy, saving me from Kevin, probably sent by his sister. Then, as the days went on, it felt like our thing. We were always together, other than dinner break, and I liked it that way. No screens to hide behind, just real Cooper. I liked real Cooper.

The last day, well, that day I was too scared. I was scared that it was too good, too fast, we were too young. I was scared that keeping in touch would derail my plans. Those got derailed anyway the second my words stopped flowing.

I'm still scared. But I think I'm more scared of missing this second chance that's been thrown our way.

"Also gone," I say.

"Pizza and finally getting your number," Cooper says as he pushes open the door, ushering me in with a hand on my low back. "I already know one of those things is worth the eleven year wait."

I'm momentarily distracted as we step inside the tiny cafe, the rich aroma of Sarah's secret sauce and melting cheeses rendering me speechless as always.

"Sit wherever!" Sarah calls from behind the counter, waving toward the dining area that's barely as big as my living room.

Before I can make a comment on the pizza definitely being worth the wait, Cooper drops his voice. "And as amazing as it smells in here, I don't mean the pizza."

I'd blame the flush creeping up my neck on the heat from the pizza oven but I'm a terrible liar. It's definitely from the man pulling out my chair for me.

Chapter Twelve
Avery

Blink, blink, blink. My cursor is once again taunting me. I should be working but an hour ago, that writing itch hit and I couldn't ignore it. As usual, as soon as I opened a new document, nothing. Not a thing. Just a blinking cursor, lukewarm coffee, and an itch I can't scratch.

I sigh and switch back over to my email. A note from Edward, my dad's assistant, catches my eye. It's just asking me to call and there's an attachment that looks like a new property to look at, which I ignore. I move on to appointment requests, including one from the corporation that owns a handful of businesses along the coast, from my favorite brewery to a hotel in Rock Beach. Interesting. Before I can contemplate why they'd be reaching out, my phone buzzes.

I eagerly reach for it, hoping it's Cooper. Logically, I know he's at work, shaping young minds, or at least trying to convince them to not practice TikTok dances in the middle of class, but I can't help but hope it's him.

Based on how quickly I'm becoming addicted to his texts, my teenage fear was valid. There's no way I would have done half the things I've done over the last decade if he would have been just a text away. I would have spent all my time swooning through a phone, just like I'm doing now.

None of that matters though because it's not him on the phone. There's a sense of dread when I see the name, but I slide the green button anyway.

"Hi, Dad," I answer tiredly. He's been pushing for me to come work out of the office during our calls this last week and I don't have the mental capacity for yet another argument right now.

"Ace! Evanston Orchards is going to be a steal, huh? Let's find another like that."

What? No. No, no, no. The one thing besides running that's kept me somewhat sane since Cooper showed up in town is Evanston Orchards. Lila might not have been my best friend growing up, but when we finally connected a handful of days ago, her story broke my emotionless robot heart. While I didn't grow up on a farm, living in Monitor Mills meant I heard the stories. Farm accidents were rare but always devastating. Amazingly, Lila's father is still alive, but he has a very long, expensive road to recovery in front of him.

"I thought we agreed that wasn't in their, or our, best interest and you were going to let me work with them on other options." I bite back the rest of my retort. I don't think I realized how badly I want to help Lila and her family until right now.

Like when I purchased The Town Mercantile, the potential with the business is there. Unlike The Merc, there's already a passionate owner behind the business, desperate to turn it around. They just need a little help.

"It's too good a deal to pass up," Dad replies, oblivious to the thinly veiled anger in my voice. I'm sure he was also oblivious to my excitement when I shared my plan. "Don't worry, I won't be going it alone. Bill Shapiro is stepping in."

Small. Freaking. Towns. Of course my dad is bringing Bill Shapiro, AKA his golf buddy, AKA my high school boyfriend's father, into this. I rub my forehead. Dad not having a second investor wasn't my concern, Lila's family was and still is my concern.

"I didn't realize you were in business with him as well," I reply much more calmly than I feel. I don't know where this anger is coming from, but I can't seem to curb it.

"*We* are," Dad corrects. "Bringing the boys on, too, remember?"

"Wait, what?" I would definitely recall a conversation about bringing on my ex boyfriend and his brother, right?

"Eli and Jordan," Dad says, like I don't know who he's talking about. "We talked about this. Their construction team? You can't still be mad at Jordan, it's been a decade."

I can hear the impatience in his voice, the same tone I associate with his and Mom's arguments. I don't want to argue with him, except...

One: We did not talk about this. Not one single time.

Two: I'm not still mad at Jordan. It's been a freaking decade and he's apologized multiple times. My "little book" more than proved him wrong.

Three: Now that I think about it, it was Dad that dubbed it my "little book," not my ex.

I take one of Tex's deep breaths. Unsurprisingly, it doesn't work. "Dad, is there something you need at the moment?"

I need out of this conversation.

"Just wondering when you're going to be moving into the office I had Edward clear out for you," he answers, solving the mystery as to why his assistant has been calling.

I look out my current office window at the tractor sitting at the edge of Cooper's lot. It showed up at the beginning of the week and hasn't moved off the flatbed trailer it was delivered on, but there it sits, mocking me. I lean forward and close the blinds. I don't know how I'm going to work in this office if my view is a constant reminder of Cooper, but I know for a fact I can't work in Dad's office either.

"I never agreed to that, Dad," I reply, keeping my voice level. "I think we've done just fine until this point with me working from here. I have my own clients here, my businesses are here, I'm not just going to drop everything."

"You can't tell me you enjoy doing wills and trusts for everyone in town," Dad scoffs. "This is your future, Avery. Our future."

"I enjoy my work," I say quietly. "All of it. My future is here."

It's not what I thought I'd be doing, but I do like it. Nice to know he thinks it's not worthwhile.

"Well, that's a disappointment. I really thought we were headed in the right direction. Now between the Evanston property and this..." He trails off with a sigh. "I thought that's why you brought Hadley on, to run your businesses there. You can't be making coffee, you're a lawyer."

Really? Hadley? She's only been my best friend for twenty years. Is he doing this on purpose? And although it's rare, I do still make coffee at The Merc some mornings and I love every second of it. The camaraderie with my employees, bantering with customers, sharing my town with tourists, it's exactly what I set out to do with The Merc.

"*Harper* does run things here and she does an amazing job. It doesn't change anything, though. Like we had discussed last week, I was working on Evanston Orchards, that was *my* deal. I saw an opportunity to help a family that has been in that community for generations, now-"

Before I can finish, Dad cuts me off.

"Bill just stepped in, I need to go. I'll have Edward send over the next few properties I have my eye on." He hangs up without a goodbye and my forehead hits my desk.

Was it really just a couple weeks ago I sat on the steps with Tex, thinking about how everything seemed to be falling into place? Telling her how Dad was really trying to work on our relationship? What happened to change that?

I sit up and scroll through my email to make sure I really didn't miss anything with Evanston Orchards. I don't find a single thing. Now what?

While I don't like how Dad just bulldozed his way through our conversation, I do see merit in his ideas and actions. Bill will be a good addition to our team and if Jordan and Eli work in construction, they could be a huge asset when it comes to some of these flips we've been looking at. It just would have been nice to be involved in the decision to bring all three of them on board.

I don't want to lose the progress we've made in our personal relationship, especially after listening to Cooper talk about his own dad, so do I brush off this conversation? On the other hand, I don't want to lose Evanston Orchards or worse, let Lila lose her family farm, which could be the case if I don't reel my dad in. And, apparently, Bill Shapiro.

Again: now what?

I try another of *Hadley's* deep breaths. Nope. Definitely doesn't work. I sit up and roll my shoulders, tipping my head from side to side to stretch my neck. Again, nothing.

I don't need a text from my best friend, I already know what I need. Run. Now.

***

"Delivery!" I call as I round the coffee counter and make my way to the back office. It's been a hellish couple days since that call with Dad and I need my best friend. Although, one glance at Tex and I'm wondering if she's had a worse week.

"Thanks," Tex says stiffly, barely looking up at me as she takes the pink mug from my hands. She sets the steaming hot tea on her desk along with the stack of mail I hand her and shuffles papers that definitely don't need to be shuffled. "How was your meeting?"

I frown at her robotic tone. "Good," I say slowly. "Basic estate stuff. Older couple just moved to town, that cottage a few down from The Glass House, with the green trim."

I sit down across from her, perching on the edge of the chair that has a shoe box full of rocks sitting on it. Colt must have been here recently.

She nods. "Uh huh." More shuffling papers.

"Everything okay?" I ask.

Even if this interaction was normal, she hasn't commented on my heels, so I already know the answer.

"I don't know, Aves, you tell me," she says, finally looking at me.

My stomach drops. "Wait, what?" What is she talking about?

"Your dad called the store. Said he couldn't find you and to let you know that y'all need to go over the new contract with Bill Shapiro before you can move forward on the second property. Anything you'd like to share?" She leans back in her chair and crosses her arms.

Shit. I never take my phone to client meetings, a fact my father knows. I close my eyes. It's not his fault. It's mine. I should have told her months ago.

"I just-" I start, but she cuts me off.

"I might not like him, I might hate how he's treated you, but I love you. I will always support you." A single tear tracks down her cheek and guilt washes over me.

"I just, I want you to be proud of me, you know? And I didn't think you would be for this. I know how you feel about him. But he's trying. I'm trying. I think? I don't know. It's a little bit of a mess right now. Maybe a lot of a mess." I bite the inside of my cheek.

It's feeling like a lot. A lot of what I don't want to be a part of. Yesterday was what Tex would dub a shit show, just a total nightmare of a day. Meeting after meeting, none of which were necessary, it was like Dad was trying to strongarm me into agreeing to his terms. He might have given me Evanston Orchards, but he made everything else a hundred times worse.

Finally, at 4:30 p.m. when my phone buzzed with a call from Edward, I'm sure another attempt from my father to convince me to reconsider the two properties I turned down, I closed my laptop, put my phone on Do Not Disturb, and laced up my running shoes.

A mess. A freaking mess. At least I've run every day this week, right?

"I'm always proud of you, Aves," she says quietly. "And I'm sorry I'm a hormonal mess lately, but I just, I just worry about you. But I'm *always*, always proud of you."

"Even if I'm working with my dad?" I ask.

"If it's something you want to do, yes." It looks like she wants to say something else, but she bites her lip instead.

I let her words roll around. Do I want to, though?

I *do* want to present Lila with the plan I set up for her family's orchards, my one win of the week, but do I want more than that? I don't know anymore. I wanted the challenge of the job, I wanted the chance to salvage my relationship with my father. Right now, it feels like the challenge isn't the job, it's the relationship.

Does my love for building businesses outweigh the stress? If this summer with Tex has taught me anything, it's that the moments in between work count. Lately, in between work I'm running away from work one mile at a time. Is that what I want?

I want more days like today. My meeting this morning in town? Easy, but enjoyable. I spent an hour helping a hard-working couple lay out their future. The hour I'll spend cleaning a rental tonight while Jessie has a back-to-school night with Colt? Honestly, I think I'm looking forward to it.

Maybe it doesn't always have to be more work, harder work, more stressful work. It's still work. It's still worthwhile. And sometimes, I don't want to work. I want to enjoy the work I've already put in.

With that in mind, I bring my eyes back to meet Tex's. "You know what I want to do?" I ask her.

"What's that?" She tilts her head.

"Ditch work and go to the beach. You in?" I ask.

"I don't know if I can." She waves her hand around, indicating the papers she's been shuffling and the sticky note to-do lists on the wall next to us. "My boss is a real hardass."

Her lip twitches and I burst into laughter. "I'm sorry, Harper. I really am," I tell her once we both stop laughing.

"Go change out of your sexy work clothes and let's go to the beach," she says, waving me off with a smile.

Fifteen minutes later, we're on the beach, Zero happily running ahead of us, chasing seafoam and seagulls.

"Nice beanie," Tex says, eyeing my headwear with a smirk. Apparently she finally figured out the origin story of my favorite green beanie.

"It was by the door," I say, avoiding eye contact and shrugging.

I'm not lying, it *was* by the door, but there were at least three other beanies by the door as well. I definitely chose this one because Cooper's been busy all week and I miss him.

I miss him. He's here and I miss him more than I did when he wasn't.

I sneak a look at my phone and smile when I see his name.

Coop:
Are you sure?

I type out a quick reply. While flattered he asked, there's no way I can help with the new creative writing club at his school.

Ave:
I haven't been a writer in years. Unless the kids need a lesson on writer's block, I'm not the one.

    His response is immediate. It must be lunch period for him.

Coop:
I'll hold out hope.

    I shake my head. There's no hope, but the fact that he thinks there is makes me smile.

    "You still owe me the story of your summer love," Tex says, bumping her shoulder into mine as I pocket my phone.

    I think back to last weekend, how easy it was to spend nearly an entire day with Cooper. How every moment with him feels charged, but also so natural, so easy, just like before. And now, having had time to think, to overanalyze, it kind of scares the hell out of me.

    "Honestly, it feels a lot like right now," I tell her.

    Unlike work, it feels like a lot of something I want more of. An alarming amount more.

    "Why do you make 'a lot' sound like a bad thing?" she asks, easily reading my tone. "Is this the spiral portion of the Triple Threat Trio?"

    Yes, yes it is.

    "I haven't dated anyone since law school! And we both know how that went. I like my life. I like it a lot! I like my cabin in the woods, I like having you here and our little routines. I like my quiet life. Then he shows up and I feel like a teenager all over again. I hated being a teenager! I'm giddy, I'm awkward and unsure, but it's also like, we just fit together. Which is weird, because we're opposites. He played college football. Football, Harp," I say with an exaggerated sigh.

    "Aves, college is over. Been over for a while now. And I don't think throwing a football really defines someone," she says patiently, having dealt with my spirals for years.

    "You know what I mean! He was like Mr. Popular, the quarterback, probably had girls falling all over him. And I'm just me.

The nerdy runner, the failing writer." I hear how ridiculous my words are as I say them. This is definitely me spiraling, but they also feel real.

"I'm going to murder him," Tex mutters.

"For playing football?" Didn't she just say that wasn't a big deal?

"Not Cooper," she replies immediately. "I like him. I like him a lot, actually. I sometimes, occasionally, maybe a lot of times want to murder the man that made you think like this, like you're not enough or that you need to change. He's been doing that shit for decades and I'm done with that bullshit.

"I'm going to respect that you're working on your relationship with your dad, I am, but Aves, 'just you' is amazing. You're a badass. Just a runner? You ran a marathon in, what, middle school or something? Failing writer? Bullshit. You were a best-selling author before we even graduated high school. You went on to graduate from college early, you got into law school at fucking Stanford, all the while investing your book money until you could buy your own business. 'Just you' didn't manifest this life you built, 'just you' badass'ed your way here. So, full stop on that line of thinking."

I'm silent. I don't know what to say. I know I did all those things, I'm proud of every one of them, but sometimes they don't feel like enough.

"But yes, you were a little awkward as a teenager, I'll give you that," Tex adds with a laugh.

I snort. Awkwardly snort, to be exact. "Still am, obviously. But like, honestly, is what I feel with him because of before? Our past? Or is it real? What do I even say? Do?" I groan. "God, why am I the way that I am?"

Zero circles around us, probably sensing my distress, and nudges my hand for a pet. She takes off in a run then looks back, probably wondering why we aren't chasing her like Colt does.

"I vote you say fuck it," Tex says. "And just go for it."

"Harper! Really?" I ask in disbelief. "That's your advice? In what world has that *ever* been how I handle anything in life?"

"Yep." She pops the 'p' sound at the end. "That's all I got."

"Wow, okay, well thanks?" I laugh. "What would I do without you?"

"Probably fall in love with a quarterback when you're fifteen and pine after him for a dozen years," she answers.

"I didn't pine!" I might have pined a little bit.

"Yearn? Agonize? Brood?" Tex lists.

"What are you, a thesaurus?" I mutter. "I didn't do any of those things."

"Wow, I thought we were past the lying, I thought we worked that out back at The Merc." Tex whistles for Zero, who circles back again, this time nosing Tex's hand for pets.

"I'm sorry I lied," I say quietly. "I wanted to tell you so many times."

"Fuck it," she says with a shrug.

I huff a laugh.

Fuck it, indeed.

Chapter Thirteen
Avery
(before)

"Hi," Cooper says, grinning broadly when I jog down the steps. His smile disappears quickly. "You okay?"

"Yeah, sorry, just," I start, then think better of it. He doesn't want to hear about my argument with Dad. "It's nothing."

I step past him and start down the path, hoping to avoid more questions. I don't need another person telling me that I shouldn't get upset so easily, especially about something like writing.

Cooper catches up and grabs my hand, quickly releasing it when I stop and turn toward him.

"Are you sure?" he asks, his dark eyes searching mine.

I just nod. "I'm sure."

I can tell by his expression that he knows I'm lying. Instead of questioning me though, he just gently tugs the bag from my shoulder and slings it over his own.

"Okay," he says.

Wordlessly, we fall in step next to each other and make our way toward the beach, carefully picking our way down the rocks. Once our feet hit the warm sand, he threads our fingers together and leads me up the beach. I study his profile as we walk. Dark hair, dark eyes, and a suspicious smile playing on his lips. He must feel my gaze because he glances over.

"What?" he asks.

"Where are we going?" I ask in reply. We've walked further than usual, away from the crowds that spill north from the creek.

"Do you trust me?" he asks, giving me that easy smile that could probably convince me to do a lot of things I normally wouldn't. Like trust someone I just met.

"Um, yeah?" I can't help the question in my voice but I think I do trust him. No, I definitely do.

Suddenly, without warning, he stops. He lays our towels down carefully along the large riprap rocks, so close that they're touching, and sets my bag on the corner. I shift my weight and look up and down the beach. He's definitely up to something, he has some sort of plan. Is this payback for the eight-mile run? He shoots me another grin and my stomach drops.

"Well, are you ready?" he asks, eyebrow raised.

"Uh..." I'm not sure I am. Usually I'm up for any challenge, even a (short) dip in the freezing cold ocean, but today? Today I'm not. I don't want to run eight miles, I don't want to climb any rock, I don't want to play football with little kids. I **do** want to spend the afternoon with Coop, though, so I nod. "I'm ready."

Cooper sinks down onto a towel, leans his back against the rocks, and stretches his long legs out in front of him. "And now we relax."

"Wait, what?" I ask as I sit down next to him. I tuck my feet under myself and sit cross-legged. There has to be more to his plan. "That's it?"

"Well, no," he says, pulling a bright green spiral notebook out of the extra towel folded next to him. "You're going to write." He pulls a pen from between the pages and holds both out to me.

"What?" I just stare at him in shock.

"You're going to write?" His voice rises into a question.

"You got me a notebook?" I ask incredulously. "And a pen?"

I cautiously take both from him, running my fingers over the glossy cover. It's just a simple spiral notebook, but it's also not. It's more.

Cooper looks embarrassed, there's a slight flush on his cheeks that I haven't seen before. "Just write, Ave."

How did he know? I haven't said a word about my writing to him. I swallow down the lump in my throat and blink back tears. I've only known him a few days and yet, he **sees** me.

"But..." I don't have words to say.

"I saw you writing the day before I met you and you were writing right before we met. You left your notebook on the deck yesterday afternoon when we left for the creek. After dinner last night you were writing on the beach while you waited for me. You stop every time I show up but I know it's important to you. I can tell. So I'll read my book. You write." He pulls a worn paperback from his towel and opens it to a dog-eared page, effectively shutting me out, even as I stare at him in shock.

Do I just...write?

"Just write, Ave," he says softly without taking his eyes off his book.

So, I write.

Cooper reads, his hat pulled down low against the bright sun above.

I write. The echo of my father's voice quiets as the scratch of my pen on the paper replaces his angry words.

Cooper stretches out, his book forgotten beside him.

I write. The weight on my shoulders lifts with every sentence, every paragraph, every turn of a page.

Cooper's hand drifts toward my calf as he rolls to his side, then settles over my ankle, warm on my skin.

I write. The knot in my chest loosens as the story within my fantasy world consumes me.

Cooper murmurs in his sleep, his thumb lazily tracing circles on my skin.

I write. The-

Cooper jolts awake, his hand tightening around my ankle. My pen leaves a strike against the page as I startle right along with him.

"Avery?" His eyes are wild until they land on mine. He sighs. "You're still here."

His voice is groggy with sleep, deeper than usual, and sends shivers racing up my spine, matching my racing heart.

Although the racing heart is probably due to the jump scare and death grip on my ankle.

I don't know what to say, so I just smile at his disheveled appearance. He shakes his head, like he's trying to rid himself of whatever dream startled him awake.

With a laugh, he jumps to his feet. "What are you waiting for? Let's go!" *He takes off in a sprint toward the ocean, tossing his shirt on the sand as he runs.*

I shake my head. I knew he'd convince me to do something stupid. I shove my new pen and my new notebook under my towel, tug off my shirt, and chase after him.

I splash through the waves and Cooper catches my hand in his. His grip tightens as we jump into the oncoming waves, moving deeper and deeper, until the water crashes over us. I'm immediately breathless, the air taken from my lungs by the cold, but Cooper just turns toward me and laughs.

I have a feeling jumping in the ocean isn't the dumbest thing Cooper will convince me to do.

Chapter Fourteen
Cooper

"At least meet with him, Coop," Megan says, her voice sounding far away.

"I can't build a house there, Meg," I repeat.

"I don't understand. You're just going to put everything on hold because there's a girl you met when you were a dumbass teenager?" I swear I hear Zoe's voice in the background.

This is not a conversation I'd like to have at work but Megan and I haven't talked since she left for the airport and I have ten minutes before my next class will start filtering in. This week is kicking my ass and I'm unsure why I thought my sister would help, but I had to talk this through with someone and she's the only one I thought might understand. I was wrong.

"She's the one, Meg. She's the reason no one else lasted. Why I barely even tried with anyone else. You were right, I never gave my heart to anyone, but it wasn't because I didn't want to take a risk. It was because she already had it."

There's rustling before Megan replies. "I swear you just said she's *The One*," Megan says, her voice clear. "I stopped doing yoga, please repeat that." That explains Zoe's voice.

"She's my dream girl. Dream Girl, Meg, capitalized. All those offhand comments, they weren't offhand. They were her." They *are* her.

Every time Megan asked what was wrong with whatever girl she was trying to set me up with, from age twenty until Brooke, I told her that whoever it was wasn't my Dream Girl. I might not have said a name, but there was a very clear person in my mind during every conversation.

"I don't think I'm the one to talk about this with," Megan says after a pause. "I'm sorry. I just, I think being back here, the house thing…it all hit me again, you know? Tyler. What he did. I should have stayed in Oregon."

"I'm sorry, Meggy." Meg and I are close, always have been, and I really did want to murder Tyler. "We don't have to talk about this at all. How's Dad?"

"You already know he's fine," Megan replies, blowing out a breath. "And it's okay, we can talk about it. I just needed a second. I'm okay, I promise. It's just, I just dove in so fast with Ty, I wish I would have spent a little more time getting to know him. So, maybe get to know the adult version of your dream girl. You moved across the country for her, the least you can do is take some time and get to know her."

"So logical," I say with a sigh, knowing she's probably right, as usual. "Although that didn't really work out with Brooke."

Meg and Brooke had been best friends since they were roommates freshman year of college. I'd known her for years, she'd spent holidays with our family, hell, our parents had become friends.

"True. I like Avery. Obviously. I can see how she'd be a good match for you and this would be like, an epic love story, like a romance book love story, which you know I love. Or used to love. But don't throw away your plans, either. She could be completely different than you remember, or, you know, having an emotional affair with her coworker."

"Meg…" I trail off, unsure what else to say. I've said it all before and I don't think I should swear in my classroom, even if students aren't present.

"I'm fine, Cooper, I promise," she says.

"Okay, I'll get to know her. See if Teenage Cooper really was a dumbass." I glance toward the classroom door. Does that count as swearing?

"Teenage Cooper was definitely a dumbass," Megan says, laughing. "God, you were so mopey for months after our trip. And here I thought it was because I was going off to college. But no, you were pining away after your summer fling."

"I wasn't mopey," I say, knowing full-well that I was one hundred percent mopey.

"Well, if this works out for you, this is my new standard. A man that would move across the country for just the idea of me." Megan sighs. "You know what? Don't listen to my advice. Or do. I don't fucking know."

"Unfortunately I don't know either," I reply.

But I think I have an idea.

***

I pause before stepping onto the deck. I haven't been to this exact spot in eleven years and the moment isn't lost on me. Despite an actual (narrow, winding) road leading up here and the immaculate cabin this expansive outdoor living space is attached to, the trees towering above make it feel just as secluded as it was back then. The view? Just as breathtaking. The woman offering me a small smile? Even more so.

"Hi," Avery says quietly. She's wrapped in a blanket, a glass of red wine on the table next to her. She tilts her head to the chair next to hers, a silent invitation to sit.

I keep the small package hidden behind me as I sink down onto the oversized rocking chair. "Hey. Sorry I'm late, my meeting ran long. Did I miss our run?"

I'd been looking forward to it all day. We've both been busy all week and, as much as I've enjoyed my new phone privileges, texting isn't the same as hearing her voice. It's not sitting next to her on the beach, it's not scrambling up a crumbling rock after her, it's not watching her eyes light up when a gigantic pizza is set in front of her. It's not watching her laugh as Colt hugs her legs, it's not seeing her bite the inside of her cheek as a flush creeps up her neck.

Just sitting next to her right now has me breathing deeper, hoping for a hint of strawberry, the stress of the work day fading away.

"Sorry, I just...." She trails off and finally brings her gaze to mine. Her gray eyes are cloudy and distant. We might not have spent much more than a week together, but I know that look. I hate that look.

"You okay?" I ask, already knowing the answer.

"It's nothing." She tugs the blanket tighter around her shoulders, like she's using it as a shield, not just against the cool evening air, but against whatever is bothering her.

It's always felt like I remembered every single second of our week together, now I'm reliving it, memory by memory.

"Well, are you ready?" I ask, wondering how long it will take for her to realize what's happening.

"Ready to run? Can't say I am." She holds up her wine glass and winces. "I'm sorry, I should have at least texted to let you know I'm bailing."

"Not what I meant." I slowly bring the small brown paper-wrapped gift from behind my back and hold it up.

"You didn't," she gasps. Her eyes dart from the present to meet mine before settling back on the gift in my hand.

"Open it."

She takes the gift and carefully tugs on the corner, unwrapping it slowly. Her cheeks pinken slightly when a flash of green appears. "But I don't write anymore."

"I couldn't resist," I say sheepishly. I don't mention the Google searches I've done this week. "I thought maybe, just in case?"

"I wish." She shakes her head as she runs a finger over the cover of the notebook. "I know we were supposed to run, but do you want to come in? I was going to make a Mediterranean quinoa salad for dinner."

"That sounds amazing," I tell her. It wasn't about the run, anyway. It was about seeing her. "But what if I make you a deal?"

"You're taking my invitation as an opportunity to bargain?"

"Hear me out," I tell her. "Please."

She stands and stretches before plucking her wine glass off the table. She motions for me to follow as she walks through a door hidden in the middle of what looks like an entire wall of glass. I pause as I carefully close the door, taking in the panoramic view one more time. The trees perfectly frame the sun as it sinks lower toward the horizon, brilliant bursts of color filtering through their swaying boughs.

"Ave, this is amazing," I say, turning to face her. She smiles, obviously pleased at my reaction, as she throws her blanket over the back of the couch.

She moves into the kitchen and sets the notebook and her wine glass on the island and starts pulling ingredients from the fridge and pantry.

"My thirteen-year-old self had the right idea, wanting to live here," she says as she reaches up to take a gleaming copper pot from a rack hanging above the island. "I can't tell you how many people told me I was making a mistake moving here, but I knew it'd be worth it."

"Definitely worth it, it's incredible. And this kitchen…" I trail off as I run my hand along the concrete counter. "This kitchen makes me want to bargain even more."

Avery raises an eyebrow. "Let's hear it."

I step forward and take the pot from her hand. "I love to cook and my current kitchen, while perfect for the time being, isn't this." I motion around us. The kitchen really is amazing. "So what if I make us dinner while you write?"

Her expression falls along with her gaze. "I meant what I said. I don't write anymore."

"But do you ever *want* to write?" I ask, watching her carefully.

"I always want to. It's always there. But then it's not. I've tried." She shifts on her feet, unwilling to look at me.

I don't need her to look up. I can see her frustration clearly. "Lucky for you, you have a teacher here to help."

"A science teacher," she says, finally raising her eyes. Amusement flickers. "For preteens."

"Let's call it an experiment, then," I say, watching her lips tip up at my quick reply. "A lab, which is always my favorite lesson to teach. Also, I'd like to point out that some of them are actual teenagers, not just preteens."

Her small smile gives me hope, now I just have to hope my idea actually works. One (or two or five) Google searches on writer's block doesn't make me an expert, but I can close my eyes and see her at fifteen, the way her hand flew across the page, the way she lit up when she finally told me what she had written, and I can't *not* try.

She gives me an unreadable look, then shrugs. "Fuck it."

"Fuck it?" This is not the Avery I know.

"Fuck it," she confirms. "It's my new thing. What's there to lose?"

I suddenly feel like there's a lot to lose but I give her the most confident smile I can muster and rack my brain. It comes up blank. I can't remember a single answer or idea Google gave me.

Avery perches on the edge of a stool and looks at me expectantly.

Fuck it, I'll start at the beginning.

"Welcome to seventh grade then. First assignment, which I gave my students their first week: write three things I should know about you, two things I should try here in my new town, and one thing you like about school. Or, in this case, writing." Before she can ask any questions, I move to the sink and wash my hands.

When I turn back around, she's tapping her pen on the paper. Not writing.

"Just keep it simple. I had one kid list his answers on a sticky note. They can be anything, from your favorite color, which I already know, to why this isn't that strawberry lotion you used to use all the time," I say, tapping the bottle of lotion next to the soap that is definitely not the same one that's sold at The Merc, the source of my emotional turmoil that first day.

"I use strawberry shamp-"

"Nope," I cut her off. "Pen to paper. Write it."

Her gray eyes lock on mine. There's no amusement flickering in her expression now, not even hope. Just hesitation. Fear. "But-"

"Just write, Ave," I say softly.

She closes her eyes, shutting me out. Her shoulders rise and fall slowly, then she opens her eyes and taps the notebook again.

As hard as it is, I turn around. I busy myself in her kitchen, starting the quinoa on the stove, slicing peppers and cucumbers. Soon, the sound of her pen on paper blends with the sound of my chopping. I look over my shoulder and catch her eye. She smiles.

I nearly slice off my finger.

"This is ridiculous," she says, her smile growing.

I turn around to face her and lean back against the counter. Even with my eyes on hers, I can see half the page is filled with her tidy handwriting. "But you're writing."

"It's ridiculous *and* I'm writing."

What is actually ridiculous is how happy seeing her pen return to the paper makes me. I don't ask to see it, I don't ask what she's written, I just watch as she starts writing again, then I force myself to turn around and finish making our dinner.

***

"Hey, Brofessor!" Micah Long calls, once again catching me in the parking lot after school.

"What can I help you with, Micah?" I ask.

"Thanks for partnering me with Sadie," he says a little breathlessly. He shakes his hair out of his face, reminding me of the "alpaca hair" reel that was going around for a while. "You're her favorite teacher."

I laugh. "Hers, not yours?"

"Can you like, put in a good word? Tell her I'm a good student maybe?" he asks hopefully.

I sigh. This kid. He reminds me a little too much of a younger me, chasing after the girl that's well out of my league. The one I'm still chasing. I soften my tone. "I think you just need to put in the effort, Micah. She wants an 'A' so there's your first chance."

Yes, I am absolutely going to use his crush on the star student to encourage him to work hard in school. Sue me.

"So, like, just work on the project with her?" he asks, obviously doubting this plan.

"Well, yeah, that is the assignment," I tell him, hiding my smile. "But you can also use that time to get to know her. See if you have anything in common."

Huh, now I'm doling out Megan's advice to unsuspecting seventh graders.

"And then what?"

"Well, since you're what, thirteen years old, I'm thinking you just start by being her friend. All good relationships are built on friendship, trust, and honesty." That's a good thing to tell the kid, right?

"And get friend-zoned?" he asks incredulously. "Bruh."

How do seventh graders even know about the friendzone? Am I putting myself in the friendzone with Avery? After dinner last night I quickly made my exit, hoping that she'd keep writing. Now I'm just hoping that wasn't a mistake.

"Micah, you're in seventh grade, you've got some time, just start with getting to know her," I tell him.

"I'm going to marry her someday," he says seriously. "So, if this doesn't work, then what?"

I am *not* qualified in the slightest to be having this conversation. 1. Are teachers supposed to be giving this kind of advice? 2. This kid is living my life and I obviously have no idea what I'm doing. I almost lost a finger last night over a smile.

"Well, again, I'd say you've got more than enough time. All you can do right now is get to know her, show her that you're a good human and that you listen to her," I tell him, hoping I'm saying the right things and that his parents aren't going to be speaking with Principal Giddings first thing Monday morning. "And maybe work on that 'A' on your project."

Micah nods, shoving his hair out of his face with his hand. Suddenly, he freezes. His eyes widen at something behind me and I can see panic taking hold.

"Goodbye, Mr. Miller," Sadie says brightly as she walks past us.

"Have a good night, Sadie," I say as Micah gapes, his mouth moving but no words coming out.

"Bye, Micah, I hope you have a good weekend," Sadie adds shyly over her shoulder.

"Bye," Micah squeaks out, then coughs to clear his throat. "Bye, Sadie."

"Also, maybe work on speaking in her presence," I tell him when Sadie's out of earshot, clapping him on the shoulder.

"Thanks, Mr. Miller," Micah says, using my real name for the first time.

Now I feel guilty. Great.

"Hey, just ask her questions, then *listen* when she answers. Really listen, not like you listen to me in class. Focus on what she's saying, learn what matters to her. But remember that you're there to work on the project, so put most of your focus on that," I tell him. "She'll appreciate that."

"Yeah, thanks, see you in class," Micah says, looking hopeful now that he has clear instructions for his project. The get-the-girl project, not that actual class assignment.

Unfortunately there aren't clear instructions for my own get-the-girl project. The Friendzone it is. And if it doesn't work? I'll go back to Kansas City with Meg, join her in her misery.

Chapter Fifteen
Avery

"The lives of two people are forever changed when they engage in a weekend-long affair."

The writing prompt that's been taunting me. And taunting me. And taunting me.

I still don't see a weekend-long affair when I read this. I see a week-long summer fling. A fling that wasn't just a fling. One that was so much more. One that forever changed me.

I tap my pen on my notebook.

What did Tex say?

"Nice feelings journal."

No, not that. I mean, yes, she did say that as soon as she saw the green notebook on the coffee table during our weekly meeting. But on the beach, what did she say?

"Fuck it."

It worked that very night, the seventh-grade assignment. One word at a time, I wrote. I did it.

I tap my pen again and close my eyes.

"The lives of two people are forever changed when they engage in a weekend-long affair."

I can't see an affair. I just can't. Instead, I see teenage Cooper smirking at me as he turns his hat backward. I see him napping on a towel next to me, the sun warming his skin. I see him running down the beach toward the waves. I hear him whispering that we're meant to be.

What if I wrote it? All of it. What if I said "fuck it" and put it on paper.

"What was that sigh?"

I look up from my notebook and find Cooper studying me closely from the other end of the couch.

He showed up after work for our run, his eyes lighting up when he saw my scribbled words in the open notebook sitting on my kitchen island. He's been sending me slightly (more like really) ridiculous assignments every day but never asks if I actually write.

I do. I haven't written more than a few pages at a time, but every day, I write. There's no cursor blinking at me, just a pen on paper, and it's been *fun*.

I've written a "recipe blog" for the special hot chocolate that Colt orders at The Merc as well as a newscaster-style report on my favorite Three Rocks community event and a trail guide for my favorite hike. I've written a running haiku, a greeting card, and, to Tex's delight, one journal entry…but with instructions to write it as if I was thirteen years old.

"Working on your Strava post?" he asks teasingly.

Even my Strava posts are now a writing assignment.

I smile but shake my head. "Just caught on a thought," I tell him, absolutely unwilling to admit what I was really thinking. "How's grading?"

"You were right. Better view up here," he replies. He squeezes my calf, then casually slides his hand down and leaves it wrapped around my ankle. He continues to work on his laptop, eyes moving left to right as he reads his students' work, oblivious to the pounding of my heart.

This. This is exactly what I pictured when I invited him to work from my living room. Me, tucked into my corner, sitting sideways, sneaking glances at his profile. Although "invited" might not be the right term. That implies I asked him to join me. What really happened is I blurted out "stay" in such a rush that he had to ask me to repeat myself. Instead of gathering myself like the adult I am and inviting him to spend the evening with me, I waved my arm around the living room. So awkward.

"You're blushing," Cooper says, running his thumb along the inside of my ankle.

I bite the inside of my cheek, wondering what he'd think if I told him the prompt scrawled in the notebook that sits in my lap. Would his mind be drawn to the same place as mine? To our unwritten and unspoken past, the subject we've both been avoiding. Would he shoot me his cocky smile? Or would it be that look, the one where his dark eyes see too much?

"Just thinking," I reply, my eyes glued to his hand that's moving back up my calf.

He pulls his hand back. "Sorry," he says, clenching his jaw as he turns his focus to his laptop.

I wiggle my toes under his thigh to get his attention. When he finally looks at me, it's that look. The one that sees too much. My breath catches.

"I'm not," I whisper.

His jaw relaxes and his hand snakes around my ankle once again, thumb lightly rubbing above the joint.

Fuck it. I might not be able to see that writing prompt, but I can see something else. It's all I see.

So I write our past, one sun-soaked day at a time.

Cooper works, his hand still on my ankle.

I start writing our present, the complicated yet very uncomplicated rhythm we've fallen into.

Cooper works, shooting me a smile every time I pause.

I tap my pen and think about our future, wondering if I can really write what I hope is meant to be.

***

Monday. Freaking Monday. I drag my eyes from my notebook to my buzzing phone. I don't want to answer. I want to live in the weekend bubble.

Tex, Zero, and I's morning walk, the fog lifting as the sun rose over the hills to the east. Cooper delivering hot chocolate and lunch, my toes tucked under his thigh on the couch, his hand on my leg. Dinner with Tex and West before a much-needed BFF sleepover complete with popcorn and gummy bears.

The morning run, Cooper's long legs keeping pace with mine as I wished I ate a few less gummy bears the night before. Hiking to the old covered bridge with Zoe and Lucas, Cooper's look of astonishment as we rounded the last bend, the waterfall finally coming into view.

Stepping in to close The Merc when Katie didn't feel well. The comfort and quiet of the dark store where I spent so many hours, the light from the fire station flickering on, Nate's silhouette giving him away as he waited for me to walk to my car as I looked over my shoulder, the nervous habit that never goes away.

But the weekend is over. It's Monday.

I stare at my phone, still not answering. I need to answer. I need to have a real, honest conversation with him, I know I do, but-

Fuck it. No excuses. It's time.

"Dad, hi," I answer. "I've been meaning to call."

"Hi, Avery," he replies stiffly. "I think I owe you an apology."

If I wasn't firmly planted in my office chair, I'd fall over. So I wasn't lying to Tex, Dad *is* trying. He's never been great at apologies which makes this even more shocking.

"Alright," I say carefully. Hopefully.

"I'm sorry for last week."

I take a breath before responding. Does he even know why I was upset last week? What about the week before?

"And the week before," he adds, like he can read my mind.

I take another deep breath. This is a start, and after listening to Cooper talk about his own dad, it feels like I should make the most of this opportunity.

"Okay," I say slowly, trying to buy time to gather my thoughts.

I know this is my chance, the time for honesty, if we both want to move forward. Anxiety builds, though. What if he's just placating me with a weak apology, like he did for so many years with Mom?

"Avery?" Dad says my name like a question.

I can hear Tex's voice once again. *Fuck it.*

"Thank you for your apology," I start slowly, still thinking. "But I think I need to be clear on what I want and need as we move forward."

I hate the hitch in my voice but I actually said it. Or started to say it. I hate the silence on the other end, too. Is this going to be the end of our relationship? I clear my throat.

"I'm going to help the Evanston family maintain ownership of their property and their business. Lila and her brother have worked on that farm since they were kids. They know it better than anyone. I don't want to be a part of any future investments that tear something apart, I want to build on the foundations already in place if at all possible."

Silence. I force myself to continue.

"Also, I'm not moving back to the valley. I don't want the office and I never agreed to that in the first place. I'm staying here. This is where my life is, including the business I successfully rebuilt, just like I want to do with Evanston Orchards. This is where my best friend lives, where my clients are. This is where I'm happy."

Still only silence.

Fuck it.

"I'm interested to hear what you have in mind with all three Shapiros, but again, adding team members isn't something I've agreed to be a part of. I won't overextend myself in any way, shape, or form. I told you from the beginning that this is part-time for me."

The only reason I know Dad's still on the line is a cough, followed by him clearing his throat. Have I ever stood up to him in this way? Set my own boundaries?

"Well, Ace, I'm sorry you feel that way," Dad says, the childhood nickname making my heart clench. I brace for whatever comes next. "I'd love to have you here, working with me, side-by-side, but I appreciate your honesty. As I always say, the person with the most information comes out on top. So thank you for telling me. I think we can continue as we have been and I'm willing to bring Bill in regarding the Evanston deal if you need additional support. See what we can do."

"What?" Again, it's a good thing I'm sitting down.

"And Eli turned down my offer for him and Jordan."

I think I'm too shocked to say anything else. Dad *is* trying. Maybe this *will* work. Maybe I can have it all: my life here *and* a relationship with him.

Where else can I apply this new fuck it theory?

***

Everywhere. I sprinkle the Fuck It Theory everywhere. Yep, it deserves capitalization.

That race I kept coming up with excuses not to run? The confirmation email is sitting in my inbox. I work a couple shifts at The Merc, just because I want to, even though it means late nights catching up on everything else. Instead of taking a meeting with the company that owns half the hotels in Rock Beach, I refer them to a law firm in Tillamook, only to find out they didn't want my legal advice, they want my store. Maybe that should be filed under the Fuck That, because no way in hell I'm selling.

The only part of my life in which I haven't sprinkled this theory? Cooper. Why? Because, much like I was a decade ago, I'm a chicken.

I've had chances. Many, in fact.

As he laced up his running shoes, declaring himself my training partner for the ultramarathon, he asked where else I was going to apply my theory. Instead of throwing myself at him, I mumbled something about The Merc.

The Merc? No. Nothing is changing there.

He just gave me a look that told me he knew that was bullshit and asked how many miles were on the training plan, completely unfazed by my obvious lie.

My next chance was when I stopped by the fire station to talk to Brian about the winter community events Tex (and my new Fuck It Theory) suggested. Cooper had just finished working out with Nate and offered to walk me home. My brain went blank the second he turned his hat backward. He suddenly looked every inch the quarterback I met all those years ago and I was every inch fifteen-year-old Awkward Avery. Nate couldn't hide his wince when I blurted out that I had a meeting and bolted out of the station without looking back.

Last night, when he sat on the couch working while I stared at my notebook, it was the perfect chance. I wouldn't have had to say a word, I could have just handed him the notebook that's now filled with our story.

It's all there. Past, present, future.

But did I take the opportunity? Nope. We stay stuck in this friends-with-PG-leg-touching benefits rut, neither of us willing to make the next move.

Tonight, that changes.

I send the last work email of the day and close my laptop. Beside it, my phone lights up.

Tex:
Gonna chicken out again?

I laugh. What would I do without her?
Probably chicken out.
But not tonight.
An engine growls outside my window, startling me before I can reply. Very few people drive up here. Confused, I open the blinds.
I fully admit I've been on some sort of endorphin high with all of these Fuck It decisions this week, but now, as I watch the tractor disappear down the narrow road, my hands shake as adrenaline courses through my veins for a different reason.
I skip the first two steps of my Triple Threat Trio and go straight to spiral.
Cooper's leaving.

124

Chapter Sixteen
Cooper
(before)

"Not much farther," Avery calls over her shoulder, gracefully navigating the steep, overgrown tsunami evacuation trail.

"I swear you said that on the death run the other day," I joke as I trip over yet another tree root.

She glances back and I smile. I wonder if she knows I'd follow her anywhere.

"There's also a tsunami trail up North Road," she says, slowing down slightly just as the trail finally levels out. "But this one gets us up higher. And it's further from town. Branch!"

I duck just in time. "I take it the goal is to be further from town?" I ask as I straighten back up.

She stops so abruptly I nearly run into her.

"And this view," she says. She motions over my shoulder but I can't tear my eyes away from her to see what view she's talking about.

No matter what she sees, the endless ocean that has left me speechless all week or the giant pillars of rocks crumbling along the coastline, it's nowhere near as breathtaking as what's in front of me.

Avery's cheeks are flushed from the exertion of the climb and her chest rises as she takes a deep breath, inhaling the sea breeze that mixes with the giant evergreens surrounding us. Little tendrils of hair blow in the breeze, framing the slightly crooked smile that slowly spreads across her face as she looks out over the trees below.

"Best view ever," I whisper. I reach forward and thread our fingers together, tugging her closer.

My breath catches in my throat when she looks up at me through dark lashes, little flecks of blue scattered throughout her gray eyes, a reflection of the clear sky above.

There's a flicker of a question in her gaze. "Coop?"

She brings her free hand to my chest and I wonder if she can feel my heart racing beneath her fingertips, not from the run up here, but from her. From this moment.

"Ave?"

If this is all I get, this moment between us, her eyes locked on mine-

*Suddenly her eyes flutter closed and she pushes to her toes, pressing her warm, soft lips to mine. It's a gentle, slow, tentative first kiss. It's everything I've been waiting for. My racing heart slows, the tightness I've felt in my chest since the first time I saw her loosens, and I know this is it. **She** is it.*

Avery pulls back slightly, just far enough to blink up at me.

"We should have done that days ago," she whispers.

I can't help it, I laugh. She's right. We should have done that days ago. I'm more than happy to make up for lost time though.

I wind my hand into her hair, and gently tip her chin up, cupping the back of her neck. Her lips part and I deepen our kiss. She tastes like strawberry chapstick, sunshine, and salty ocean swims.

"We definitely should have done that days ago," I whisper when we break apart.

Avery laughs and circles both of her arms around me. I pull her tight to my chest and wonder just how I'm going to let her go in a few more days.

Chapter Seventeen
Cooper

I stare across the road at my plot of land, half-heartedly stretching my quads, as I wait for Avery. The tire tracks the trailer left behind make me shake my head. I don't know why I even had Rick bring the tractor up here in the first place. I should have told him the second I knew Avery lived next door that my plans were on hold. He sure made quick work of moving it after my call though.

I bring my attention back to the closed door in front of me. I check my watch. I'm early. Of course I am. She's probably finishing up with work so I resist the urge to knock. Instead, I sit down on the steps.

I'm not the impulsive teenager I once was, I have a plan, the problem is that my plan isn't working. The "get to know her" plan. The Friendzone Plan. Or maybe it worked too well? Either way, I know her, and I want more. Seven mile run after work? I'm early. Grading assignments from her living room? Yes, please. Waking up early just in case she's at The Merc? Alarm is set.

Looking back over the last few weeks, it's like we've been inching toward our future as we simultaneously retrace our past. The slightly awkward first encounter followed by immediate sparks. Our run to the top of the rock. Sunset. Our inseparable weekend. The notebook. The conversations. The ease between us. We're headed in the same direction we were back then, toward something big, something life-changing, I can feel it.

The stakes are so much higher now, though. This isn't just a week. This is me, moving across the country. This is my job, this is my entire savings account wrapped up in the now-empty lot next door. This is my entire life.

And sitting here, just a few feet from the spot where my life changed so many years ago, it hits me.

This is it.

This. Her. She's it for me. I'm not just here for our run, I'm here for her. I've never been more sure of anything. Why wait? Why play it safe? There's nothing safe about this.

Fuck it. Isn't that her new theory?

I'm going to tell her.

I knock.

Nothing.

I check my phone.

Nothing.

Maybe she got caught on a call, in a meeting. I sit back down on the step and wait. I've waited eleven years, what's a few more minutes?

A few minutes turns into fifteen. She's late. She's never late.

Is this a sign? A sign to stay in my lane? In the friendzone?

I resist the urge to knock again.

Now what?

***

"Just felt like a fucking awful workout?" Nate asks an hour later, wiping sweat, or maybe rain, from his brow.

"Football," I grunt, flipping the tractor tire. I step back. "Old habits die hard."

"Sure." Nate steps up. Flip.

Something in his voice makes me pause before I step forward to take my turn. We're not exactly friends, but we're not *not* friends either. We've worked out a few times. We squat, we bench, we bullshit, we go home. I know he's one of the paid firefighters in town, I know he made my sister laugh, I know he works out a shit ton. Beyond that, no idea. He might be the most guarded person I've ever met.

I take the last flip, the tire finally back across the lot just as it begins to rain in earnest. My eyes drift to The Merc. Still no sign of Avery.

Nate juts his chin toward two worn sandbags just inside the open station doors. "Mile?"

Without waiting for an answer, he cleans one of the sandbags to his shoulders and starts toward the bridge. I quickly haul the other one up and jog to catch up.

I've been in weight rooms since middle school, I played college football, I'm no stranger to hard workouts, but when Nate starts running, not a nice easy jog, but *running*, I start wondering what kind of mistake I've made.

A big one.

This bag is heavy. So fucking heavy. My legs are shot from tire flips because who thought *that* was a good idea? Oh, right. Me. I awkwardly shift the bag to my other shoulder, unable to balance it on my back like Nate seems to be doing.

"Fuck," I mutter, catching it as it slides once again.

Nate doesn't slow down when he sees me fighting the sandbag. He might even speed up. "You know what your problem is?" he asks as we round the corner onto my street.

"I'm not a fireman?" Seriously, why won't this bag cooperate?

"Quarterback, right?"

I grunt in response.

Nate stops in the middle of the street, right in front of my house, and turns to me. "Stop waiting for someone else to call the fucking play."

I drop my sandbag. His hits the street next to mine.

"What are you talking about?" The entire day catches up to me and I put my hands on my knees, hunched over, trying to catch my breath.

Nate's a pretty average-size guy, not as big as West or even myself, so how he lugged his sandbag without sucking air, I don't fucking know.

"Just fucking run it in." He stacks the two sandbags at our feet on top of each other and heaves both to his shoulder.

"What the hell?" I ask, straightening up. I might have been struggling but I'm not about to quit.

"Good luck, man," Nate mutters, turning back the way we came.

What the actual fuck? Does he really think I can't make it?

Nate lifts a hand from the sandbags that are somehow both balanced on his right shoulder and waves. "Hi Avery," he calls.

I whip my head around.

Avery sits on my front porch, the dim light flickering overhead creating a halo over her head. Even from here, I can see she's shivering.

I close the distance between us, drinking her in. Without a coat, her wet, cream colored shirt sticks to her skin, showing a hint of pink underneath that I have to drag my eyes from. Her black, wide leg pants make her long legs look even longer and her heels put her closer to my height when she stands. Most breathtaking? The glare she's giving me.

"Where's the tractor?" she demands. There's a fire in her eyes I've never seen that leaves me momentarily speechless.

"Uh, hi? Do you want to come in?" I motion toward the door.

"Where. Is. The. Tractor?" She places one hand on her hip and completely ignores my question. I see goosebumps on her exposed forearms.

"You're cold, please, let's go inside." I motion again but she stays firmly planted on the porch.

"Cooper, I just need to know. Are you leaving?" There's a tiny break in her voice and she looks away, her jaw clenched in anger.

I guess we're doing this. Here and now. On a random weeknight on my porch in the rain.

Nate's words echo. *Just fucking run it in.*

I wait until she looks up at me, her gray eyes searching mine in the faint porch light, and hope this isn't the end.

"I can't do it, Avery." I run my hands through my wet hair and take a shaky breath. "I can't live next door to you."

Silence. She shifts her weight to her other hip and fidgets with the key fob in her hand, all while biting the inside of her cheek. Her eyes never leave mine though.

"Even if whatever this is between us, if this stops here, if friends is all we ever are, ever will be, I'll always wonder," I say quietly. "I'll always want this to be more."

Utter silence. She stills completely, no shifting weight, no fidgeting. The only movement between us is the rise of her chest as she inhales a shaky breath.

"Fuck it," she whispers on a quiet exhale.

A thread of hope starts winding itself around my heart as she steps forward. Her hand lands on my chest, cold through my thin tee shirt. My heart pounds.

"Ave?"

"What if this is more? What if this is meant to be?" Her words land one at a time, throwing me into that memory.

"We're meant to be, Ave, I know it."

There's a split second where we stare at each other. Her head tilts, her lips part. The thread of hope tightens, strangling my heart as it races wildly in my chest.

I don't know who moves first. All I know is that her lips are on mine. They're just as soft as I remember, with that sweet hint of strawberries I'll never get enough of. It's not a tentative first kiss though, it's the kiss that I've been waiting more than a decade for.

Eleven years. I've waited over eleven years for this moment. For her. I was a fool to wait so long. I should have found her sooner. Been here sooner. I should have kissed her the second I saw her across the fire.

I wrap my arm around her, sweeping her into me. My other hand moves to the back of her neck, gently tilting her chin up. I need more. Our tongues tangle together and she nips my bottom lip, breaking the last of my restraint. I tighten my grip on her waist and she melts, molding perfectly to me, rolling her hips into mine. I back her into the door until I'm caging her in and she moans, a sound I'll never forget, one that I want to hear over and over and over again.

Headlights flash as a car crosses the bridge and we pull apart, both of us shell-shocked. Her key fob clatters to the porch but neither of us move to pick it up. Instead, we stare at each other. My heart hammers in my chest. There is no coming back from that kiss. Ever.

"We should have done that weeks ago," Avery whispers breathlessly.

"We definitely should have done that weeks ago," I reply immediately, thinking of that day. The day I've never forgotten.

A small smile plays on her lips. "You remember?" she asks.

"Ave, I remember everything about that week, but *especially* our first kiss." I slant my mouth over hers once more, unable to resist.

She slides her hands under my shirt and I gasp, they're not just cold, they're icicles. I force myself to pull away. She looks up at me through dark, wet eyelashes and I can't stop myself from reaching out and smoothing rain drops from her cheeks before dropping my forehead to hers.

"You're cold," I whisper against Avery's lips as a shiver wracks her body. "Come inside?"

She responds by raking her fingernails down my ribcage and pressing her mouth to mine once more. One of her hands disappears behind her back and I hear the click of the door handle. We trip inside as it falls open, mouths fused together, a tangle of limbs, and I kick it closed.

I fumble for the lightswitch before pressing her back against the wall. I want to throw her over my shoulder and carry her to my bedroom like a caveman. I want to learn every inch of her, make up for all the years we've lost.

"I tried to find you," she says, wrenching her mouth from mine. "Years ago."

"I wanted to come back," I tell her, burying my face in her neck, breathing her in. "When I graduated. I wanted to come back and find you."

"There was a cheerleader." Her icy cold hands are under my shirt, tracing my abs.

"No one compared to you, Ave." I kiss my way down to her collarbone. "I tried to find you, too. I only found your words. Your books."

"I hoped you would," she says. She arches into me, silently asking for more.

"I devoured them," I whisper.

My words unleash a storm. She kisses me with an urgency I've never felt and a raw need courses through my veins in response. Eleven years of waiting, wanting, dreaming. I reach down, lifting her, and she wraps her long legs around my waist.

"I've dreamed about these legs for years," I tell her between frantic kisses, squeezing her thighs. "*Years*, Ave."

Her head falls back against the wall and her hands wind around my neck. "Coop?"

I pull back, holding her steady with one hand on her thigh, the other gripping her waist, and search her eyes. There's a dark mark under her eye that I only notice now that we're in the light. When I bring my thumb up to rub it away, another dark streak appears.

I look down. "Fuck," I breathe. "No, no no."

Not only are my hands, and now her cheeks, dirty from the tire flips, but my clothes are an absolute mess, which means her clothes, too. Black streaks, everywhere. Handprints, even.

She bites her lip as she looks down at her blouse. "I think I like it, your handprints on me."

I groan. I don't think I should tell her how much I like that, too. In fact, I want to mark every inch of her as mine.

"Between the handprints and the heels, fuck, Ave." I really am a caveman, about to carry her off to my bed without another thought.

She must like something about the desperation in my voice because she pulls me back in for another searing kiss. I spin us, her legs still wrapped tightly around my waist, and then pause.

I really am a mess. None of this furniture is mine. Fuck. Can I drag her into the shower with me?

Sensing my dilemma, Avery loosens her thighs and I take the hint, letting her slide back down to the floor. She takes a step back and looks me up and down, heat in her eyes.

"You can't look at me like that." I tilt my head back and take a deep breath, reminding myself that two minutes ago I was in the friendzone. I might have waited eleven years for this, but that's all the more reason to slow the fuck down.

"What exactly did Nate do to you?" Avery asks. She looks back down at her clothes, which are definitely ruined. No doubt about it.

"Unfortunately this is my own doing," I sigh. I rub my hand over my face before realizing what I've done. "Shit. This was definitely not my plan."

Didn't I have a plan at some point?

Avery tries to hide a smile. "I'm not going to lie, you have a line of dirt, or whatever that is, down your face."

"I probably shouldn't tell you where else I left marks then." I motion to the circular mirror on the wall behind her.

She spins and winces as soon as she sees her reflection. She brings her hand up to trace the line of dirt underneath her eye.

"Sorry?" I say, hoping she's not actually mad.

"Well," she says as she tilts her head, taking in the full extent of dirt and grime I've left on her cheeks. "Maybe this is a sign."

"A sign?" I tug her back against me, figuring I've already ruined her clothes, a little more won't hurt, right?

She leans into me, her back against my chest, and studies our reflections in the mirror. I slip my hand under her now-untucked shirt. Her skin is soft and cool, and probably now dirty.

"A sign I should go," she says quietly, her eyes glued to mine through the mirror, watching my reaction.

My heart falls. "Oh."

I can feel her tensing under my fingertips, I'm not sure why. I loosen my grip on her but don't let go. Why is she suddenly nervous?

"I spent too long pacing, well, spiraling, convincing myself to come down here, if we're being honest," she says in a rush, pulling her gaze from mine and turning away from the mirror. "I have contracts to finish before morning and a client waiting on updates to their trust and I want to stay, but, I'm sorry. I have to go."

"Okay," I say slowly. My mind races. What the hell just happened?

"I'm sorry," she repeats.

I use my hands still resting on her hips to turn her to face me. "Can I see you tomorrow? Take you on a real date?"

Finally her eyes find mine. I pull back just slightly, just enough to see her better. To search for an answer. She bites the inside of her cheek as she studies me. I wait. And wait.

"Ave?"

"I thought you'd be mad," she whispers.

"That you have to work?" I'm not mad, I'm just confused. Not confused that she has to work, but at her reaction.

She just nods.

"Definitely not mad," I tell her. There's a story behind this fear, but I don't think right now is the time to press her.

"Oh." Her voice is small and she blinks rapidly.

"C'mon, I'll walk you to your car." I hold my hand out but she doesn't move.

"It's raining."

"I've learned it does that fairly often here," I say lightly, finally drawing a smile from her. "Come on."

She puts her hand in mine and we walk to the door and out onto the porch. I pick her key up and we make it just a few steps off the porch before she tugs me to a stop.

I turn to her in confusion. "You okay?"

Instead of answering, she kisses me. The rain pours down, but all I feel is her lips on mine.

Chapter Eighteen
Avery

I jolt awake when I hear the back door open and half a second later a cold dog nose is in my face.

"Honey, I'm home!" Tex calls.

I sit up and something falls off the couch. My laptop. I give Zero the pets she demands before I stretch. I didn't mean to fall asleep on my couch, I just couldn't stop writing. The last time I checked the time, it was nearly three in the morning.

Tex saunters into the living room and hands me a bright pink Team Merc coffee mug. "Thanks," I murmur, blinking sleep from my eyes as I take a cautious sip of what I hope will be a mocha.

"It looks like I should have brought you breakfast, too," Tex says. "How long have you been awake?"

"Um," I clear my throat. "Approximately thirty seconds. It was a late night."

"Is a certain quarterback the reason for your late night?" She wiggles her eyebrows up and down with a smirk.

Instead of answering, I set my mug on the coffee table and fumble for my laptop. I hold it up.

"Shut up! You're writing?!" She sets her own pink mug down and scrambles across the couch to hug-tackle me.

"It's nothing!" I exclaim, trying to wriggle out of her hold. "It's not a book, it's just, well, not a book!"

Fuck it. It's a book. Or at least the start of one. One I've been trying to write for years.

Tex finally lets me up and leans back against the cushions. "I don't care if it's a crazed manifesto, you're writing and you're happy, I can tell. And here I thought it was that quarterback."

My skin prickles. It *is* that quarterback. Or at least partly him. I've replayed last night a thousand times. It took forever to get my work done after I got home, my mind kept drifting back to him. When I finally finished, sleep wouldn't find me, but writing did.

"It feels good. It's just, it's like nothing I've ever written. But definitely not a crazed manifesto, which, by the way, you should care if it's ever that!" I pick my mug up and take a sip, letting the rich coffee and dark chocolate soothe me. I love the routine of my morning coffee, especially after a night of very little sleep.

"I love this journey for you," Tex sings in her Alexis Rose voice, making me laugh. "But really, Aves, I do. You're writing, that's amazing. I had hoped that's what you were doing all summer."

"I tried," I tell her quietly. Guilt washes over me once again. For my failure. For my lies. "I tried for *years*. I couldn't. It's part of what led me to start working with my dad. I was tired of failing. I needed something fresh. Take my mind elsewhere."

She nudges my knee. "It seems to have worked. I'm happy for you, Aves."

I smile because, holy shit, she's right. It worked. It freaking worked. *Finally*, it worked. And it feels *good*.

"Although I still think maybe that quarterback has something to do with it," she adds after a pause.

"He did, or does, obviously, but it's more than Cooper." I tap the side of my mug, trying to figure out how to explain it. "Remember what you said on The Merc steps that day? That it wasn't just West, it was this place?" I ask.

She nods.

"It started with a writing prompt," I tell her. "About how decisions and people can change your life, how just a few days can change your whole life trajectory. And Cooper did that, before. But I thought about how that applies in other ways, things that happen, friends, places. All the things that led me to be here, now."

"'Here' is pretty good," Tex says quietly, her thumb moving to her scar, gently rubbing the wave tattoo that rises above the jagged line.

Even though we're sitting in my living room, I have to fight the urge to look over my shoulder. I wonder how our lives were changed that night, would we still be sitting here if it never happened?

"I realized it during ice cream breakfast with Zoe. I even tried to put it into words that weekend, but it didn't click until…like 1 a.m. this morning I guess, how this town has changed so many people's life trajectory. Not just mine. That's really what the story in my laptop is. The story of this town. The magic of it all."

"This place *is* magic," she agrees before looking up at me and smiling. "And I can't wait to read it when you're done."

"Thanks, friend," I say. I open my laptop and pull up the document that kept me up all night. I toggle to the prologue and paste it into a new document. "Want to read now?"

"Gasp!" she gasps.

"Did you just say 'gasp!' as you gasped?" I laugh.

"You never let anyone read though," she says, eyes wide. "Are you sure?"

"I let Cooper read," I say quietly. "Before."

"Gasp!" She covers her mouth in exaggerated shock.

"Oh my god, stop saying 'gasp!' like that!" I shake my head, unsure where this mood of hers came from.

Without looking at her, I stand and take my coffee mug to the kitchen where I know she's dropped a week's worth of mail. I hear her sniffling in no time. While it's still surprising how emotional she is these days, it's much better than the constant nausea she's been battling. I hadn't really planned on letting her read what I wrote, but fuck it.

Her sniffles grow louder so I toss a tissue box in her direction before stacking the important mail neatly. Brian, the truce-making liar, has snuck in another thank you card, which I add to the growing pile that all remain unopened.

"Get in here, you terrible person!" Tex calls, her voice trembling. She blows her nose loudly.

"Terrible person?!" I grab the stack of thank yous, thinking they'll cheer her up, and walk back into the living room.

"You made me cry with your words!" she says, yanking me down next to her. I nearly land on her dog, who has curled up in the corner of the couch on the blanket I leave there for her. "You're an amazing writer. I love that you're writing again. I love that you wrote about us."

"I mean, if I'm going to write a love story, it should be ours, right?" I ask with a laugh. I gather the cards that fell when she pulled me down and put them on the coffee table in front of us. "You and this place, the two constants in my life."

"Wait, you should do that, write a love story," she says excitedly, wiping her tears with her sleeve. "Small town romance. Pleeeease?!"

"That is so far out of my wheelhouse I wouldn't even know where to start," I tell her. I can feel a flush creeping up my neck.

"Well, one, I can tell you're lying, and, two, I bet your quarterback could help you with that," Tex says, nudging my shoulder with hers.

Now I'm on fire. I sneak a glance at the green notebook, which of course Tex catches.

"Oh my god, did he *already* help you with that?!" she shrieks.

I bury my face in my hands. "Can we not?"

"No, we *cannot* **not**." She tugs at my hands.

"Harperrrr!" I moan, drawing out her name.

"Okay, okay." Her hands are up in surrender when I open my eyes and peek through my fingers.

"I like him," I whisper. It feels like a whole different confession this morning.

"Uh, yeah, I know. You've told me. I like him, too. But I'm not writing secret romance stories about him." Her smirk grows even bigger. "Are you going to tell me what happened last night? I *know* you didn't chicken out again."

"I almost did," I say with a wince. "I was working and-"

"*Not* the details I want!" she interrupts, rolling her eyes.

"Okay, okay. We were supposed to go for a run but I looked outside, like right when you texted me, and the tractor was gone. The one that's been sitting on his lot. No work done, just *gone*. I kinda freaked out, thinking he was leaving." I close my eyes and lean back against the couch. "Kinda really freaked out."

"You did the Avery spiral, didn't you?" Tex asks quietly. I can feel her eyes on me, even though mine are still closed.

"One hundred percent. I skipped our run. I think he knocked on the door, I don't even know, I was locked in my bedroom. I paced and paced. Then I finally said fuck it and stormed out of my house in the rain, still in my work clothes-"

"You hate work clothes!"

I open one eye and look at her. "And the heels from my earlier meeting in town."

"Gasp!" She covers her mouth and widens her eyes, making me laugh.

"And showed up on his doorstep, shirt soaked through, total mess, and he wasn't even there." I shake my head.

"Well that did not go where I thought it was going to go." Tex sighs.

"Nate must have seen me drive past the station, because suddenly they were both there, in the street. Nate, like, delivered him to me." I laugh, remembering the smirk Nate gave me.

"And then?"

"And then I threw myself at him." I admit, bracing myself for her reaction.

"Yes!" she cheers. She fist pumps exactly like Colt does. "And?"

My cheeks heat as I remember his hands on me. His mouth. How he easily lifted and pinned me against the wall.

"Avery Anne!" Tex shoves my shoulder. "Did you *sleep* with him?!"

"No!" I bite the inside of my cheek.

I don't tell her that I would have. I definitely would have. As soon as his lips touched mine, it's like any hesitation, any doubt I had was gone. I wanted everything.

And also, my body was on fire. Head to toe. On. Fire. I don't know how all of our clothes stayed on. I've never had that reaction to anyone. Making out with Cooper was better than any and all previous sexual experiences. Which probably says something about my exes, but also something for the chemistry Cooper and I have.

"No? Then what's that look?" she demands. She knows me way too well.

"I didn't!"

"But you wanted to," she says with a smirk.

I don't respond.

"Soooo?" She draws out the question.

"So, I had a small amount of panic about my reaction to him, remembered all the work I needed to get done and used that as an excuse, then freaked out that he was going to be mad and nearly ruined it all." I tip my head to rest on her shoulder.

"No," she groans.

"Yes."

"Avery Anne Moore!" she scolds.

"I'm a mess," I groan, making her laugh.

"You're never a mess, Aves. So if you happen to be a little bit of a mess now, it's about damn time."

"I think this is big," I whisper.

"I hope it is. Like I said, I like him. And someday you'll tell me about before. Because I know that was big, too, by the way you never said a word about it." She shrugs her shoulder, jostling my head, so I sit up and look at her. She's giving me the best friend look. The one that deserves the truth.

"It was," I say simply. I'm not ready to share *before* with anyone but Cooper and my green notebook.

That notebook. The story inside. This morning, more than ever, I hope it really is the story of us, the story of what's meant to be.

Zero whines softly and wiggles her way out from her corner and across my lap, until she's between the two of us.

"Hey," Tex says after stroking Zero's ears for a few minutes. "Wanna ditch whatever this is and go get breakfast? Almond croissants?"

"An almond croissant does sound amazing."

"Come on, Z," Tex says, pushing the nearly ninety-pound dog off our laps.

"Let's take the cards, Lucas and Marabelle can open some of them," I suggest, knowing they're the two employees at The Merc this morning. "And let Zero stay here, it's too cold for her to wait on the porch."

As if she can understand my words, Zero carefully climbs back up into her spot, curls into a little ball, and tucks her nose under her paws. I drop another blanket over her. I've never been a dog person, but this oversized lap dog has grown on me.

"Are you kidding me?" Tex moans as I follow her out the door. I automatically look over my shoulder.

"Wasn't it raining when you came up?" I ask, confused by her reaction.

"This!" She plucks an envelope from under the corner of the doormat.

Laughing, I tuck it into the stack in my arms and follow Tex into the rain.

***

"Thank you for installing the little library, without it, I never would have found my love for red-hot firefighter romances and the men they use as cover models," Zoe reads, tears of laughter streaming down her face. "There's a hand-drawn illustration that just says 'smolder' above it!"

She holds up the card and sure enough, there's a shaky drawing of a faceless man with six-pack abs and flowing hair, flames escaping a window of the square house behind him.

"I'm betting that one is-" Tex starts to guess but is cut off by Lucas.

"Betty. That is absolutely Betty," he declares.

Zoe nods, laughing too hard to speak. She's not working today but happened to be visiting Lucas when Tex and I showed up with the unopened stack of thank you cards from my kitchen counter.

"I cannot believe Brian did this, why haven't we been opening these?!" I exclaim.

"I mean, he did drop off an overwhelming amount of cards," Tex says, reaching for another. "And the first ones just had his signature or nothing at all."

"I feel like such a jerk, I haven't thanked a single one of these people for this!" I moan, waving my hand at the opened stack.

These cards aren't just from Brian and the firefighters like the first dozen or so we actually opened, with their names barely legible on generic cards, these are from the entire town. Tourists who wrote the dates of their stays, summer residents who have already packed up and headed inland for the winter, weekenders and full-timers alike have all written cards for my entire staff.

"I'm going to visit Kelsey next week, I'll take her some!" Zoe volunteers.

"You guys, this is amazing," I say for the third time. I cannot believe Brian.

While I wish Kelsey was here, as she was a huge part of Team Merc all summer, part of me is glad we waited to open these cards. It feels like everything I've been working toward is coming together and this is the perfect way to spend the morning. Or, well, early afternoon.

"Another for Marabelle!" Lucas declares, holding up the card he just opened. "Specifically for the strawberry scones from the Fourth."

"Well deserved! Those were soooo good!" Zoe says.

Marabelle tuts from behind the counter, shaking her head when Lucas waves it in her direction. She might be even less of a fan of compliments than me. Zoe is right though, those were amazing scones.

Tex must have a longer note in the card she just opened, her eyes fly back and forth, her brow furrowed.

"Another drawing!" Zoe holds up a crayon drawing of Rejection Rock.

"Oh, this one is sweet, it's from that family that stayed at the house on the golf course just a few weeks ago," Marabelle says. "It says their daughter and son-in-law announced their pregnancy when they were here. They're already planning to come back when the baby is born, they want it to be their new summer tradition."

"I love that!" Zoe squeals, shimmying her shoulders.

Opening these cards would warm my emotionless robot heart no matter what, but Zoe takes it to a whole new level with her reactions.

Meanwhile, silent tears stream down Tex's cheeks. I reach over and gently wipe them away. Of course that thank-you would make her cry.

"Aves," she whispers. She swallows hard and looks up at me, her face white as a sheet.

"Oh no," I groan. "You were feeling so much better!"

Without dropping the card, she bolts for the back. I stand to follow her, already pulling a hair tie from my wrist, ready to reclaim my position as hair-holder-backer, but movement at the door catches my eye.

A man stands in the doorway, running his hand through damp, dark hair in a familiar gesture. His eyes find mine and my knees nearly buckle.

"You," I gasp.

I might not have seen Cooper coming back into my life, but this man? This man I've been waiting for. Searching for. Looking over my shoulder for.

Chapter Nineteen
Avery

"Avery," the stormy-eyed man says.

"Avery!" Sam calls. "Have you seen Harper?"

"I thought she was with you," I reply, looking back toward the bonfire.

A barely visible silhouette fades into the treeline just beyond the haphazard line of trucks in the distance. I've caught glimpses of stormy eyes hidden behind messy, dark hair, but every time I turn around, he disappears into the shadows.

"You," I repeat, finding my voice, my anger.

I step toward the man who has lived in my nightmares for over a decade. The reason I look over my shoulder. The reason for Harper's scar.

I feel movement behind me and track Lucas out of the corner of my eye. It only takes a slight shake of my head to stop him.

"Avery," the man says softly, holding his hands up in surrender. "I'm sorry but I had to find you."

I have to find her.

Something is wrong. Icy dread flows through my veins, goosebumps cover my skin, and I shiver.

I have to find her.

I don't realize I'm moving until I'm in the trees, disorienting shadows cast by the moonlight dancing in my peripheral vision.

I have to find her.
"Harper?" I call. "Harrrrper!"

Harper. Where is Harper? Anger turns to panic.
I have to find her.
"Avery." Harper's voice floats through the air, far away yet right beside me. "Avery, stop."
She's here. I turn, my eyes landing on hers.
"I saw him, Harper, that night, he was there, in the woods." I barely get the words out before my panic takes over. My vision blurs and my heart races.

My heart races, pounding against my ribcage in an unsteady rhythm. Panic starts to overtake my senses, clawing its way up my throat until I can't breathe. I swallow the metallic taste of adrenaline and gasp, but there's no oxygen. My vision blurs.
"Breathe," I order myself.
I breathe.
*Cool night air fills my lungs, one shaky, uneven breath at a time. I strain to hear anything, anything at all, other than the muffled shouts from the partygoers behind me. A stick snaps close by. I spin, thrown off balance by the dark. Something, **someone**, falls to the ground.*
"Harper!" My scream pierces through the night, bouncing through the trees. There is no chance of calming my panic now, instead it escalates until I can't do anything other than run.
I scramble through the forest, tripping over pinecones and tree roots, holding my arms up to protect my face from the branches that are closing in around me. I can just make out a shaking figure huddled on the ground. Harper.

"Harper, he was there." My voice shakes as I blink away the image of her on the ground. She's here. Not there. She's okay.
"He's your brother." Harper's voice is muffled. Are we underwater? Is that why I feel like I'm floating?

I realize I'm swaying. Lucas reaches out and grasps my arm. His mouth moves but I can't hear a word he's saying. I only feel the pressure of his hand on my arm. I order myself to breathe.

I breathe.

The man in the doorway nods, at what, I'm not sure. At Harper? Why is she smiling at him?

"Wait. What did you say?" I spin out of Lucas's gentle hold to face Harper.

"Your brother," she says, holding up an envelope that has my name scrawled on the front. "Just look at him."

I look back at the man. He's tall, lean, and has a very familiar stance. His eyes are a darker gray than mine, tinged with the same midnight blue specks that my father has. He pushes his hair back, that familiar gesture, the exact same way Dad does, and I know.

"My brother assaulted my best friend," I whisper.

Lucas is back beside me in an instant, this time wrapping his arm around me, supporting me, holding me up.

Sam is beside me in an instant, holding me up. He tucks me under his arm, his eyes scanning the dark forest. "Did you see anyone, anyone at all?" he asks urgently.

I shake my head silently, angrily wiping tears, knowing that if I try to speak, a sob will escape instead. Then I stop.

The guy with brown hair and stormy eyes.

"No, Avery." The man, my brother, shakes his head. "No, that wasn't me."

I turn to Harper, focusing only on her, not the man at the door, not Lucas beside me, holding me steady, not Zoe, whose arm is wrapped protectively around Harper's waist, or Marabelle, frozen in the background. Harper's thumb finds her scar. I have to blink away the image of blood dripping from her hand.

"Harper," I tell her, my voice low and urgent. "He was there. I saw him."

Lucas's hand clenches into a fist, but he stays at my side, looking between Harper and I, waiting.

"It wasn't him," Harper says, shaking her head.

"He. Was. There." Now my hand turns to a fist.

"Aves. It wasn't him," she says. "I don't know if he was there, but it wasn't him."

"I was there," the man, my brother, interjects. "But please just…please let me explain."

I ignore him. Like so many times in my life, only Harper matters to me right now.

"It wasn't him," she repeats.

"It wasn't me," he says quietly.

No one moves. I can feel his eyes on me, but mine are still on Harper. She gives me a small shake of her head and steps out of Zoe's hold.

"Hi, I'm Harper, known around here as Tex," Harper says, squeezing my hand as she moves past me. She offers her hand to the man at the door. My brother.

"Alex," he says so quietly I can barely hear him over the echoes in my mind. He clears his throat. "I'm Alex."

"Nice to meet you, Alex. Your sister is the best person I know, and if you tell her a single lie or hurt her in any way, I will crazy murder you." In typical Harper fashion, she's smiling pleasantly as she threatens his life.

Zoe snickers behind me and unsuccessfully tries to cover it with a cough. "Sorry," she whispers.

"I'm sorry for showing up like this, but I'd really like a chance to talk. I can explain everything, I promise." He looks over Harper's shoulder at me.

I don't see the icy glare our father uses as a weapon, I see kindness and understanding. I see hurt, too. He walked into my store after trying to find me, if the card Harper holds is any indication, and was met with my immediate accusations.

My hands shake as my adrenaline slows. I give a small nod. "Okay."

He nods, swallowing hard, his eyes darting around the store, looking anywhere but at me.

"She's scary sometimes, but she's got nothing on your father," Harper tells Alex. "He's the fucking worst."

"You have no idea," Alex mutters.

Suddenly Harper's distrust and dislike of Dad seems a bit less unwarranted. I have a brother that I never heard a single word about. If Alex found me, he must have found our father first. And whether that was yesterday, a week ago, or Alex's entire lifetime ago, I should know I have a brother.

Zoe steps forward and introduces herself but Lucas doesn't leave my side.

"Are you okay?" Lucas asks quietly. "Want me to call Jake?"

"I'm okay," I tell him, touched by his offer to call his best friend, a police officer in Rock Beach. "Thank you."

"You don't owe him anything," Harper says, moving to stand beside me as Marabelle shakes Alex's hand. Lucas nods his agreement. "Not even a conversation. But keep this." She tucks the card in my pocket.

I nod robotically. I have a brother. A brother. What am I supposed to do? I look around the store like the answer will be on a shelf down aisle three.

"The man looks like a younger version of your dad, he's definitely related, no question," Harper says quietly. She gives me a quick side hug and then raises her voice. "I'll go wipe down the tables for you. It's a little chilly but with a nice, hot coffee, it's the perfect place to sit."

Alex watches her with an amused smile, probably remembering her threat, and then turns to me. Marabelle, Zoe, and Lucas all melt into the background and we're left staring at each other.

"Alex," I say, clearing my throat when his name comes out as three jumbled syllables instead of two. "Alex. Hi. I'm Avery. I guess I'm your sister."

"Hi, Avery," he replies. "I really am sorry for showing up like this, but I tried to get a hold of you. I even spoke to Edward."

Aware of the fact that my three employees as well as two customers who just walked in can hear our every word, I tip my head toward the door. "Anything in particular you'd like Lucas to bring out?"

"Whatever you're having is great."

Lucas nods to tell me he's heard, already knowing what I'll want, and I follow Alex, *my brother*, out the door.

***

I'm gripping my pink Yeti so tightly that my knuckles are white. I can't stop staring at the man across from me. The small talk is over. I know he's married to a woman named Ava and they have a son named Jack. I saw pictures of their wedding, the wedding that I missed, and so many of Jack, the nephew that I've never met. But I still don't know how we ended up sitting here staring at each other, strangers through and through. My heart already aches and it's bound to only get worse from here.

Alex blows out a slow breath. "The beginning?"

"Yes, please."

"Okay, well, I was born and raised in Wheaton, not far from Monitor Mills. No other siblings, it was just Mom and I. Her name is Bethany."

Bethany. Somehow, in some long-forgotten memory, I've heard her name. I know it.

"I, of course, questioned her about my dad, but all she would say is that he wasn't ready to be a father. As I got older, that wasn't enough for me." He shakes his head. "So, I took matters into my own hands. He wasn't listed on my birth certificate, but that didn't stop me. I found some things I shouldn't have ever seen. An envelope, hidden in the very back of my mom's closet, with an uncashed check, which I stole, and a letter from a lawyer."

"Oh no," I whisper. I can picture this so clearly, I don't even need to know what the letter said.

"Yeah. So I had his name. A starting point. A little more digging and I realized you existed. Not just existed, but you lived with him, he was actually your dad, you know? He wanted to be your father, but not mine. I wasn't good enough." He sighs and my heart sinks even lower.

"That's not..." I trail off as Alex shakes his head.

"I spent my teenage years proving him right. I started small, like fights at school, stealing a pack of gum from the gas station, dumb shit like that. I escalated over time, did some things I'm not proud of. Finally tried to cash the check I stole, obviously it didn't go well. Your dad, *our dad*, I don't even like calling him that, was not pleased, to say the least."

"If you don't get him under control, I will do it for you. You do not want that option, Bethany."

I gasp as the memory hits me. Dad's whispered threats as I opened his office door to tell him dinner was ready. The anger on his face, rage in his eyes, it was a version of him that, despite his and Mom's constant arguments, I had never seen before.

"When was this?" I ask, already knowing the answer.

"I was fifteen."

I nod; I was right. I was thirteen. Eighth grade. How had I forgotten about that day in his office?

"Mom wasn't mad, she was *scared*. But I didn't see that." He drops his gaze to his lap. "I blamed her, I thought she did something to make him leave her, leave us. I continued to be a teenage asshole, especially to her. It was just so much easier, you know? She was there, much more satisfying to lash out at her, to see the hurt I could cause. God, I was such an asshole."

"Alex," I say quietly. I wait until he brings his eyes back up to meet mine. "I'm so sorry you went through all of this."

"Don't apologize," he says immediately. "None of this has anything to do with you."

I open my mouth to argue but he silences me with a shake of his head. I motion for him to continue.

"Finally, one day Mom snapped. No yelling, she just cried and cried. Sobbed." There's no mistaking the heartbreak in his voice. My own heart breaks for her. "She asked if I had ever thought about the fact that maybe growing up without him was preferable. That the kind of father that threatens the mother of his unborn baby isn't a father at all. That your life wasn't as perfect as it seemed. You were being raised by a man that lied and cheated and no amount of money could make up for that."

A derisive laugh escapes before I can stop it. "Although I pretended otherwise and they sometimes managed to put on a good show, I think everyone knew my parents weren't happy. Small towns."

"I'm sorry to say I went full stalker for a few months. I came to your race your freshman year, when you won districts. I was there. Your dad wasn't. I saw him with another woman once, a much, much younger woman. Another time I overheard your best friend say something not too nice about him."

"I'm guessing it wasn't just 'not too nice,' she's never been a fan of his," I say. "And she's not one to mince words when it comes to me. She's a little overprotective."

Now it's my turn to look at my lap. The one thing I pushed Harper's feelings aside about again and again and she was more right than anyone would have guessed. God, how many times have I defended him over the years to her? The last few weeks, even?

"Okay," Alex says, blowing out a long breath. His foot shakes, rattling the table. I steady it with my hand. "Now the hard part."

Because this hasn't been the hard part.

"We don't have to do this right now," I tell him quietly.

We study each other across the table once more. Even though it's only been a short time, I no longer see a younger version of my dad starting back at me. I see Alex, my brother. Alex, with warm, friendly eyes that crinkle at the corner, whose wide, flat, barely-upturned smile matches mine.

"Do you want to know?" he asks.

I nod, even as dread settles in my stomach. As soon as he admitted he was there that night, I didn't just want to know, I *needed* to know.

"So, backing up, in his threats after my dipshit check-cashing attempt, your dad said I wasn't to have any contact with you or there would be legal action. He said that you knew about me and that you didn't want me to screw up your life. You were going places, you were going to be a lawyer one day, and I'd bring you down."

Rage. Fury. Anger. I try to mask all of them. Alex isn't the person to direct these emotions at, our dad is. *My* dad. Alex doesn't want to claim him, understandably, but he is my father. Not only that, I work with the man. I *choose* to have him in my life.

"I didn't know." Somehow, my voice is steady.

"I know that now. And obviously I skirted that line. So, fast forward through me being a little shit, the threats, Mom finally gets through my thick skull, and I do a little light stalking. I see she's right. Maybe you're not better off with him in your life. Then I start to wonder if you even know about me. If you do, I wonder what you've heard. I've turned myself around, I'm about to start college, leave town, what do I have to lose?" He shrugs. "Small towns, it was easy to find out about the party. Friends of friends, you know?"

It's my foot that shakes the table this time. Bile rises in my throat. I don't know if I can do this. I glance through The Merc window and see Harper sitting with Zoe. I try one of her deep breaths. It works. Sort of.

"You were sitting in a chair with Harper, laughing, looking completely carefree, when I showed up," Alex continues. "Did that make it the perfect time or the worst? You'd have her support, so maybe it was a good time. For about thirty seconds, I was determined to walk over there. But then someone said something about Harper moving. It was your last night with your best friend. I couldn't ruin that with my existence."

"I hate this already," I whisper. I try another breath and nod for Alex to keep going.

"But I stayed. You guys were drinking, it was like my first chance at being the older brother, looking out for you, even if you didn't know. I talked to some of the guys I knew through basketball, tried to stay on the outskirts in case you saw me, in case you did know about me." He stops. He rubs his forehead and clenches his jaw.

I brace myself, knowing, but not really knowing, what's coming. My stomach rolls. Another breath.

"I was getting ready to leave, it seemed like things were winding down, you had a designated driver, but then everything changed. I saw Harper walk away. There was a guy, an older guy closer to my age, that had been watching her all night. He followed her. It didn't feel right. I saw you with your boyfriend, arguing maybe? Someone else approached you. You looked right past me, into the woods, and just took off. I followed. You screamed, or maybe Harper did? This part is blurry. There were shouts from the bonfire. Then you screamed Harper's name."

I close my eyes and hear her name echoing, bouncing among the trees.

"I swear I can still hear it in my mind," he says. He pauses, his jaw clenched, and takes a deep breath before continuing. "I started running toward your voice, but then someone was running at me. Without thinking, I tackled him. I just *knew*. I knew he did something. I got in one good swing but then he yelled that the cops were coming, we needed to run."

"You punched him?" I stiffen.

"I'm sorry," Alex says, hanging his head. "I had him and I let him go. He said the cops were coming and all I saw was my past troubles, my future college plans. I panicked. I let him go."

Rage. Fury. Anger. I can't mask any of them.

"Where. Did. You. Hit. Him?" I know exactly who had a black eye the next day.

Alex looks me in the eye and nods. "It was him. That's why I'm here. Why I had to show up like this."

The bile burns my throat. I think I might throw up.

"And there's more." Alex barely gets the words out.

"No." I shake my head. I see Zoe and Harper through the window, both of them looking at me. I already know where this is going.

"Whispers started. Rumors. Again, small town. I put it together. You and your mom had disappeared, I'm guessing here, to the beach? Harper had moved. So what option did I have?"

"No." I scoot my chair back. I want to stop him, but I know I need to hear. I need confirmation.

"I went to him that same week. He listened. He asked questions, took notes. And then he very clearly told me that he would handle it. But me? I didn't see anything. In fact, I assaulted someone. My best course of action was to get myself out of town. *Finally*, my dad was looking out for me, protecting me. Both of us."

I stand up so fast that my chair tips back.

"I'm sorry, Avery."

***

Avery,

I know this letter goes against your wishes and for that I am sorry. A phone call seemed too abrupt, an email too impersonal, and Edward might have hinted that you've always loved "real" cards.

While I've always wished we could have a relationship, I understand why you couldn't. But now, I am hoping you'll reconsider. I grew up without you in my life, but I'd love for you to be in my son's.

Please consider this an open invitation to write, call, or even show up in my life, today, tomorrow, any time.

With Love, your brother, Alex

Chapter Twenty
Cooper

Like a scene from a movie, the sun breaks through the clouds, a slice of sunlight shining directly on The Town Mercantile as I turn into Three Rocks. Despite the temperatures steadily dropping, the hanging baskets are still bursting with color and the flags flanking the porch steps wave in the light breeze.

Unfortunately it's not a movie and Avery doesn't appear, although Tex's Jeep is in the lot so their weekly meeting must be over. I lift my hand in a wave to Nate, who is in full turnout gear, using the giant tire as a box, stepping up and back down in the fire station parking lot across the street.

I don't think, not even for a split second, about changing into workout clothes to join him. All I think about is asking Avery to dinner. All I've *been* thinking about is that. A date. Finally, a real date with my Dream Girl.

I glance at the time as I pull into the small driveway of my cottage. Between being eager to see Avery and the fact that it's finally Friday, I got out of school quicker than usual. I pull my backpack over one shoulder and start up the walk. When I drop my keys as I fumble with the lock, I'm reminded of last night. Avery's keys hitting the porch. That look in her eyes. The hitch in her breath. The way she felt. The way she tasted. Everything.

I set my keys on the table inside the door and check my phone. Still no notifications from Avery. I never even got a reply to my good morning text.

Where is the line between understanding and respecting her workload and making sure she's not panicking over what happened last night?

Run it in.

Fifteen minutes. If she hasn't replied in fifteen minutes, I'm going to show up at her door, flowers from her own store in hand, and ask her to dinner.

Decision made, I start across the room to put my bag in the bedroom but I've barely made it two steps in the right direction when the door flies open behind me. I turn just as Avery stumbles inside. There's a muffled thud and I realize I've dropped my bag, my laptop taking the brunt of the impact.

"Ave?" It only takes a glance to know something is wrong.

Adrenaline pumps through my veins, narrowing my vision, until all I can see is her. Her trembling hands and red-rimmed eyes, her palpable panic rising with each erratic breath.

"Avery?"

She slams the door behind her and leans back against it, tears streaming down her cheeks as she wordlessly slides to the floor. I cross the room in three strides and slide down in front of her.

My heart pounds against my ribs like it's trying to escape, trying to make its way to her. I lay my hand on her knee and she flinches, *she flinches,* at the contact. I pull my hand away quickly and watch helplessly as her whole body shakes.

"He fucking let him go," she says between hiccuping breaths.

"Ave," I say quietly, struggling to keep my voice level. "Avery, look at me."

"Oh my god, I have to tell her." Avery focuses on me, her eyes wild and panicked like a cornered animal. "I have to tell Harper what he did."

What he did?

"Who?" I ask. There is no chance of keeping my voice calm as anger and confusion swirl. "Who did this to you?"

Avery tips her head back against the door and closes her eyes. I cautiously reach out again, selfishly needing the reassurance of her touch. This time she doesn't flinch. I thread my fingers through hers and she grips my hand tightly, like a lifeline.

Finally, after a shuddering breath, she opens her eyes. "My brother."

Her brother?

She doesn't have a brother. It's one of the first things I learned about her all those years ago.

I can't help my rising panic. "Ave, you don't have a brother," I say, trying to keep my voice steady.

Silent tears fall from her eyes as she looks at me once again. There's no fire in her eyes anymore, not even a flicker of anger or the panic I just saw. Now it's pure heartbreak. She pulls something from her pocket and holds it out. An envelope.

"Turns out, I do have a brother. His name is Alex." Sobs wrack her body and I do the only thing I can. I pull her into my arms.

Despite all the years of practice I've had holding other people together, it doesn't make it any easier. Instead of waning since there isn't a physical threat, my adrenaline keeps pumping, growing with every single one of Avery's sobs. My hands shake as I stroke her hair.

As she cries into my chest, I mentally flip through the contacts in my phone, debating who could find this brother of hers the quickest. I murmur quiet, reassuring words while swallowing down the metallic taste that burns my throat. My mind runs through the ways I can destroy this man.

After what feels like a lifetime, she stops shaking. I stand and lift her, carrying her to the couch, where I resettle us without letting her go. I feel her phone vibrate against my hip, lost in her pocket somewhere I'm sure. She ignores it.

"My whole life is a lie," she whispers as she burrows into me. "I thought everything was finally coming together. How was I so wrong? The entire fucking thing is a lie."

She starts shaking again and I can feel her tears through my shirt. I tighten my hold and focus solely on comforting her, not my own questions, my own fury.

Her phone buzzes again. And again. Then mine starts.

I don't look.

Hers again. Then mine. Hers. Mine.

I look.

It hasn't been a lifetime, it's been seven minutes and five missed calls and three texts since I stepped in my front door.

Tex:
Please just tell me she's with you

Tex:
Somewhere, anywhere. She's with you?

Tex:
Answer me

"Ave, can I at least tell her you're here?" I whisper against her temple.

All I get in response is a shuddering breath and a nod. I tighten my hold and text with one hand.

Cooper:
Yes my house

Two minutes later, my front door flies open.

"Oh, thank god," Tex says, stepping inside and shutting the door behind her.

Her eyes narrow as they move from her best friend to me. I give a shrug because I actually have no idea what the fuck is happening. Tex crosses the small room and sits down on the couch next to me and pulls Avery's legs over her lap.

"Hey," Tex whispers. "Count with me."

Neither of them actually count, but after a minute of quiet sniffles, I realize that Avery and Tex are breathing in sync. Their steady, even breaths are the only sound in the room. Avery's hand snakes through my arms and finds Tex's hand.

"So, is it weird if I say your brother is hot?" Tex asks, her voice laced with humor. "Like, it's a good thing he wasn't around when I was about fourteen years old. I would have been so madly in love with him. Best friend's brother. Maybe you should write that trope."

What the actual fuck? Why is Tex joking about the man that left Avery a scared, panicked mess? What piece of this fucked up puzzle am I missing? I tighten my hold on Avery but she huffs a laugh.

"I'm telling West you said that." Avery's voice is muffled in my chest, but at least she's talking.

"Okay, he'll be here in ten minutes, tell him then," Tex says.

My mind races. I have a million questions. But I stay quiet. My hand rubs up and down Avery's back as we sit in silence. Tex tips her head to rest on my shoulder.

"Harper, I know who did it," Avery whispers just as I hear West's truck pull up. "That night. I know who it was."

Tex stiffens, lifting her head off my shoulder, but doesn't say a word.

"It was Eli."

Tex sucks in a breath and blows it out slowly.

"And my dad let him go. He fucking let him go."

Tex goes rigid.

***

"I'll be shocked as shit if she comes home tonight," West remarks, taking the pan I hand him. He's leaning back against the counter and his eyes don't leave the two women on the couch. "Her or her dog."

Once West showed up at my cottage, the four of us came up to Avery's house where Zero was waiting. We started on the deck, Avery and Tex sharing the two-person lounge chair that looks custom-made, I'd guess by the man drying dishes next to me, and Avery quietly told the three of us about her conversation with her brother, Alex.

West, sitting to my left, remained eerily calm throughout the entire story. Zero, on the other hand, did not. As soon as tears started silently streaming down Tex's cheeks, Zero was climbing onto the chair, pushing her way between Avery and Tex, and settling on both of their laps. I just sat in shock the whole time as the story got worse and worse.

Cheating on your wife? Denying paternity? Threatening the woman carrying your child? Can't get worse than that, right? Wrong.

Matthew Moore failed both of his children their entire lives and that doesn't even touch on what he did to his daughter's best friend.

"I don't think the three of them have been further than two feet apart since we got up here," I comment.

They haven't. When we finally moved inside, Avery announced she needed to cook. Tex planted herself on a barstool at the island, Zero curled up at her feet, and watched as Avery started chopping the vegetables that had magically appeared on the doorstep at some point. After the soup was simmering, the two of them disappeared into Avery's room, Zero trotting along behind them, returning quickly with matching fuzzy socks and freshly scrubbed faces. During dinner? Tex's foot was resting on Avery's chair the whole time. Zero was under the table. They've been on the couch together since, heads tipped together, the dog under a blanket next to them.

"Why now?" West asks suddenly, keeping his voice low. "Why, after all these years, did he decide to show up?"

"I had the same thought," I say quietly.

West crosses his arms. "I don't trust him."

"I don't either," I say, rinsing the last pan. "But I did get a text from Lucas, saying he called his buddy. Jake?"

West nods. "Good."

I hand him the pan and rinse out the sink one last time as I try to think through this whole scenario. I don't necessarily doubt Alex's story, but it's just so much and everything is so interwoven, that it seems not impossible, but improbable. Although, when it comes down to it, if his story is true, does it matter *why* he showed up? The fact of the matter is, Matthew Moore is the villain of the story, no matter how it's told.

"Maybe not the best time to bring this up, but Avery was the first person here in Three Rocks that I gave a damn about, and that gave a damn about me in return," West says.

I take the towel he hands me and dry my hands, already knowing where this conversation is going. She didn't have a brother before today and West has been filling that role. I get it.

"I won't hurt her," I tell him, easily meeting his assessing look. I have no intention of hurting her. In fact, seeing her hurt today has killed me.

"She-" He's cut off by his better, or at least smaller, half.

"West!" Tex calls. She doesn't even turn to look over her shoulder at us. "Stand down."

West shakes his head, shooting an amused look at the back of Tex's head. "But-" he tries again.

"Nope. Done. We're being kicked out anyway." Tex stands and stretches before offering her hand to Avery. Avery shakes her head.

I thought Tex would be staying. No, I thought they both would be. All three of them, actually. I stand frozen as Tex walks our way. She tilts her head, I think to tell me to go to Avery, but she shakes her head when I move.

West pushes off the counter and makes his way to the couch instead. He crouches in front of Avery and speaks in a hushed tone.

"Do. Not. Leave. Her. Alone," Tex says quietly, deliberately accentuating each word as she joins me in the kitchen. "She's going to take some time to process all of this, then she's going to spiral. Maybe a little avoidance thrown in. Push people away. It's her thing."

"It seems like that's a normal reaction to something like this," I reply. But honestly, what do I know? Has there ever been a situation like this?

"Probably, but listen to my words. Do not leave her. If she kicks you out? Sit in the driveway, call me, and I'll come back. You think West is scary? I'm scarier."

"Tex, I knew the second I met you that you were the crazy one." I make sure my voice is loud enough that Avery can hear us. West raises his eyes over the back of the couch but instead of a glare for what I just said to his girlfriend, he smirks.

"Scary. I said scary." Tex gives me the glare that West didn't.

"Huh, must have come out wrong." I shrug.

She laughs. "I knew I liked you, quarterback."

Before I can say anything else, she returns to Avery, leaning over the back of the couch to whisper something in her ear. When Tex stands, her eyes are shining with tears. I can't read the look she gives me as West walks her toward the door, Zero on their heels, but I can read his.

Don't fuck this up.

***

I reach toward Avery to pull her back into me and find the bed empty. Cold.

The room is dark and I grope blindly for my phone. 3:37 a.m. Did she ever fall asleep? After nearly an hour of rubbing her back, it seemed like her breathing had evened out, like she was sleeping, but was she?

Tex is going to murder me.

I pull my tee shirt on and follow the soft glow of light down the hall. I find Avery in her office, staring at the large monitor in front of her. She clicks, highlights, clicks again, then runs her hand through her hair.

"Hey," I say softly, leaning against the doorframe of her office and crossing my arms.

She spins her chair to face me, obviously startled. "Sorry, I couldn't sleep. Thought I'd get some work done." Her eyes drop to the floor and I know what that means.

"Work, huh?" I'd bet my empty lot next door on what kind of work she's doing. "Want help?"

"It's three in the morning." Her leg bounces under her desk and I wonder if this is the spiral that Tex was talking about.

"So is that a yes?" I ask, undeterred. Maybe this is the pushing away portion. Which was supposed to be first? Is it a strict order?

"Are you sure? This is a lot." She studies me closely and I wonder if she's asking about more than middle of the night research.

I cross the room and lean down, placing my hands on the armrests of her giant desk chair. Her eyes widen as I cage her in. "I've never been more sure of anything," I whisper before brushing my mouth over hers in a light kiss. She sucks in a breath and I pull away. "C'mon."

"I thought you wanted to help?" She looks back at her screen, unwilling to leave.

"I do. So let's go to the couch. It's where we work." I leave the office, hoping she'll follow.

I'm relieved when she takes her spot at the end of the couch and tucks her feet under my thigh, her laptop balanced on her knees. I loop my hand around her ankle and look at her expectantly.

"Eli Shapiro. AKA the one who assaulted Harper. AKA my high school boyfriend's older brother. AKA the guy my dad offered a job to a couple weeks ago, which, by the way, is why Alex decided to show up." She hands me her iPad.

"Wait, what?" I ask, wondering if I'm still half asleep. "Alex showed up because of Eli?"

Avery nods and rubs her face. I can see her exhaustion in the dark circles under her eyes. "He was going to leave it at the letter, just have the offer out there for me to reply, but then he was on the phone with Edward, telling him the letter failed, and overheard my dad welcoming Eli and Jordan into the office in the background. Probably the day he talked to them about joining our so-called team."

"Huh." I don't know what to think of this. Again, not impossible, but improbable.

"I know it seems…" Avery tilts her head back and forth, trying to decide on her words. "Fuck it. It seems impossible. All of it. But however it happened, whatever brought him here today, or I guess yesterday, here we are."

I nod. Here we are.

It's surprisingly easy to find him. A link to his company is the first thing that pops up. I trace up and down Avery's calf as I scroll, not nearly as distracted by her bare skin as usual. Eli Shapiro makes an interesting research subject.

More than interesting. Shocked, I sit back.

I stare out the window into the night. How could someone that has the ability to assault a teenage girl in the dark end up where Eli seems to be? I'm all for second chances, believing in the power of change, but not in this case. Not when he wrecked multiple lives in a matter of minutes.

My blood boils when I think of Avery and Tex retelling the story, how Avery's voice shook and Tex's thumb rubbed along a small tattoo on her finger. How, with barely more than a glance, Avery walked Tex through the breathing exercise they had done earlier on my couch.

I need a second take on him. A second opinion. And what tells the true story of someone's life better than social media? Basically anything, but that's what I have.

It takes a *lot* of scrolling, but from what I can gather, just a few weeks after he assaulted Tex in the woods, instead of going back to college, he moved to Washington. The partying pictures stopped, and a single photo of a broken glass, the Space Needle in the background, is all that's posted for nearly a year. There's no caption.

The first photo after a year of silence is a field, woods to the left and a river down below on the right. *"It's going to be harder than you want it to be."*

Photos come in rapid succession now. A church. Construction. A flyer for rec league basketball. More construction.

I see him literally rebuilding his life, construction site by construction site, but I still can't accept it.

I research sexual assault and feel physically ill when I see the statistics. I knew they'd be bad, but did I really *know*? I look up the statute of limitations, which is ridiculous because I'm sitting next to an actual attorney. But the rabbit hole is endless.

"Hey Ave?" I tip the iPad in her direction, offering her what I've found.

No reply.

Somehow, I didn't notice Avery had fallen asleep. I pluck her laptop from the edge of the couch where it's tipped precariously toward the floor and set it on the coffee table. She stirs as I reach for the blanket that's slipped off her legs.

"Hmm?" she asks sleepily.

"Just sleep, Ave," I whisper.

Chapter Twenty-One
Avery

I wake up to a cold dog nose in my face, a repeat of yesterday.

Yesterday.

The day I wish would cease to exist.

I pull the blanket over my head, effectively shutting Zero out, as well as the low voices coming from the kitchen.

Undeterred, Zero climbs onto her corner of the couch and lays directly on top of my legs. I move my feet out from under her and curl into a ball, wishing I was in my bed, hiding.

The couch dips and a familiar hand lands on my hip.

"If you don't come out, I'm coming in," Harper threatens.

"Okay, okay," I sigh. I bring the blanket back down and have immediate regret when I meet my friend's worried stare. "Nope, stop. Give me two minutes before you start that."

"I wasn't doing anything!" She holds her hands up in surrender but I know better.

"There were like twenty-seven questions in your eyes." I pull the blanket back over my head. I'm not ready to face her, not because of her questions, but because of, well, everything.

"Okay, yeah, there were. But the only one that matters is, are you okay?" The wobble in her voice makes me pull the blanket right back down.

I shrug in answer to her question. She nods. I raise an eyebrow, my own question. She shrugs. I nod.

"So weird how you guys can do that," West mutters from above us. He holds out one of the Team Merc pink Yetis. "She forgot this in the truck."

"Thank you." I sit up and gratefully accept his offering.

Mocha, extra whip, only a few sprinkles. Marabelle must have made it.

I tilt my head from side to side and roll my shoulders. Falling asleep on the couch, as comfortable as it is, wasn't the best idea. I should have gone back to bed, let Cooper wrap me in his arms again, cocooning us against the real world.

Cooper. Where is he? I glance over the back of the couch but he's not in the kitchen. I wouldn't blame him for making a run for it. It's a lot to go from kissing in the rain to shuddering sobs on the floor to internet stalking in the middle of the night.

"Went home to shower and change," West says, reading my worry correctly.

I take a second look at my coffee-wielding, mind-reading, giant of a friend. He looks like hell. Harper looks better than he does. Before I can ask him anything, he leaves the room. Not just the room, the house. I hear the door slam shut. His truck doesn't start so my guess is he's glaring at the cloud layer that's hanging low in the trees. He did that a lot when he first moved here, glaring through the trees between hammer swings as he built my deck.

"Yeah, sorry, he's not okay," Harper says, biting her lip. "I think he's trying to be calm and stoic like he usually is, but you can see how that's going."

I remember how still West sat last night on the deck, barely moving a muscle as I recounted the entire conversation with Alex. Only his hand moved, fisting and unfisting, otherwise he was completely still, his eyes unmoving from Harper. It's why I sent her home instead of selfishly keeping her here with me. She might think he calms her, but really, it's her that calms him. Or it goes both ways, I guess.

"I'm sorry," I tell her.

Like that covers it. A simple apology for my boyfriend's brother assaulting her. For my father sweeping it under a fucking rug. For a decade of anxiety and panic attacks.

"What did Jessie say that morning at The Merc? Sometimes things are just a lot."

"A-freaking-men." I take another sip of my mocha.

A lot. Understatement of the century.

It's my turn to glare at the trees through the window. Maybe I need to swing a hammer. I should ask West to help me extend the deck. We could both swing hammers.

"And none of this is your fault," Harper adds. I feel her staring at me but I keep my eyes glued to the windows, watching the trees rustle in the morning breeze.

I tip my head back and forth. It sure feels like my fault. It's *my* father that didn't protect her. Us.

I sigh. "Now what?"

"Now you tell me how you are. How you *really* are. How last night went." She's still watching me. I'm still watching the trees.

I take another sip of my mocha, wondering if I should put alcohol in it. I'm guessing not. But maybe?

"It went," I finally tell her.

I only have vague memories from last night. Sending Harper home. Nodding robotically when Cooper told me he'd take the couch. Awkwardly handing him a spare toothbrush from the guest bathroom. Cooper pulling the comforter over me. The panic that buzzed through my veins when he stepped away after kissing my forehead. Grabbing his hand. Whispering for him to stay. Pleading. My mind finally settling as his hand rubbed lazy circles on my back.

"Cooper said he left everything on the iPad. Want to look?" Harper nudges the iPad laying on the coffee table with her foot.

"No." I take another sip. "But yes."

My search found nothing, if you could even call it a search. I stared at my laptop screen, telling myself to find something, anything, in my father's finances, that would unravel it all, leaving him with nothing. I couldn't even focus, I just stared at blurry numbers. I hope Cooper had better luck.

Harper reaches forward and types in my passcode. Eli Shapiro smiles at us from the screen. She drops it on her lap with a quiet gasp, making Zero whine.

I take it from her and scan quickly. Construction for a cause. Disability remodels. Home repairs. Domestic violence. I frown in confusion. Obviously I knew Eli was in construction, it's why Dad wanted to bring him on, help with flipping properties. But this...

I click around the website some more. Nonprofit. An interview with Jordan.

I freeze. Why didn't this occur to me sooner?

"Did Jordan know?" I whisper.

I finally look at Harper. Now she's the one staring out the window. I don't think she even heard me.

"I remember hearing that Eli dropped out of college, that he moved to Washington," she says. Apparently she did hear me. "Wasn't that just, like, a month or two after?"

"It was before Jordan and I broke up, right around Mom and Dad's divorce, so I didn't really..." I trail off.

Those months blur together. That night. Harper moving thousands of miles away. Throwing myself into writing. Finishing my manuscript in Three Rocks. Looking over my shoulder. Wishing Cooper would appear on the beach. Mom and Dad arguing more often than not. Harper being too far away. Looking over my shoulder. Getting my book offer. Jordan scoffing at my dreams. Mom and Dad's divorce. Looking over my shoulder. Jordan and I's breakup. Harper still too far away. Looking over my shoulder.

"Do you think he did all that," she waves at my iPad, "because of that night?"

"Do I think Eli started a nonprofit construction company because he assaulted you?" I ask, trying to keep my voice steady despite the fury that's burning deep inside.

Harper nods. "Like you said, like you wrote, all the things that change your life trajectory."

I don't know what to say. Maybe he did start his nonprofit because of that night. Maybe he didn't. Either way, he still assaulted a teenage girl, so does it matter?

"I think that even if he did, that does not make anything okay. But I also think the real question is, what do *you* think? What do you want the outcome of all of this to be?" I ask carefully.

I've waited to find justice for my friend for years. If not justice, revenge. Preferably both, if I'm being completely honest.

"It made me who I am today. Every single thing in my life, every experience, led me here. And this is where I'm supposed to be. Here. With you. With West. And if it led him somewhere good...like, he's doing good in the world, I...I don't know."

Out of the corner of my eye, I see her thumb on her scar before she lays her hand over her belly. Zero whines again from her end of the couch.

I really want to point out that sure, all of that might be true, but it's also true that some actions deserve consequences. But I don't, because I know my friend, and that's not what she needs right now.

"Now what?" I ask, setting the iPad back on the table.

"Now we make sure West didn't murder anyone," Harper says jokingly.

"He better not have left without me." I'm not joking. And I don't mean because I'm his lawyer.

"Aves, I'm okay, I promise. I'm more worried about you." She leans her head on my shoulder, like she's done so many times.

"What? Why?" I ask, tipping my head onto hers.

"Let's see, your actual long lost brother walked into your life yesterday and dropped a fucking bomb, but you're so focused on me, on that night, you haven't even called your mom. What do *you* want? This isn't just that one night. This is your whole life."

My whole life. All a lie. Suddenly, the enormity of that hits.

"Harper?"

"Yeah?"

"Wanna ditch life and hide under the covers?"

Without a word, Harper pulls the blanket back up over our heads.

***

"Pretty glad I was tasked with this," Cooper says, staring slack-jawed at the view in front of us.

As soon as the sun broke through the drizzle, Harper and I emerged from our blanket fort. A leftover bowl of soup was waiting for me as well as my mud-caked hiking boots.

Standing on the bluffs overlooking the Pacific, white-capped waves as far as the eye can see, the wind whipping my hair beneath my beanie, might be just what the doctor ordered. Or West, I guess. I think he's taking credit for this idea.

"Thank you for being here," I tell Cooper quietly.

He tugs my hand until I'm standing in front of him, then he wraps his arms around my waist and rests his chin on my shoulder. I lean back into his chest, listening to the waves break against the rocks far below.

This moment is exactly what I need. I need to pretend, just for this moment, that we're lost in our own world. That the story written in my notebook, the story that started almost a dozen years ago, is real life, and that the nightmare of the last twenty-four hours is just fiction.

"Nowhere else I'd rather be," he replies, tightening his hold around my waist.

I feel his chest rise and fall with each breath he takes and when I close my eyes, I can feel his heartbeat. My mind slowly quiets the longer we stand.

Too slowly. No matter how hard I focus on his steady breath against my neck, the roar of the ocean below, or his arms snug around my waist, reality still creeps in.

I willingly aligned myself with a monster. My finances are tied to his. My name is with his, signed in ink, on so many contracts.

Lies.

So many fucking lies.

Sometimes things are a lot.

And sometimes they're too much.

I need the quiet.

"Hey Cooper?"

"Hey Avery?" His tone is teasing but his expression is serious when I turn in his arms.

I flip his hat backward, wrap my arms around his neck, and press my lips to his. Cooper responds immediately, his hand gently cupping my neck, while his thumb traces my hammering pulse. The remaining thoughts racing through my mind come to a crashing halt, the ocean fades into a distant hum, and the vice grip the last twenty-four hours has had on my chest loosens.

Every nerve in my shell-shocked body vibrates as he tips my chin up, deepening the kiss further, his tongue tangling with mine. I need this feeling to consume me, to erase everything else within me, until it's only now, only us. Nothing else.

But then, all too suddenly, it's nothing. Cooper pulls away and looks into my eyes. I close them. He'll see too much.

"Ave," he whispers, resting his forehead on mine.

"No." I don't want the real world. I want this. I want the quiet.

I slide my hands to his chest and feel his heart racing beneath my palm. His lips find mine once more, but he's tentative. Soft. Sweet. When he pulls back again, I don't only feel his hesitation, I can see it in his eyes as they search mine.

Everything comes racing back. Nausea builds. Noise builds.

"Are you questioning this?" I ask, fighting the panic that's wrestling for control. "I mean, at this point, I wouldn't blame you. This probably isn't what you signed up for."

This isn't what anyone signed up for, or would ever sign up for.

"Ave, no," he quickly replies, brushing his thumb along my cheek. "I just know it's been a lot, to say the least, the last couple days, and I don't want this to be more."

I shake my head, nothing makes sense. I can't believe myself anymore, let alone anyone else. "That's exactly what I was hoping this was, what I thought it was. More."

"Hey," he says, tugging me closer once more. "This *is* more, this is everything. I'm just trying to take things slow, for both of us."

I stare at him, trying to make my brain make sense of what he's saying. It feels like my mind is either working overtime, too many thoughts racing all at once, or in slow motion, unable to keep up, always a step behind. I just want it quiet.

I need it quiet.

"I'm sorry," I whisper, tucking myself into his chest, my new favorite safe place. I inhale his scent and once again, everything slows.

"I got to sleep with you wrapped in my arms last night, do you know how long I've waited for that?" Cooper runs his hand down my back, much like he did last night, and I melt against him, my body molding to his.

"You quieted the noise," I tell him.

His hand freezes. "What?"

"The noise. My mind. My brain. It wouldn't stop, but then, you were there. And it got quiet."

"Ave," he says, waiting patiently for me to unbury myself from his shirt. Once my eyes meet his, he smiles. Everything quiets. "That's all I want. To quiet your noise. So let's just go slow, no rushing. I want to savor all the little moments, even if they're stolen between really hard, really heavy things. I'm here for it all. I'm here for you, whatever way that means."

He's so steady, sure of himself, sure of us. Meanwhile, I'm the opposite. Unsure of everything.

"Okay," I whisper. I just want this quiet to last.

I stay wrapped in his arms, unthinking, just being. I don't know how long we stay on what feels like the edge of the world, his hand slowly rubbing up and down my back, but when he finally releases me, I let him take my hand and lead me back down the trail.

***

Surprisingly, my mind stays quiet. I stay quiet. I sit on my couch, Zero on one side, Harper on the other, and stare at the trees. I nod when Harper asks if I need her to look at my schedule for the next week. I shake my head when Cooper asks if I want to go for a run. I eat the dinner West sets in front of me.

I don't miss the worried looks they're giving each other, I just...don't care? I can't find it in me to do anything other than exist. There's so many things I should do, talk to my mom, confront my father, call my brother.

Call. My. Brother. My brother.

"Hey," Cooper says quietly, crouching down in front of me. I try to give him my attention but I can't.

My brother. Whose wife I've never met. Whose son doesn't know I exist. I move that, *meet my nephew*, to the top of this mental list of things to do that I just...can't.

"Ave?" Cooper places a hand on my knee.

My eyes finally focus on him. "I want to meet Jack."

"Yeah?"

"Yeah. Someday soon." I look around. "Where are Harper and West?"

"They left a while ago," he says gently. He offers me his hand. "Let's go to bed."

I nod. I stand up. I follow him through my bedroom. I let him gently push me into the bathroom, one of his tee shirts in hand. I pee, strip out of my clothes, and put on the tee shirt. I watch as he puts toothpaste on my toothbrush for me and I brush my teeth. I let him lead me to my bed and I stare at the ceiling.

"Roll over," Cooper whispers.

I roll onto my stomach. His warm palm rubs circles on my back. His steady, deep voice fills the deafening silence. I don't hear his words. I close my eyes. I sleep.

Chapter Twenty-Two
Cooper

"You quieted the noise."

Those words, an echo of my own reality years ago, is all I hear when I look out the window and see Avery huddled under a pile of blankets.

I know that feeling, that desperate search for quiet when it feels like you're drowning in a sea of chaos and commotion. It was her voice, flowing through her books, that finally broke through, that silenced it all.

"You quieted the noise."

Those words, the only thing reassuring me right now.

I was worried last night. Really worried. After we got back from our hike, Avery just…existed. I don't know if she spoke more than a handful of words to us the rest of the day. I thought I had broken her. That I said or did something.

But maybe that's exactly what she needed. Needs.

Quiet.

Which is why I'm standing here, trying to ignore the glare Tex is giving me from across the kitchen island, while Avery's outside in the rain.

"What?" I finally ask, setting the cheese grater in the sink and rinsing my hands.

"Why are you so good at this, quarterback?" Tex answers with a question, still glaring.

"Cooking?" I know everyone jokes about her cooking skills, but grating cheese?

"All of it!" She waves her arm in a circular motion.

"Yeah, you're going to have to narrow it down, sorry." I check the giant pot on the stove, turning the burner up slightly when I see it's not at a rolling boil anymore.

"You're domestic as hell, you don't seem at all put off by the shit show of the last couple days when most guys would be running, and why aren't you more concerned about her right now?" Tex looks on the verge of a breakdown herself, which is understandable. West is at his shop for an appointment, so it's just me with two barely-hanging-on best friends.

"One, cooking is a basic life skill and I did a lot of it to help out my parents for a while, then my ex worked later hours than me, so," I stop and shrug. "I cooked. I figured out pretty quickly that I like it."

"I hate her already. Not because she didn't cook, I hate cooking, but, as Avery's best friend, I'm required to hate your exes."

I laugh. "She's Megan's best friend."

"That sounds like a story." She tilts her head, like I've piqued her interest, or at least distracted her slightly.

"It's a pretty boring one. Two, I'm not put off by this 'shit show' because I just found Avery again, why would I run?" I shrug again.

I don't add that I've lived this before. I know how life can change with a single conversation. I know that sometimes, even when you want to fix everything, the only way you can help is by making dinner.

So you make dinner. You do the dishes. You stay.

"Stay."

I can hear Avery's quiet voice that first night, asking me to stay. The shaky sigh she let out when I slipped into bed with her. How I could very slowly feel her tension draining with every circle of my palm over her back.

"Acceptable answer." Tex is no longer glaring, but she's still watching me closely.

"And I'm not worried about her right now because she's writing." I jut my chin toward the window.

"What?" Tex whips around and squints.

"Didn't you see her take her notebook with her?" I didn't even have to give her a prompt, she just picked up her notebook and walked outside.

"No." She shifts on the barstool, trying to see if I'm right. "But it's raining."

"Which is why West and I rigged up a temporary patio cover and set up the second heater earlier," I tell her patiently.

We also discussed which one of us gets first shot at Eli and how to best destroy Avery's dad's life. And face.

I wasn't sure West and I had much in common, but I think we'll get along just fine, which will be handy if we end up in prison together for aggravated assault.

"Oh." She turns back to face me, an unreadable expression on her face. "Okay."

"Now, want to learn how to make lasagna?"

I'm not sure if this is a great idea, based on what I've heard about her cooking, but I don't know how else to keep her busy and away from Avery, who obviously needs some alone time.

"I can't eat cheese." Her glare returns.

"Which is why I picked up vegan options and goat cheese; we're going to experiment."

I'm really glad I remembered she can't have dairy when I was at Safeway earlier. Like we confirmed the other day, she's the scary one.

"Damn, you are good." Tex gives me a smile and hops off her stool.

After she washes her hands, we work next to each other, making three different lasagnas, two of which are vegetarian, two kinds of garlic bread, and one giant salad. I'm not sure how the vegan cheese will taste compared to my usual recipe, but Tex seems excited. There's also ice cream and some sort of non-dairy frozen dessert in the freezer, dropped off by Mrs. G, Kelsey's mom, earlier.

"I see you guys are done putting up with me," Avery comments when she walks through. When I frown in confusion, she adds, "Tex's cooking. Attempted murder?"

"Ouch, uncalled for," Tex says, using the dramatic flair she seems to save for Avery or Instagram. "I haven't poisoned anyone in years!"

"It was an accident, right?" I stage-whisper to Avery.

Avery laughs at the two of us and disappears into her bedroom, green notebook tucked under her arm. Tex watches her go with a critical eye.

"You were right, quarterback," she admits, lifting a shoulder when she turns back to me. "She needed that."

"You didn't trust me?"

"I trust like two people and my dog. But I'll admit it, you were right."

I sigh in relief. At least I got one thing right.

Later, during dinner, Tex declares our lasagna experiments a success. Two things right.

***

"Trust me," Tex says a few evenings later.

I look at the warehouse in confusion. Why is Tex standing in front of a warehouse in Rock Beach instead of sitting on a couch back in Three Rocks with her best friend?

"Trust you not to murder me in a back alley?" I ask, taking a closer look at our surroundings.

"I was running errands for The Merc, don't worry, West is with Aves, and I saw this place. I knew we had to try." She nods with conviction.

I wasn't worried, I knew she wouldn't leave Avery alone, I'm just confused about why we're here. I look at the sign hanging crookedly above the door.

I blow out a breath. "You're sure?"

"No. But we're doing it anyway. Come on." She reaches for the door but I get there first, opening the heavy door and ushering her inside.

I follow Tex into the graffitied building and am met with rows and rows of gleaming weapons. Knives, throwing stars, and pick axes line a wall and a shriek echoes down a hallway to the right. This is not what I expected when Tex called and gave me an address.

Honestly, she might be onto something. While Avery hasn't slipped back into the zombie-like existence from the weekend, she hasn't recovered, either. She doesn't want to run and she hasn't been to the beach with Tex and Zero. I don't think she's worked at all; I don't think she's even left her cabin all week.

I woke up alone this morning, not surprised in the least, but instead of finding her in the office staring blankly at her computer screen, I found her sitting on the deck. She was wrapped in a blanket, no laptop, no notebook, no coffee.

"What if I can't?" she had asked, without turning toward me.

"Can't?" I questioned. With everything she's accomplished, I didn't know this word was in her vocabulary.

"What if I can never make it better?" She glanced over her shoulder, her gray eyes filled with tears as she looked pleadingly at me. "I tried; that first morning I tried. There was nothing there, nothing to use against him. My own father. I can't believe he did this to her. I have to make it better. For everyone."

I crossed the deck in three strides and dropped to my knees when she didn't look at me, catching her watery eyes at her level. "Ave, that's not what she needs. Or expects. She just needs you."

All I got was a sad smile and silent tears. She stayed buried in her blankets as I made the coffee and sent an SOS text to Tex. When I left for work, they were both out there, Team Merc mugs wrapped in their hands.

So, if Tex thinks rows of gleaming weapons might be the answer, fuck it. Let's try.

The door opens and I turn to see that same sad smile. Behind Avery, West glowers. So at least one of them is at their normal baseline.

"A rage room?" Avery asks doubtfully, eyeing the massive space.

"I need it, I figure you might want to give it a go, too," Tex says.

Without waiting for confirmation from Avery, Tex grabs West's hand and tugs him toward the check-in counter.

"Were you in on this plan?" Avery asks me as she takes in the cavernous building.

"Innocent bystander, bullied by your best friend," I tell her, stepping closer. Needing to be closer. It's not enough, so I ask the dumb question. "You okay?"

She gives me a half-hearted smile, tipping her chin up to blink up at me with cloudy gray eyes. I thread our fingers together.

"No, but I'm better now," she says. "Seeing you."

"Yeah?" I ask. I can't help my smile, my relief.

"Yeah." She nods, searching my eyes.

"I'm glad your friend is a relentless bully, then."

Avery laughs.

She *laughs*.

I lean down.

"Brofessor!" a familiar voice calls just as I'm about to press a quick kiss to Avery's strawberry lips. She jumps back like we're the middle schoolers in this scenario.

"Micah!" I hold up my fist for a fistbump. "What are you doing here?"

"My parents own this place," Micah replies. He tugs his backpack strap.

The assignment. I look between him and the high schooler shrinking under West's glare at the counter. "I guess I know why you put this down. That your brother?"

"Yeah," Micah tells me. "At least he gets paid. I'm not old enough to work." He looks at Avery and his eyes widen.

"Micah, this is my friend, Avery Moore. She's an attorney and she owns The Town Mercantile in Three Rocks," I tell him.

He continues staring at her and I don't blame him. Even when her world is falling apart around her, she's beautiful.

"Hi, nice to meet you," she offers with a polite smile.

"Do you know Sadie?" Micah blurts out.

"I don't think so," she says, shooting a glance at me. "Does she come into The Mercantile?"

Micah pries his eyes off Avery just long enough to fumble his phone out of his pocket. He immediately drops it. He scrambles to pick it up, his cheeks bright red. "Uh, no, but bruh, those cinnamon rolls are fire."

"Micah!" A curly-haired woman calls. "I need you to get room three reset!"

"Aw, man. See you tomorrow, Teach." He gives Avery one last glance and starts swiping on his phone.

"Bye, Micah," I tell him, trying to hide my amusement at his awkwardness around pretty girls of all ages. I don't think he hears me, already lost in his phone.

"Did I just get called 'bruh' by one of your students?" Avery asks, another laugh spilling over as she watches Micah disappear.

"Yep, you definitely did. Welcome to my world. Now, are you ready for Tex's world?" I ask.

Avery looks past me and I follow her gaze. West is attempting to fit into what I assume is the largest size of coveralls they have while Tex laughs.

"Anything and everything," Avery says, shaking her head.

She repeats the sentiment once we're signed in and I'm placing a hard hat on her head.

"Always!" Tex calls from inside the rage room, bouncing impatiently on her toes.

I must still look confused because West shakes his head at me and steps through the door, leaving Ave and I in the hall.

"It's Harper and I's thing. We'll do anything and everything for each other, always," Avery explains. "Which apparently means this." She nods toward the room, watching Tex balance a glass bottle on a stack of tires.

"Want to bail?" I ask. "Make a run for it before she starts swinging?"

Avery chews on the inside of her cheek, still watching her best friend. She shakes her head and sighs, grabbing my hand and pulling me through the doorway with her.

"Might as well get it over with," she mutters.

I reach for one of the lead pipes waiting in the corner and flip Avery's face shield down for her. I hand her the pipe.

"Get it over with, then," I tell her.

"Harper?" Avery says, trying to hand the pipe to Tex.

Tex crosses her arms. "No way, you first."

"West? You always want to hit something," Avery tries.

West glares. Avery sighs. Tex smirks.

With a quick glance over her shoulder at me, Avery steps forward. She takes a careful, measured swing at the beer bottle balanced on a stack of tires near the center of the room. Glass shards fly.

Then, silence.

Tex and I exchange a glance. West's jaw clenches.

"Holy shit," Avery breathes. She turns to Tex first, then me, then West, her eyes wide.

"Yeah?" I can't help but smile at her reaction.

"Yeah." She swings the pipe in a circle.

"Hell yeah!" Tex fist pumps.

West stays silent, but he does almost smile. Almost.

"Again." Avery's bouncing in anticipation now, waiting for me to balance a chipped glass vase on the tire stand. There's no hesitation, only a hard swing of the pipe as soon as I step away.

A cracked ceramic cookie jar is next. Another beer bottle. A bright red vase. Tex tosses a wine bottle in the air and Avery times it perfectly, the baseball bat I just handed her slicing through the air with a satisfying *whoosh*.

"Why does that feel so fucking good?" she asks, pushing her face shield up.

There's a wild gleam in her eye, a glimmer of Avery before her world crumbled, and I want to kiss the hell out of her. Too bad she's holding a weapon.

Tex flips Avery's face shield right back down, steals the bat from her, and points it at West. He lines up three bottles. There's nothing tentative about Tex's first swing.

"We're going to need more bottles," Tex says without even turning around.

"How about a laptop?" Avery says, digging a battered MacBook from the pile of destroyed objects in the center of the room and setting it on the tires.

"Hell yeah!" Tex says, winding up.

The laptop goes flying and we close the place down.

***

"Cooper," Avery whispers in the dark. "Thank you."

"You're welcome," I reply, kissing her shoulder as I pull her closer, wrapping myself around her, breathing her in. "But also, for what?"

"For staying," she says, shifting her hips.

I grit my teeth, trying and failing to ignore how fucking good she smells, how warm she is tucked in my arms, how few clothes she has on. It's my sixth night sleeping in her bed and until this moment, I've been able to see it for what it is: comfort. But right now, with her lean legs tangled with mine, after an evening where she smiled and laughed, it's more of a struggle.

"Such a hardship," I tease, trying to bring us back to playful footing instead of whispered words in the dark.

It doesn't work. She turns in my arms, rolling to face me. She reaches up, tentatively tracing my jaw, her touch featherlight, and suddenly my hand is on her waist, under my shirt that she's wearing, tracing her smooth skin. Even in the dark, I know her strawberry lips are just inches from mine.

"I mean it, Coop. No one wants this." The crack in her voice tells me there's tears welling in her eyes.

My hand stills. It's no longer a struggle to see this for what it is.

"I want this, Ave," I whisper.

"I'm a mess. I can't even…" she trails off.

I'd bet anything she's biting the inside of her cheek.

"Well, when I couldn't even…" I say gently and mimic her pause. "You were there, you just didn't know it. I told you that your books helped me, but it was more than that. It was your words. Your voice. It was like you were there with me, quieting the mess, the noise, the absolute chaos that I felt."

"Really?" she asks quietly. Doubtfully.

"Really." Really fucking really.

"But-"

"I want *you*, Ave," I interrupt, unwilling to let her list any doubts. Reasons we aren't meant to be. "All of you, even the mess. Especially the mess."

Her breath hitches but she doesn't say a word. Did I go too far?

"Coop?" she finally whispers.

Her hand slides around to the back of my neck and her hips shift toward me. My grip on her waist tightens.

"Yeah?" It's taking everything in me not to kiss her, to erase her doubts a different way.

"I need you to quiet the chaos for me."

"Ave?" What is she asking me?

Instead of saying another word, she presses her lips to mine. I barely hold back a groan when she slides her tongue into my mouth. I bring my hand up her side, lightly tracing her ribcage, then when she shifts, still ticklish, I drop it back down to her waist, pulling her even closer.

She hooks her leg over my hip and I don't think I can do this. I can't resist her. Years waiting. A decade. More. Completely worth it for this moment. Our bodies are flush, no space left between us, her body molded to mine.

"More," she pants, rolling her hips.

My fingers slide under her tiny sleep shorts and I pause.

More.

I want more. I want everything.

But.

Fuck.

"Ave," I whisper between kisses. "You-"

The buzzing of her phone startles me.

Avery freezes. "No," she whispers.

Her phone buzzes again.

She doesn't move.

I roll us until I'm hovering over her, nestled between her thighs, so I can see who is calling out of the corner of my eye. Tex.

I place one last kiss on Avery's lips and lean over. In one quick motion I unplug her phone from its charger and hand it to her. I sit back on my heels, skimming my hands over her long legs that rest on either side of my hips.

"Harper?" Avery's voice is an octave too high as she answers.

All I hear on the other end is jumbled words. The light of the phone screen illuminates the stricken expression on Avery's face. I shift back to my side of the bed, adjusting myself and reaching for my sweats on the floor.

Avery grabs my hand. "Stay."

That same whispered plea.

I stay.

She curls into me, the little spoon to my big spoon. "Is West home?" she asks into the phone.

I know for a fact that if he isn't, I will be going to pick Tex up and bring her back here to take my spot in this bed, even if they both argue with me. But I also know for a fact that West wouldn't leave Tex alone, not after the last few days.

"I think it's normal, right? To have a nightmare after all of this," Avery says quietly. There's a muffled response that I can't make out. "Oh. I don't think I'm the one you should be having it about."

Completely unsurprising that Tex is most worried about Avery, and vice versa. I thought Meg and Brooke were close, but Tex and Avery are a whole different level.

"He's here. Yes, I promise. I'm okay. Mm-hmm." Avery shifts, hooking her foot over mine, bringing my attention back to her.

I lay my hand on her waist and give a light squeeze. I'd give anything to take this away from her, from both of them.

"Love you," Avery says softly. There's a small pause. "Always." Avery hits the red circle to end the call and shakes her head. She leans over and plugs her phone in before collapsing back onto the bed with a sigh.

"You okay?" I ask. Dumb question.

She just shrugs. She's not okay.

"Coop?"

"Yeah?"

She rolls onto her stomach. "Will you tell me about your dad?" she asks quietly.

I absentmindedly start rubbing her back, tracing the race logo on the back of her shirt. She shimmies sideways, closing what little space is between us, until her shoulder is pressed into my chest and her cold feet tuck under mine.

"What do you want to know?" I ask.

"I just…" she trails off.

I think I know why she's asking. I just don't know if I should tell her what a great dad I have.

"Are you sure?"

I feel instead of see her nod. So I slip my hand under her shirt, splaying my palm across her back, and start talking. I tell her about our card games, our family dinners, our ridiculous matching Halloween costumes, the evidence of which Dad held over my head as a general threat the few times I brought a girlfriend home. I tell her about his fight. I tell her about the hospital pranks, the Beach Boys playing during every chemo treatment, our FaceTime calls after every single one of my games.

"He sounds amazing," she whispers. "I'm glad you told me."

My heart cracks but I continue tracing circles over her warm, soft skin. Her breathing slowly evens out and finally, she sleeps.

***

"Mr. Miller?" Sadie peeks around the open doorway looking hesitant.

"Hi, Sadie, what can I help you with?" I ask, motioning her in.

"Micah says you know the owner of the store in Three Rocks, Ms. Moore?" Her voice rises into a question and I nod. "I just wondered, she's a lawyer, right?"

"She is," I confirm, wondering where this is going.

"Leadership class is doing a project," Sadie continues, her eyes on the floor. "About future careers, and, do you think she'd talk to me?"

"I think she'd love to," I tell her, which brings her eyes back up to mine. I feel a slight twinge of guilt; adding something, even something small, to Avery's plate right now doesn't feel right. "I know she's really busy right now, but why don't you send her an email? If she doesn't get back to you, just let me know and I'll see if she can at least refer you to someone else. How does that sound?"

Sadie swallows hard and nods. "Okay," she says quietly. She doesn't make a move to leave, just shifts her weight.

"Do you need her email address?" I ask. "And I'll send her a text right now, give her a heads up."

"I have it, I found it on her website," she replies. She stares at my phone as I send Avery a text before I forget. "Just, what's she like? Is she nice?"

I smile, unable to help myself. "Ms. Moore is the reason you're stuck with me as a teacher. I met her the first time I visited Oregon, when I was just a few years older than you. She's very nice and she's also really down to earth. She loves hiking and running, her best friend is her store manager and they always have a ton of fun at work. You'll like her. You guys are actually pretty similar, you're both smart and driven."

Sadie's eyes widen and she mumbles something under her breath and bolts out of my classroom. Apparently I said the wrong thing. Before I can figure out what it was, the bell rings, and students start trickling into my classroom, their noise drowning out any thoughts other than the lesson plan ahead.

That's a lie. I still think about Avery. Just a lot less than I want to.

Chapter Twenty-Three
Avery

Who knew spending hours shattering glass and taking a baseball bat to a broken laptop would feel so good? Micah's parents, apparently. Did it bring me any answers? No. Did it solve any of my problems? Also no. Do I wish I had a lead pipe in my hand right now? Yes.

I spent the last handful of days sitting. Just sitting. I'd sit on the deck, staring out over the trees. Then I'd move to the couch, notebook in my lap, not writing. I don't sit in silence. I mean, I do, I love silence, but I don't sit and stare. I sit and do. Until now.

Some shattered glass fixed that, though. Now I'm ready for the fight.

"Did you know?" I ask bluntly, staring at Jordan over the tiny coffee shop table. I don't acknowledge the man sitting next to him.

"Know what?" Jordan asks.

"He didn't know," Eli says quietly. I don't look at him. "Doesn't know."

"Doesn't know what?" Jordan looks between his brother and I.

"*I* didn't know," Eli adds. "Until just now."

"Excuse me?" I ask in disbelief. There's no way he thinks he can lie his way through this.

I finally look at Eli. Really look at him. He's pale and his hands shake but he looks me straight in the eye without flinching.

"Didn't know what?" Jordan asks again, glancing around the crowded shop.

"I didn't-"

"I know who gave you the black eye," I say, interrupting Eli's bullshit. "I heard his story. So don't give me that, don't lie."

"Black eye?" Jordan asks. "Avery? Are you okay?"

I ignore him. Eli does, too.

"I deserved the black eye then and I deserve your rage, and hers, now," Eli says quietly. "And so, so much more."

"A little late for that," I snap. "Don't you think?"

Recognition dawns on Jordan's face. "What the actual fuck, Eli?" he hisses. "I thought you asked if the rumor was true because you *liked* her! You were just, what, trying to protect your-fucking-self?!"

"It's complicated," Eli says. He keeps his attention on me, not his sputtering brother. "I admit it now, today. I tried to admit it back then. But I swear, I didn't know what really happened."

Jordan's chair clatters loudly to the floor as he stands and the entire coffee shop looks our way. Jordan looms over his brother. "Stand up," he demands.

"What do you mean you didn't know?" I ask as Eli stands.

Now it's my turn to look in confusion between my two tablemates. Eli holds his hands up in surrender as Jordan steps toward him. There's a blur of a fist. A crack of cartilage. Eli stumbles back, a hand over his face. A barista gasps, as do half the patrons.

Jordan storms away, shaking his fist and swearing loudly, every widened pair of eyes in the place tracking his movement. When he's nearly to the door, he turns back.

"Sir!" A man stands from his own table, moving to intercept Jordan.

"I'm leaving," Jordan says loudly. "But she can't stay with him."

"I'm calling the police," the man says as he pulls out his phone.

"No need," Eli says thickly as he tries to catch the blood flowing freely from his nose in his cupped hand. "I'm fine, that was deserved. I'm leaving."

"Are you okay?" Jordan asks me, the man still standing guard between us, preventing him from coming closer.

I nod, which is a lie. I'm far from okay.

A drop of Eli's blood hits the table as he picks up his wallet and all I can see is Harper's blood, dripping from her hand, as Jordan carried her through the trees.

My vision blurs. The sounds from the coffee shop sharpen, then fade.

"Breathe. In through your nose, out through your mouth," Eli whispers, grabbing the napkins from the table. He drops a business card on the table. There's a smear of blood on the corner of it. "I'd like to talk, but, obviously, only if you want."

I just stare at the blood, unmoving.

"Avery, breathe."

I breathe.

In through my mouth, out through my nose.

Again.

"Miss?"

I look up. A dark-haired barista is hovering over me, her eyes on the bright red spots on the table.

"So sorry," I tell her with a practiced smile, my mask of indifference firmly in place.

"Are you okay?" she asks.

"Yes, sorry," I say automatically. "That was, well, unexpected. I'm so sorry for that scene." I tip Jordan's chair back up and take my phone from the table.

"Don't forget your mocha!"

My freaking mocha. I hadn't even gotten my drink from the counter when I spotted the brothers sitting in the corner.

"Of course, thank you," I say with another automatic smile.

I feel the stare of every single person on me as I weave through the tables, making my way to the counter. Their eyes, along with their silence, follow me to the door. Fuck it. I tip my to-go cup in mock toast to my audience and push the door open with my hip.

And then I bolt.

"Eli!" I call, chasing after the man who assaulted my best friend, silently thanking the girl who slid a drink stopper into my lid as I grabbed it from the counter.

I catch up to him in the small parking lot. He's holding his shirt to his nose, stemming the flow of blood, beside the open driver's side door of a truck. Jordan is leaning against the rear bumper, arms crossed.

"I need to know," I say, when both men look at me. "I need to know what you meant."

Eli nods, bringing the shirt down. "Can I change first?"

"No, you fucking cannot," Jordan snaps, moving to stand next to me.

I look at him, at his hand that's once again clenched in a fist. He is no longer the sweet, kind teenager I once knew. I mean, he might still be sweet and kind, but right now, anger radiates off him in palpable waves.

I turn to Eli. "Yes, change."

Jordan shifts angrily.

"I don't want to see the blood," I say quietly.

Eli opens the back door of the cab and reaches inside. He digs a shirt out and I turn around, facing Jordan.

I was surprised when Jordan answered my call at 7 a.m. this morning, even more surprised that I caught the brothers in our hometown instead of Seattle. I wasn't sure I would be able to walk into the coffee shop despite being the one to set the meeting, but now that I'm here, I can't walk away.

"Jordan, I need to hear this. All of it. I get your anger. Trust me, I do. But I need to hear it. You need to back down."

Jordan studies me for a moment. I wonder what he sees.

Whatever it is, he nods. "I'll be quiet."

"Here?" Eli asks, looking around the parking lot.

"No. There."

Both Jordan and Eli stare at me, shocked.

"But you're riding with me," I tell Jordan.

***

"I never came back here," Jordan says, staring out the windshield at the river below. "After that night, I couldn't. Didn't matter who was throwing the party."

"Me either," I reply.

Not that I went to any parties at all after Harper left. After that night.

"Fuck," he whispers. "I seriously thought you called us to convince us to work with your dad. I was confused when Eli was so adamantly against that offer."

Now it's my turn to whisper "fuck." I have a very bad feeling about this.

A light rain starts to fall as we step out of the car. I tug my beanie, Cooper's beanie, down over my ears and zip my fleece. I should have brought a jacket.

Eli doesn't move as we walk up behind him, he just continues leaning against the tree, looking out over the river.

"I don't remember a thing from that night, past about 10 p.m.," he starts, not looking at us. "I only remember waking up with a black eye the next morning and this deep sense of dread. Kyle thought it was hysterical that I got in a fight I couldn't remember. I laughed along with him but it didn't feel funny at all."

"Kyle was the worst," Jordan says. While I agree with him, I cut a glare in his direction anyway. "Sorry, I'll be quiet."

"I won't lie, I partied hard that whole year as I'm sure many college freshmen do," Eli continues, like Jordan didn't say anything. "But I went way too hard. Fake ID, easy classes, dumbass friends. Not that I blame them, those decisions were mine. They were just easy to make when I always had a buddy willing to go with me. Then I got home for summer and had all my high school friends, my little brother…and I just kept going.

"That night, I got you guys the keg, but I was drinking from a flask. I remember laughing, watching you and Harper together in a chair by the fire. She was flirting with Sam. You, of course, had Jordan, but you always gravitated back toward each other. The last thing I remember is taking a couple shots with Kyle when I realized I had no chance of getting Harper away from you."

I bite the inside of my cheek so hard the metallic taste of blood floods my mouth. I swallow it down, along with the ball of emotion, adrenaline, anger, *something*, that's choking me.

"You couldn't have her, so you-" I stop. I can't even say it.

Eli finally looks at me and his eyes are bloodshot. "The last thing I remember is taking the shots. I swear on my life, I don't remember anything."

Now I can't *not* say it.

"You had a fucking knife to her ribs, Eli! You somehow tore the hell out of her finger, she bled all over your brother as he carried her back to his truck." I shrug off the steadying hand Jordan lays on my shoulder. "Her shirt was missing. She was a shaking, bleeding mess in the woods when I found her."

"Fuck," Eli says in barely a whisper. "Fuck, that's so much worse than I even thought. My knife? What the fuck?"

"Yeah, Eli, what the fuck is right! How could you not fucking remember that?" I'm shouting now and Jordan is holding me back.

Holding me back from what, I'm not sure.

"Was she, did I…" Eli can't say it.

I wait. I'm going to make him ask. Make him say the word.

"Did I rape her?" Eli whispers.

I shake my head slowly.

"Thank fuck," he mutters.

"Really?" Jordan snaps. "Because I was there. She took one look at me and *cowered*. She fucking *shrank* at the sight of me. An hour before, she was laughing and begging me to dance."

"I-" Eli starts but is immediately interrupted.

"She had panic attacks for years. *Years.*" I feel Jordan's grip on my arm tighten.

I gasp. How does he know that?

"I just-" Eli tries again.

"There was a bloodstain in my truck when Dad sold it," Jordan cuts him off.

His words and the tightened grip on my arm make me pull against him.

"Let her hit me," Eli says, his dark, haunted eyes finding mine.

"I'm not going to hit you," I retort.

I really want to hit him.

Instead, I storm down the narrow switchback path carved in the hill as soon as Jordan releases his grip. I sit down on the rocks, the river inches from my shoes, and let the rain soak me.

Why am I here? What did I hope to get out of this? Sure as hell not this, Eli not knowing. Not remembering. Now what?

Cautious footsteps approach and I tense, wondering which brother it is. Which one I want it to be.

"Here," Jordan says, sitting down beside me.

I take the jacket he offers and pull it on. "Where is he?"

"Back there." Jordan tilts his head toward the path.

I don't know if he means he's behind us or he's up the steep embankment. I don't bother looking.

We sit without speaking, the river flowing peacefully past, the sound of raindrops filling the silence. It's too quiet. Too peaceful. The opposite of every emotion swirling inside.

I pick up a rock and hurl it into the water. It makes a gentle splash, nowhere near as satisfying as I hoped it would be. I can't decide between throwing every rock on this riverbank into the water or dunking myself. How many times did I jump in this river after a run, the cold water washing away the sweat? Could it wash away *this*?

"How did you know she had panic attacks for years?" I finally ask.

"You and I might not have lasted all that much longer, but you think after that night, I'd not check on her ever again?" Jordan asks incredulously.

"She never told me," I say quietly.

She didn't. Like a true friend, when I told her Jordan and I had broken up, she cursed his name. Many times, in fact.

I can feel him looking at me. "What?"

He shakes his head with a small smile. "You two. Always protecting each other."

"But I didn't protect her. I was too late," I whisper.

I'm still too late. I angrily wipe the tears that fall.

"I'm sorry, Avery. If I would have even thought he was capable, if I would have had any idea it was him…" He shakes his head again, this time without a smile.

I can see the anger in his own eyes, the fresh wound of knowing it was his brother.

"I need to know the rest," I say quietly.

"Me, too." Jordan pulls his phone from his pocket and sends a text.

Two minutes later, Eli appears.

"I need to know the rest," I tell him, repeating my words.

He nods and sits a few feet away from Jordan and I, staring at the dark water. I wait.

"A few days later, I heard the rumors. I didn't know what to do. I asked Jordan if anything had happened. He'd know, right? He said no."

"She had begged us not to say anything," Jordan says.

I confirm with a silent nod.

"I don't know how no one saw you get her out of there, but it stayed a rumor," Eli says.

"Someone yelled the cops were coming. Nearly everyone scattered. Sam made sure," Jordan says robotically.

I nod silently again.

"But still, that bad feeling. I didn't remember a fight. The guys that I'd normally scuffle with, not a scratch on them. Jordan was adamant that nothing happened, but there was a flicker of a lie. Avery, you had left for the beach, Harper had moved to Texas, I didn't know who to ask." Eli finally turns to look at me. "But then I knew where to go. A family friend who happened to be a lawyer, whose daughter was best friends with the rumored victim."

"Fuck," I whisper.

"It took a week or so to get up the courage, but I walked into your dad's office and just blurted out that I thought I hurt her. He listened and said he'd call me the next day. I had immediate regret. I won't lie. *Immediate* regret. I thought I had just thrown my life away. I went out and got shit-faced with a couple buddies. Completely blackout drunk. Again."

I remember that night. Jordan called me when he was driving to get them, then again after he got them home. He told me his brother was in a real mood. Combative.

"I was hungover as hell when your dad called me but ready to face whatever I did." Eli's eyes find mine again. "He said nothing happened to her. I trusted him."

I see red.

"What. The. Fuck."

Rage isn't just red. Rage is the fire burning in my veins, it's the metallic taste of adrenaline. Rage is pushing to my feet and as soon as Eli follows suit, kneeing him in the groin.

Chapter Twenty-Four
Avery

"You went to confront Eli?" Harper asks as she unclips Zero's leash. "Alone?"

We watch as Zero takes off up the beach to chase the tiny sand pipers along the water's edge, happy in the way only beach dogs can be.

"Yeah. Well, I mean, Jordan was there, too," I tell her, kicking a rock that the ocean has left behind.

Harper's eyes follow her dog running ahead of us in a ridiculous waterproof doggy jacket as she silently considers my answer. Sheets of rain roll in off the ocean and I tighten my rain jacket hood over my beanie, wondering why I thought a beach walk was a good idea.

We could be sitting in front of the fireplace right now. Although, after days and days of sitting on the couch, this really is what I need.

"Just say it," I finally say, bumping her shoulder with mine.

"Sometimes things are just a lot, you know?" she says, parroting Jessie's wise words. "Like, what do I even say right now? You said you had a meeting in town, then I find out it was with him? Them? You should have told me."

Guilt creeps in. Should I have told her? Probably. Would I do the same thing again? Yes.

"I mean, it *was* a meeting, but I'm sorry. I didn't know if I'd even be able to go inside the coffee shop and I didn't want you to worry," I say.

"I've been worried about you since I opened Alex's card," Harper replies, her eyes still following Zero. "Since he walked in that door. Since you bolted from The Merc before he even drove out of the parking lot. Also, since we were seven years old. You're my person, I'm always going to worry."

"But I don't want you to worry *more*. I mean, this is a lot for you, too, right? *And* you're pregnant. You don't need to worry about me. I'm okay." Maybe if I say I'm okay often enough, it'll be true.

"You're definitely not okay," Harper snorts. "But it's okay to *not* be okay." She loops her arm through mine as we walk.

"I hate not being okay," I sigh.

"We can hide under blankets again," she offers.

"I think I'm past the blankets," I reply.

I'm definitely past blankets.

"Rage room?"

"I think it worked too well," I say. "I kneed Eli in the balls."

Silence.

Two beats of silence, followed by what might be a sob.

Shit. This is not the reaction I thought I'd get. That I'd hoped to get. I just wanted to reassure her that I'm okay, that I'm ready to face reality.

"Harper?" I stop and look at my best friend.

She's laughing. Full-on hysterically laughing. Zero circles back to check on her, that's how hard she laughs.

"You didn't!" she gasps.

"I did." A trickle of satisfaction creeps in at her reaction. I bite the inside of my cheek, trying to hide my smirk.

"That falls under 'anything and everything' I guess?" Harper asks, laughter starting all over again when she catches my smile.

I snort. "Yeah. I guess. Maybe I should have kneed him harder though. Like, I really thought it'd make me feel better. It did, don't get me wrong, but it didn't solve anything. So we're back to the same question…now what do I do?"

"Aves, you don't have to do anything. It's not your job to fix any of this," she says gently. "And-"

"Yes, it is," I say, cutting her off before she can continue. "It's my actual job to find justice. I'm a lawyer. It's what I do."

It's laughable, really, that I even think there's justice. There's not. Not for any of this.

Harper's thumb moves to her scar. "That's not-"

That fucking scar. That's what makes me lose it. Watching her rub the scar.

"Years, Harper. For years, I looked for the truth. Years of barely being able to say your name. Years of letting you down, never finding him, and he was right fucking there!" I'm yelling now, scaring Zero, who circles us, worriedly nosing our hands.

"Avery." She's not yelling. Her voice is calm, measured, and everything I do not feel right now. "I will tell you this over and over again: You did not let me down. I am okay."

"But I-"

"No," she says loudly, cutting me off. She looks at me with rain droplets in her lashes, her finger still on her scar, determination blazing in her eyes. "You did not let me down. I am here today because of you. If you want justice, do it for *you*. For your brother."

My brother. Another person I've let down. I haven't reached out, not even a text, since my hasty exit from our conversation on The Merc's front porch.

And while we're at it, let's add my mom to the list. I can't even look at her contact picture on my phone, let alone call her.

Maybe I'm not ready for the fight. Maybe I do need the blankets.

"What if I can't?" I whisper. "What if I can't find even a shred of justice for *any* of this?"

Harper shrugs. "Then I guess it'll be my turn to kick someone in the balls."

I can't help but laugh at her serious expression. "Thanks, Harp."

"And it's probably going to be your dad," she adds.

"While I appreciate that, I don't know if that will be enough for me," I say tiredly.

I do know. It won't be.

***

"You really went to confront him…and you went alone?" Cooper asks, an unreadable expression on his face as he echoes Harper's words hours later.

I've noticed the two of them have similarities so I brace myself for his reaction when I confirm that I did go to confront Eli and I did go alone.

"Avery?" he says.

"I just needed to," I say quietly. I fidget with the hem of my shirt.

I don't want to do this right now. I don't want to explain myself all over again. I shouldn't have to.

"Ave, look at me." He moves around the counter and waits patiently for me to look up. When I finally do, I'm startled by his smile. "That's amazing."

"Wh-what?" Of all the reactions, this was not one I expected.

"That's courageous and brave and honestly pretty badass," Cooper says. "You're amazing."

I don't know if I'd use any of those adjectives, but my cheeks flush. "It didn't feel like any of those things at the time," I admit. "It just felt like something I needed to do."

It felt like something I couldn't *not* do. Like I needed to make up for the days I spent sitting. Staring. I needed answers so I could move forward.

"Did it help?" he asks. "Seeing him?"

"I don't know," I say honestly. "I might be more confused now."

I'm definitely more confused. I got answers, but no solutions. So I'm still stuck, not moving forward.

"And Harper?" Cooper questions. "How is she?"

I know they've gotten closer over the last week. They basically trade off babysitting me. Cooper has nights, Harper has days. Their paths always cross at least once a day. Well, until today. Now, instead of the two of them whispering about me, it's my turn to give him a report on her.

I sigh. "She asked if I thought Eli had changed, made up for it, I guess."

Her quiet questions as we walked in the rain did little to calm me, but she seemed happy with my answers. Happy with where Eli is now. I just don't think I'll ever feel the way she does and I'm not sure how to deal with that.

"And? Has he?"

"Jordan says he doesn't drink, that he leads the non-profit side of their company, that he's a good man," I recite robotically.

"Do you believe him?" The edge of doubt in Cooper's voice tells me exactly what he believes. This is apparently something he and Harper *don't* have in common.

"I believe the first two, sure, but he assaulted a teenage girl in the woods with a fucking knife. I don't think 'good man' is the right description." I clench my jaw and look away, trying to fight the tears of anger suddenly pooling in my eyes.

I know people can change, I do. I've seen it with Liam, haven't I? But I also thought I saw it with my father, and, well, now we're here. Now fucking what?

Cooper reaches his hand up and cups my jaw, rubbing the pad of his thumb over my cheek, wiping the single stray tear that spilled over. He waits for me to look up at him before he asks, "And how do you feel now?"

"Like I should have kneed him in the balls harder." A lot fucking harder.

Cooper's hand on my cheek freezes and then drops. "You kneed him in the balls?"

Really? I've seen both him and West, their hands fisted, fury radiating off them, and I'm going to be judged for my literal knee-jerk reaction?

"Jordan broke his nose, so I didn't even do the most damage. And-"

"Can I take you to dinner?" Cooper interrupts me.

"What?" I stare at him like he's lost his mind. I think he might have.

"Right now. Can I take you to dinner?"

I motion to the ingredients that I found in a grocery bag on my doorstep after my walk with Tex, now scattered on the kitchen island. "I thought we were going to make stir fry?"

"I think facing the man who assaulted your friend and kneeing him in the balls deserves a celebration," he says as he quickly starts to put everything on the counter away. "Pizza from the cafe. Wine. Strawberry ice cream for dessert."

It's my turn to laugh. That was not at all what I was expecting.

"You're serious?" I ask.

"Dead serious." Cooper closes the fridge and steps back around the island to wrap me in a bear hug. "You're amazing. You deserve pizza."

I lean into him and wrap my arms around his waist. My mind quiets as I breathe him in. It feels like I've waited all day for this. I might have woken up this morning and chosen violence, but right now, I choose him. I choose quiet.

"Are you smelling me?" Cooper asks, not loosening his hold. He buries his face in my neck. "Because I could smell your strawberry shampoo every day and never be sick of it."

I laugh again, both from his words and the way his scruff tickles my skin. "Harper teases me for it."

"For your shampoo?" He places a soft kiss in the crook of my neck.

"Yep. And it's why she stocks that lotion at the store. I don't even use it, it's just there to tease me for my teenage years."

"That damn lotion," Cooper mutters. He pulls back and drops his forehead to mine. "It hit me like a ton of bricks the second I smelled it, my first ten minutes in town."

"I'm sorry," I whisper. I don't know if I am though.

He slowly shakes his head. "No apology needed."

Before I can say another word, Cooper tilts my chin up and threads his hands through my hair. He slants his mouth over mine in a slow, tender, leisurely kiss. The kind of kiss that makes heat bloom from head to toe, my heart down to my core. The kind of kiss that makes me forget reality.

"Ave?" Cooper whispers against my lips. "Pizza?"

"Pizza?"

I should probably be worried about how quickly I get lost in him, how quickly I've come to count on him, but I just...can't. I've waited eleven years for him, my life is crumbling, what is there to lose?

"C'mon," Cooper says.

And with one last, light kiss, he pulls his beanie off, a black one with his college team's logo, and tugs it down over my head before we head out into the rain.

***

Despite the pep talk Cooper gave me over pizza, bile rises in my throat as I smile into the camera. There is not a single fiber of my being that wants to see my father in any way, shape, or form, yet still, I smile.

It's ironic that it was my father who conditioned me to hide my emotions behind a mask of indifference as this skill will somehow, in a yet to be determined way, lead to his downfall.

I might not feel the same way as Harper, I don't know if I ever will, but I'm more than willing to shift my focus from Eli to my father. We both agree he has sins to pay for. Right now, I just need more time to come up with an actual plan.

"Everything looks great on that contract, but I'm hesitant on moving forward with anything new, it's the slow season for me," I say, my voice laced with regret. "Trying to tighten up the finances."

Suddenly I'm a liar, an excellent one at that. Apparently I just have to have a massive amount of rage bubbling inside, leftover pizza in the fridge, and almond croissants on the counter to be able to pull off any and all lies.

It *is* the slow season, that's not a lie, but thanks to Team Merc, the store is holding its own and we even have a fairly steady stream of renters.

Evanston Orchards will be the last deal I ever sign with Dad, and that's only if I can't push him the rest of the way out. I just have to hope he doesn't realize what I'm doing.

I send the text I already had written. The reply is immediate.

Edward:
Done.

"You sure?" Dad asks, frowning as he looks to the side of his screen where I'm sure Edward's message is appearing.

"It's just not the time for anything new," I tell him, trying to look disappointed.

"Right, right." He nods, obviously distracted, exactly as planned.

I might not have a solid plan, but one thing is clear, I need to separate my finances from his. I can't do that alone. First thing this morning, I called Edward, now my co-conspirator.

"I'm sorry!" I blurted out as soon as he answered, realizing at the sound of his voice what I had done.

"Avery, you should know by now that I'm an early riser," he chuckled.

"No, for everything else," I said as emotions welled up, making me take an unsteady breath.

"Does this mean what I think it means?" he asked carefully.

It meant I was an idiot. Edward has worked for my father for years and years. Before law school, who was the one that would check in weekly, just to see if I needed anything? It definitely wasn't my dad. Whose handwriting was on every single birthday card? Again, not Dad's. The flowers at The Town Mercantile on opening day? Edward.

"It means that I know about Alex. I know you were trying to get a hold of me to give me warning. It means I know that you've always been in my corner, even when Dad wasn't."

It meant that I wasn't just an idiot, I was the emotionless robot my father molded me into.

"I always hoped, Avery, that he would see what an amazing person you are, and when it seemed like he was finally noticing, I was happy to step back. Well, not happy, because I've missed you, but willing, because I will never stop wishing the best for you."

"Honestly, Edward, the opposite should have happened. I should have realized how terrible he is, was, and always will be." I swallowed down the lump in my throat. "And I've missed you, too."

"People change, Avery. And the fact that you held out, hoping for that change, says more about how amazing you are than anything else," he said gently.

I closed my eyes and pictured his warm smile and kind eyes. I sighed and shook my head even though he couldn't see me. "Well, obviously he cannot change. And now that I know about Alex and the things Dad did that go way, way deeper than just, you know, refusing to acknowledge his child, it's time to change things for him."

And change they will. Starting now. I bring my focus back to the man on the screen.

"It just seems, if you're easing back, that Evanston is the one that will take the most work," Dad says. "If we have Jordan on board though, his construction experience, the work that needs to be done…" He lets the thought hang in the silence.

Jordan. My second call this morning at Harper's suggestion.

"What about Eli?" Jordan had asked.

"There's only one man I have my sights set on now," I replied.

The one giving me what's supposed to be an easy smile through the screen. Now I see it for what it is. Manipulative. Just like all his other smiles.

"Let's fucking go." Jordan's exact words just a couple hours ago replay in my head as I tilt my head like I'm confused.

Let the games begin.

"Did I forget to tell you? Shoot, must have slipped my mind. Jordan took a look at the barn inspections already," I say with a smile. "Special favor, you know?"

"Already talked to him about it, huh? Finally put the past behind you?" Dad asks, his smile turns into a smug grin. "Knew you two would figure it out."

Hook, line, and sinker.

"I didn't want to say anything…" I give an embarrassed shrug. "There's a reason I want this one to myself."

Dad lets out a deep laugh, shaking his head. "I knew there was a reason. Just can't hide a thing from me."

I smile and bring my palms to my cheeks, trying to hide the fact that I'm gritting my teeth in frustration. How am I going to pull this off if I can't make it through one conversation?

"Well, I just got a ping from Edward with a new opportunity, let me look through it more carefully, but would you be willing to do partial?"

Another thing that will never change: his inability to hear no.

"It just feels like I need to keep a close eye on things here," I say. I make a show of moving papers around. "I'll see what I can come up with. Reconvene tomorrow?"

He nods and cuts the call without another word. My hands shake with adrenaline as I reach for my water. How long will I be able to fake it like this?

Chapter Twenty-Five
Cooper
(before)

As I stare into the flames, I wonder, for the millionth time, how this week is going by so fast. I didn't even want to come. A beach you can't swim at? What's the point? Being stuck with my sister and her friend? No, thank you. Missing Zeke's birthday? It's on a party barge, our entire class is invited. No fucking way.

But now, I don't want to leave.

But now, Avery.

The girl I can't get enough of. The one tucked into this little niche in the rocks next to me, lost in her notebook. She's been quieter than usual, something seems to be bothering her tonight. Her pen has moved slower, she's paused and crossed things out.

Right on cue, she sighs and taps her pen against the page before striking an entire line out with a quick stroke.

I lean over and press a kiss on top of her head, just because I can. Just because next week at this time I'll be stuck in a car somewhere in California, listening to Meg's terrible music, getting texts from my teammates, asking if I'm ready for camp, wishing I was back here. With her.

"What are you thinking about?" Avery asks.

I didn't even realize the scratch of her pen on paper had stopped. What am I thinking about?

Her. Always her.

"You," I say simply.

Her cheeks flush. "Is it because I'm bad company tonight?" She closes her notebook and looks up at me. "I'm sorry."

"Absolutely not. I'd sit here all night with you, even if we didn't say a word."

It's not a lie. Just having her warmth pressed against me, anchoring me to this moment, the crackling fire, the distant rhythmic waves, it's a different kind of happiness. A kind I've never experienced. Stillness. I've never been good at being still until her.

Avery moves her gaze to the fire. Silence settles between us. Her head rests on my shoulder, my hand is on her thigh. I really could stay here all night.

"It's a book," she finally says. "I'm writing a book."

"A book?" I'm shocked. Not that she's writing an entire book, but that she finally told me. I had started doubting that I'd ever find out what was in there.

"I've never told anyone that before. Ever." There's a hitch in her voice, like she's nervous.

"That's amazing, Ave. Seriously. You're writing a book!" I squeeze her thigh gently.

"Thanks," she replies quietly.

"I can't wait to read it. To tell everyone that I know the author."

"You don't even know what it's about!" she immediately protests. "Or if I'll get a book deal!"

"Don't need to know and I know you will," I say, never more confident about anything.

If whatever is in that notebook is half as incredible as her, best-seller, for sure.

She shakes her head. "Well today it seems like an impossible dream."

"That's why I'm here, to hold you together when you don't think you can do it." I push aside the reality of us: two days left. "So, can I help?"

Avery huffs a small laugh. "I think writing is usually a solo process."

"Sounds like you need a team behind you."

"Sounds like a quarterback thing to say."

She doesn't have to be looking at me for me to know she's rolling her eyes.

"You gonna let me quarterback this then?" I ask.

She laughs. "What does that even mean?"

"It means that whatever in that notebook has you stuck, let's work through it."

"You're serious?" She drums her fingernails on the cover of the notebook. I bet she's biting the inside of her cheek, too.

"Absolutely."

"Okay," she says, finally turning her head to look up at me. There's a small smile playing on her strawberry lips. "Yeah. You can quarterback it."

Chapter Twenty-Six
Cooper

"I can't do this," Avery whispers the second I walk into her office.

When I walked past on my way out to The Merc, she was typing quickly and methodically. Now, she slumps in her chair, like the fight and fury the rage room brought to the surface has finally drained away.

"You're shaking," I say quietly, setting her new Team Merc mug down and the plant Jessie handed me next to it. I lean my hip against her desk. "Have you eaten yet?"

There's an almond croissant with one bite taken out of it next to her laptop and an unopened protein bar peeks out from under a haphazard stack of papers. At least there's calories in the mocha, right?

"I think so?" she answers, eyes still glued to her laptop.

I've been waiting for this moment. I thought quiet Avery was spiraling, but I think this is it. All weekend she stared at documents, trying to find something, anything, that would annihilate her father.

While I'd also like to see his life blown up, I don't want it at the expense of Avery. And it feels like we're precariously close to that happening.

"Hey." I move around her desk and into her space. "Ave?"

"I'm sorry," she says, finally looking up at me. Her eyes are filled with tears. "Hi."

I smile gently and reach to cup her cheek. She sighs and leans into my touch. A single tear spills over and I swipe it away with the pad of my thumb. She tips her chin up and I lean down to brush my lips across hers.

"You okay?"

Why do I keep asking the same stupid question over and over again? As usual, no, she's not okay. Obviously.

"I'm better now, seeing you," she says, her new answer ever since the rage room.

I smile at this new little thing we have between us, something that breaks the heavy moments, that makes asking the dumbest question worth it.

The corner of her lip quirks. "I mean, you did bring me coffee."

"I'm glad I'm good for something."

She huffs a laugh. "Coffee, hikes, pizza dates, pep talks, and just, you know, holding me together when I fall apart."

The memory hits just as hard, just as clear as every other reminder of our past does. I lean down, resting my hands on the arms of her chair, caging her in.

"That's why I'm here, to hold you together when you don't think you can do it." I whisper the same words I said to her so many years ago.

Avery looks up, bringing her lips within an inch of mine. "You said that before."

"Meant in then and I mean it now." I watch her eyes flick down to my mouth.

"You think you can just quarterback all this?" she whispers.

"I love a challenge," I tell her, which makes her raise an eyebrow.

She pulls away, leaning back in her chair and crossing her arms, a smirk playing on her lips. "And just how do you think you're going to quarterback this mess?"

Well, shit. How am I going to quarterback this? There's no plan. None.

I stand up and glance around, like the answer is just going to be sitting here. Except, it actually is.

Thank you, Jessie.

"Like I recall telling you many, many years ago, it starts with a team." I nudge the tiny planter Jessie sent with me toward her.

Avery leans forward. "What's that?" she asks. "Is that…"

I wasn't sure it was a good idea when I watched Jessie set it gently on top of the new sage green Team Merc mug that I'm sure Tex special-ordered, but now, it might be just what Avery needs.

"Jessie said sometimes things are a lot, then handed me the planter and asked me to deliver it." I glance at the plant inside the miniature planter and grin.

"It looks like…" she trails off and narrows her eyes.

"A dick?" I supply.

Her lip twitches and she looks at the planter again. "A dick," she confirms. "You brought me a dick plant."

"I'm just the delivery guy!" I say, holding up my hands in mock surrender.

Avery laughs and suddenly, I have a plan. I glance at my watch. I have less than ten minutes before I have to leave for work.

"Come on," I tell her. "Bring your new mug."

"Freaking Harper," Avery mutters as she follows me down the hall.

I'm sure she just realized the mug is new.

"I don't get credit for that, either, or, well, this." I sweep my hands wide.

She gives me a blank look. "What are we looking at?" she asks, looking around the kitchen.

"You don't see it?"

She shakes her head so I turn the wine bottle sitting in the middle of the kitchen island.

"Brian?" Avery only needs a glance at the custom "thank you" label to know who sent the wine.

"Brian," I confirm. "Anything else?"

She studies the kitchen more carefully. She nods toward the mason jar that holds a bouquet of pens. "Those have Harper written all over them."

"Technically they have curse words written all over them."

Creative curse words at that. Glad I noticed 'douchecanoe' on the one I grabbed last night before I took it to work.

Avery's eyes fall on the pastry box in the corner near the knife block. "And the croissants?"

"I was sworn to secrecy." I raise an eyebrow, a silent challenge for her to guess anyway.

"Marabelle?"

"Bingo."

"Green smoothies? That has Zoe written all over it," she says, spotting the notecard-size recipe book propped on the blender.

I just nod.

Avery shakes her head and leans forward to wrap her arms around me. I tuck her under my chin, relishing the way she molds herself to me. How she fits. How her breathing slows until it matches mine.

I might not be able to fix anything, but I have this.

"Hey Cooper?" she says softly.

"Yeah?"

She wiggles out of my hold just far enough to peer up at me. Her eyes are clear, no stray tears, just happy little flecks of blue. "Thank you."

My heart hammers as her hands slip under my shirt, her touch gentle but sure. "Like I said, I'm just the delivery guy."

"Just the delivery guy?" she asks innocently, like she's not sending fire licking up my ribs with her touch.

I send a silent thank you to her friends, to the community she helped build, for this moment. Because the smile playing on her lips isn't because of me, it's because of them. I really am just the delivery guy.

Her fingers stray along my ribcage but her sparkling eyes stay glued to mine. "I'd say you're a lot more than that. You really are holding me together. You know when I need the chaos quieted, you know when I need to be reminded of the real world. Of *my* world, here. You know when I need pizza and a pep talk. But right now, I need this."

She pushes onto her toes and presses her lips to mine. It's not one of the quick kisses we share before I leave for work, it's not a soft goodnight kiss after she whispers for me to stay, it's not a kiss to dry her tears.

It's everything else. It's strawberries, a hint of chocolate, and Avery. It's long-legged, Dream Girl Avery. It's the years we lost, the ache in my chest that never went away. It's all consuming. *She* is all consuming.

I bury my hands in her hair, tilting her chin up, silently asking for more. In typical Avery fashion, she goes above and beyond. She nips at my lip while her fingers dance their way up my ribs. When she traces my abs before slipping her fingers into my waistband, I groan.

I have to go to work. I know I do. But I don't want to. Really, really don't want to.

"Ave, wait," I murmur halfheartedly, sliding my hands beneath her shirt, needing to feel her soft skin, before kissing her again.

"Hmm?" she hums, the sound vibrating between us.

I force myself to pull back. Her cheeks are flushed, her strawberry lips, swollen from kissing, are tilted into a dazed smile, and she has that fire in her eyes, that same look from the night in the rain, before her world was crumbling, and I'm stunned silent. I don't know what it is, but fuck, that look does me in every time.

I see the clock on the stove out of the corner of my eye.

"Fuck." It comes out as a rumble. A sigh. A painful utter.

I don't want to stop. I want to carry her to her bedroom and lay her on her bed. I want her spread out before me, my Dream Girl in every sense of the world. I don't know if I'd even get that far. The couch. Fuck it. Right here.

I can't.

We can't.

But I really fucking want to.

"Coop?" She tilts her head, studying me.

"You're beautiful," I tell her. It's the only thing I can say.

She smiles and shakes her head. "I'm a mess."

"My favorite mess," I correct. "A beautiful mess. *My* mess."

"How do you always know what to say?" she whispers as a phone buzzes beside us.

Her hazy smile freezes and her eyes close. "I can't deal with him yet." She leans sideways to grab the buzzing device from the counter. "Oh. Yours," she says. The relief that just washed over her vanishes, replaced with a frown. "Your dad."

"Great fucking timing," I mutter as I swipe my screen to answer. "Hi, Dad, everything okay?"

I don't hear his reply. I just hear Avery gasp.

"Timing. That's it. That's fucking it."

She's out of my grasp, off the counter, and running for her office.

***

I'm trying to text Meg back one-handed, coffee in my other hand, when I round the corner to my classroom. I stop short.

A student sits on the floor, his back against my classroom door, hood pulled over his head, which is dropped onto his knees. Everything about his body language screams distraught teenager.

I pocket my phone. Megan is going to have to wait.

Micah gives me a halfhearted chin nod as I approach. His eyes are bloodshot and he looks away quickly.

"Hey Micah, everything okay?" I ask, even though the answer is obvious.

I really need a new question to ask when someone is very much not okay.

"No," he replies, standing without another word.

I push open my door and motion him inside. Micah trudges in and lets his backpack fall to the floor. I wince, wondering if his laptop survived.

Before I can even turn the lights on, he drops into one of the chairs in the front row and buries his face in his arms.

"Shrimp tacos, Mia," he mumbles. "Or wasting singer's ex."

"Didn't quite catch that," I say, unable to translate his mutterings into actual English.

He raises his head and glares at me through red eyes. "She won't even talk to me! Or answer a single text!"

Only one person could leave Micah this upset. "Sadie?"

He doesn't answer, he just drops his head back to the desk.

I don't know what to say. "I'm sorry, Micah," I tell him when I can't think of anything else.

"So now what?" His voice is muffled, but at least this time I can tell what he's saying.

"Well, did something happen between you guys?" I ask gently.

Micah raises his head and resumes glaring at me. "I can't tell you what happened."

Anger radiates off him and I'm at a total loss. I don't recall any professor going over this during college but I do remember one joking that middle school teachers should minor in psychology. Now I'm wondering if it really was a joke.

"Well, if I don't know what happened, I can't really help. I'm sorry, Micah," I tell him. I do want to help, I just honestly don't know how. Story of my life. Dad, Meg, Avery, and now Micah. "Maybe she just needs a little space."

"I promised I wouldn't tell anyone," he says after a beat of silence. "So you can't tell."

"As a teacher, and as someone who cares about Sadie, if it's something serious, something bad, I am required to report it. As her friend, I'd hope you'd want it reported," I say, watching him carefully.

I'm reminded once again how much my students go through that we have no idea about. It could be as simple as having an argument with her mom, who I only "know" through emails, but, especially at this age, little things can feel really big. And sometimes it is something big, which I really, truly hope is not the case.

"No, nothing like that!" Micah looks horrified. "It's just, she got mad when I told her I was going to stand up to her...someone for her."

"It's hard to know where to draw the line sometimes. Do they need a friend to stand up for them or do they just need someone to listen?" I nod to encourage him to continue, not even surprised at this point that his life is mimicking mine, it has been since I met the kid. I'm guessing Sadie is like Avery, she'd rather stand up for herself.

Micah's eyes shift around the room, I'm pretty sure if he had a pen in hand, it'd be twirling between his fingers before hitting the floor.

"Remember when she asked you about your friend?" he asks.

"For the leadership project?"

He nods. "Sadie's not in leadership class. I am."

What? I glance at the clock. "Micah, I'm not following this at all and it's two minutes until I need to open the door for tutorials."

"Sadie never heard back from her."

"Avery? I mean, Ms. Moore?"

Shit shit shit. I should have helped Sadie find someone else to email since Avery's life is crumbling.

Wait, didn't he just say Sadie's not in leadership?

"About her dad." He gives me a look, like I should be following. I'm not.

What does Sadie's dad have to do with Avery?

"I don't-"

There's a loud knock on my classroom door and Micah jumps. He kicks at his backpack and a book peeks out from the broken zipper.

"What book is that?" I ask, crossing slowly to the door.

"Sadie gave it to me," he says.

He pulls the book out. Of course.

I laugh. "It's a great book," I tell him as I open the door.

A handful of students file past, giving me fist bumps as they file in.

"Yeah, I hope Sadie has the next book, too," Micah says, shoving Avery's book back in his bag.

He drops his phone, which lights up. A picture of him and Sadie is his lock screen. Sadie's laughing as Micah looks at her like she hung the moon.

It's adorable. But also...I tilt my head. There's something familiar about...

I'm guessing Sadie is like Avery, she'd rather stand up for herself.

Sadie *is* like Avery.

Her barely-upturned smile. The way she tilts her head and bites the inside of her cheek. Her swinging ponytail.

Suddenly I know.

How did I not see it before?

About her dad.

Shit. Shit. Shit.

Now fucking what?

"You're a good friend, Micah," I manage to get out. "Just keep supporting her."

He gives me a defeated shrug as more students file past, needing my attention.

When I turn to face the classroom though, he's gone.

Chapter Twenty-Seven
Avery

"The fucking timing is wrong," I mutter to myself as I click back through the entire Evanston Orchards file.

I knew this property was the key to, well, something. I fucking knew it. Something is still missing though. Some tiny, unknown piece. It's too early, and I might be too far off the mark, to ask Edward. I just have to think it through.

Again.

The very first email from Lila thanks us for *still* being interested in the property. *"The timing is incredible."* Her exact words.

I thought Dad stepped in with an offer to purchase Evanston Orchards when Lila's dad, Dan, had an accident. Nice guy, right? Helping out local farmers.

Fact: he's not a nice guy.

According to Lila's email, he actually tried to muscle his way in *before* the accident.

Why?

Why this property, this massive operation? He invests in properties and businesses and anything he can get his hands on, but only if he can be completely hands-off. Evanston Orchards is obviously a well-run operation…run by the Evanston family. Without them, it's not a well-run operation. It's a money pit.

Matthew Moore does not throw money away. Ever.

What is it about this farm? And why bring me on? Does this timing revelation even make a difference? I could walk away from this deal and my finances would be completely fine. It'd be a hit, it would sting, but I would be fine. And I'd be free of him. Nothing would tether me to him.

But then he'd win. Again.

What would he win? I have no fucking clue.

Fuck it. I'm going to figure this out, if only to piss him off.

I start over.

He tried to buy Evanston Orchards, seemingly out of nowhere.

They didn't want to sell.

Dan's horrific farming accident, barely two weeks later.

Dad steps in again. Brings me along with him.

Balks when I want to save the farm, not portion it off.

Brings in Bill Shapiro when I continue to argue logistics.

Why is he refusing to let go?

I shuffle the papers scattered across my desk. I feel like I'm losing my mind, circling and circling, finding no new information. Nothing.

This is absolutely the third and final step of the Triple Threat Trio. Where is Harper when I need her?

"Stop spiraling. Move on," I demand.

The words echo around my empty office.

This isn't the way to revenge, to justice, to whatever middle ground I can find. This is me, spiraling. I just need some red string and I could put together an evidence board on my wall, star in my own conspiracy theory docu-series.

"Honey, I'm home!" Harper. The sanity I need.

Zero's paws race down the hallway. I spin my chair to face the door and brace myself. I hear the side door slam shut and Harper mutters something incoherent just as Zero flies into my office and shoves her head in my lap, demanding attention.

"Hi, Z," I murmur. I pet her soft ears as she leans into me, making my chair scoot backward across the floor. "You here to rescue me from myself?"

"Hey," Harper says, leaning against the doorframe.

Her eyes widen as she scans the room, looking at me, my desk that can't be seen under scattered papers, my tiny dick plant, and back at me.

"Hi?" Despite clearing my throat, my voice still rises into a question.

I quickly rub under my eyes, where I'm sure mascara has smeared, and run my fingers through my hair. I don't even bother with my desk. It is what it is at this point.

"Wow, okay. Uh, how's it going?" she asks, biting her lip.

"Good, great. It's going goodly. Well, I mean. It's going well."

Pull. It. Together.

Harper's lip twitches. "Nice try. Even if you and your desk didn't look like a tornado came through, Cooper sent me a text before he went to work."

Of course he did. Wait. I didn't even ask him about his dad, their phone call. I'm an asshole emotionless robot. I should text him. Except…where is my phone?

I look around for my phone. It's nowhere.

Did I mention that I'm spiraling?

Harper clears her throat.

"Fine," I sigh. "Shitty. It's going really, really shitty. I think I'm obsessing over this one investment, which doesn't even matter to my finances that much, like I could walk away and be fine, but I just…can't. Am I spiraling? Is this a classic Avery spiral?"

"I mean," she pauses and motions around the room, "this isn't exactly the office of Attorney Avery. There's definitely a borderline obsession going on right now, possibly a spiral."

"Definitely a spiral," I mumble. Zero noses my hand again so I stroke her soft ears. "I'm sorry, did you need something business-wise from me?"

She shakes her head. "Just checking on you."

"I'm sorry. I'm okay. I'm going to move on and…" I trail off.

And what? What can I do? My regular work? Pretend everything is fine?

"And skip work and go to the beach with me?" Harper asks.

I look at my laptop. Or the half of it that's not buried under a property survey.

"I already checked your schedule; you don't have meetings," she adds.

I raise a single eyebrow at Harper, who is unsuccessfully trying to hide her smirk, and cross my arms.

"Come on, Aves, you need to step away from this and I could use the fresh air," she says, disappearing from the doorway, leaving a whining Zero in her wake.

I shake my head, knowing my best friend is right, both about the lack of meetings and that I need a few hours away from everything spread out in front of me. Zero dances out of the room ahead of me as soon as I stand. At least one of us is excited.

I'm pulling on my boots under both Harper's and Zero's supervision when my phone buzzes in my pocket. Yep, it's been in my pocket this whole time. A Rock Beach number I don't recognize flashes on my phone. I frown, undecided. I can feel Harper roll her eyes as I swipe to answer.

"Avery Moore," I answer briskly, like I haven't spent the last two hours spiraling.

"Mr. Miller's friend? That Avery?" a young voice demands.

"Uh, yes? Can I help you?" Why would a kid be calling me? Did something happen to Cooper? Is my sleep-deprived, spiraling brain making this whole thing up? "Is everything okay?"

"No! It's not okay! Sadie just wanted to meet you! Now she's grounded and it's my fault!" The kid practically yells at me. No, he does yell.

"I'm sorry, who is this?" I ask. I hold a finger up, asking Harper to give me a minute. She flings her hands up in exasperation and walks outside, Zero on her heels.

"Micah. We met at the rage room. Not that someone like you would remember."

Ouch, safe to say Micah isn't my biggest fan, although I don't know who Sadie is. The name is ringing a bell, I just can't figure out why.

"I do remember you, Micah. But who is Sadie?" I ask gently.

"She's my best friend," Micah says quietly.

"And, wait, is she the one that wants to be a lawyer? Coop told, I mean, Mr. Miller told me a student would be emailing me."

The last week is a blur, but I do remember checking and not seeing anything from her. Don't I?

"She doesn't want to be a lawyer," he says flatly.

"Are you talking about someone else? Mr. Miller said it was for a career project." I slide my other foot into my boot.

Silence.

"Micah?"

Silence. I look down; our call is still connected.

"Can you please check?" he whispers. "It's important."

"I'll check right now," I promise.

"I can wait," Micah responds, his voice a little steadier.

Persistent. I like him. I move to my email and check all folders. Nothing. Wait.

I scan the email and somehow manage to not drop my phone, even as my heart sinks into my stomach and the bitter taste of acid fills my mouth.

I take one of Harper's deep breaths before speaking. "Micah, I just found her email. She will hear back from me very soon. You're a good friend."

"Mr. Miller said the same thing."

This time I do drop my phone.

Cooper knew? What, exactly, did he know? Why did he tell me it was for some career project? Did he not want to tell me? Did he see my slow and steady spiral and try to spare me? He wouldn't do that. Right?

I pick my phone up off the floor but can't think of a single thing to say.

"Thank you. Goodbye, Ms. Moore," Micah says. He hangs up before I can formulate any other words or even say goodbye.

I stand frozen, staring at my phone.

One thing at a time. I swallow down the fear that's building, the anxiety that rises when I think of Cooper feeding me lies, and read the email again.

I blink. The words remain the same. The name remains the same.

Sincerely, Sadie Hope Howell

Sadie Hope Howell.

Hope Howell.

Howell.

I close my eyes and flip through memories, searching for the answer. My mind is moving too fast, though, a blurry kaleidoscope instead of a neat and tidy photo album.

Photo album.

I don't need to stand here with my eyes closed, physical proof is two rooms away.

I tear into my bedroom, my unlaced boots nearly tripping me, and fling open the closet door. I don't even turn the light on.

"Shit," I whisper, hopping on one foot and grasping my ankle in my hand when I stumble over my running shoes.

I glare at the photo album that juts out from the haphazard stack of childhood mementos, just out of my reach. Even without the twisted ankle, the shelf is too high. Instead of finding my step stool, I jump one one foot and try to tug the photo album loose.

If I cared about anything other than getting it into my hands as quickly as possible, I might rethink this high-stakes Jenga. But I don't.

An entire stack of memories falls. A stuffed animal, a shoebox full of medals, notebooks filled with stories. I barely manage to catch a wooden frame before it hits my face. The last thing I need is a black eye or a trip to urgent care for stitches.

I set the frame on top of the pile that now sits at my feet and jump again, tipping the photo album into my hands. I sink to the floor.

Page after page of photos. None the one I need. I know it's in here. I flip faster.

Sadie Hope Howell.

Hope Howell.

Howell.

I know this is it.

"Holy shit," I breathe, flipping the pages one last time.

I turn on my phone's flashlight and stare at the picture. My stomach turns.

I snap the album closed.

That's the answer. That's the Evanston Orchards clue. The missing puzzle piece. The straw that is breaking this camel's back. The needle in the haystack. The last pin in my evidence board.

I stare at the photo album in my lap.

Holy shit.

"Uh, Aves, what are you doing?" Harper asks from behind me. She flips the lightswitch. "What *is* all this?"

I blink at the sudden onslaught of light and look around at the mess of my past surrounding me. Zero lets out a high-pitched whine.

"I thought you lost that!" Harper nods to the frame next to me, the one that almost hit me in the face.

I turn it over. My fingers trace the words slowly as tears fill my eyes.

"Anything and everything, always," I whisper.

I also thought I lost this. Closing my eyes, I see Harper carefully cross-stitching next to me on the couch, my grandma smiling at us as we giggled over this time-forgotten hobby.

I tilt the frame and my memory shifts. Harper and I are still giggling, but my dad is huffing his annoyance in the corner, upset we're spending an extra night at the beach house.

I spin in a circle, still sitting on the floor, and really take everything in. A writing award I won in middle school after my English teacher encouraged me to enter a creative writing contest. Track ribbons, cross country trophies, and Team MVP plaques. A carefully taped (and retaped) recipe card, a blend of Harper's and my handwriting, chocolate stains on the corner, from the summer we decided to perfect our hot chocolate recipe. Dozens of spiral notebooks filled to the brim with my words, my stories.

With Harper's cross stitch in one hand and the green notebook Cooper gave me that day on the beach so long ago in the other, I have a bright white flash of clarity. I see the pattern to these things that I hid here in the dark.

These are the things my father deemed unworthy.

He molded me, not into an emotionless robot, but into an attorney. A damn good one, yet did I ever want to take this route? No. I wanted to write.

Without realizing it, I let him take that from me. Wasn't it him that demanded a pen name? Wasn't it him that cut down my writing as a "hobby" time and time again? Wasn't it him that chimed in with the "solution" of law school when my writers' block hit?

I hated watching my mom bend to his will but all along, I was as well. I let him take so much from me.

That ends now.

I am done.

I don't care if my finances go down in flames, if I have to sign everything over to him just to get out from this partnership. I don't care what road I have to take, but it will lead away from him. He will not get another second of my time. My energy.

"Fuck it," I whisper.

"Aves, you okay?" Harper asks.

I smile, gripping the cross stitch tighter. "I'm really fucking good."

"Really fucking good," she repeats as she takes in everything she just walked in on for the second time this morning.

AKA me talking to myself. AKA my fuck it. AKA the pile of memories surrounding me. AKA the wild look I'm sure is in my eye.

I nod and stand, a running trophy falling from my lap. "Really fucking good."

"Okay…" Harper doesn't look convinced. "Are you sure?"

"Look at this, all of it." I sweep my arm and Harper ducks so I don't hit her. "This is it. This is the answer."

"Uh huh," Harper nods, still obviously unconvinced that I haven't lost my damn mind.

"This is what he did to me. The things I love most, hidden." I nudge the trophy with my unlaced boot. "Running, he was never even there. Writing, he was so ashamed of it he convinced me to write under a pen name. Why? Because there were 'romantic undertones' and I was, what, sixteen?" I somehow use air quotes despite still holding the framed cross stitch and notebook.

Harper's nodding along, encouraging my rant. I'm pretty sure if she had more warning of this closet epiphany, she'd have a glittery poster in hand, cheering me on from the sidelines, like all those unworthy races she attended.

"I see it now, Harp, what you saw all these years. He's fucking awful and I'm fucking done. And it feels really fucking good."

I take a deep breath. Done. It does feel good.

"Hell yeah!" She cheers. Then she tilts her head. "But why are we in the closet in the first place? Could we maybe celebrate somewhere else? Like, you know, the beach?"

Fuck. The reason we are in the closet. The reason I *can't* be done.

With shaking hands, I set down the notebook and cross stitch and pick up the photo album. I look up at Harper as I open the cover.

"Because-"

Zero barks, interrupting me. Footsteps approach, then Cooper peers around the corner.

Despite the rush of disappointment I felt when I realized he knew, my heart doesn't sink. Instead, my hammering heart steadies as my eyes meet his. My hands stop shaking. The weight pressing against my chest feels lighter. Everything becomes quiet, clear.

I look directly at him as I answer. "Because I have a little sister."

Chapter Twenty-Eight
Cooper

The second I peer around the closet door, I know it's bad. I haven't heard a word of the conversation, I don't know why they're standing in a closet, I don't know who made this mess, I don't know what Avery is holding in her hands, I only know this: she already knows.

Avery's hands are shaking when her gray eyes meet mine. But then something happens. Something changes. She stills. A calm settles over her. A quiet spark burns in her gaze, which doesn't waver from mine as she says, "Because I have a little sister."

Before I can say a word, Tex makes a strangled sound. "Wait, what?" Her mouth gapes open and she looks from what I now see is a photo album to Avery, then back.

"Ave-" I start, but Avery holds up her hand, stopping me.

"Wait." A single word request.

So I wait.

Avery flips through the pages. "Remember when your parents threw that huge neighborhood party? We were like twelve, thirteen years old maybe?"

"What in the actual hell is going on?" Tex shakes her head. "Backup. *Sister*? What's next? An entire clown car of siblings?"

From what I've pieced together about her father, that would not surprise me. I was barely able to focus on work, my anger toward this faceless man growing every second Sadie didn't show up for class. Had she spoken to him? What had he said to her? Done to her? Was she okay? Thank god for emergency subs and an amazing school counselor.

"Look." Avery shoves the photo album toward her friend.

Tex looks at the photo and tilts her head, frowning, before tugging the entire album from Avery's grip.

"I don't know what I'm looking at," Tex says. She tips the page toward the light. "I remember this party, but...I don't get it."

"This is why my dad won't let go of Evanston Orchards," Avery says, starting to pace back and forth in the small, confined, very messy space.

I want to reach for her. To offer her comfort. But I wait.

"Lila's family's farm? I thought that was a done deal." Tex is still studying the photo.

"I thought it was, but it wasn't. And I couldn't figure out why. But look." Avery stops pacing and points to the right side of the photo.

"What is happening with my hair? Why did you let me get this cut?! This is not a style, this is an abomination!" Tex exclaims, squinting at the picture. "This is not a good look."

"No, look. Lila's sister!" Avery resumes pacing, only to trip over her untied shoelaces. She kicks her boots off with a frustrated huff.

I can't wait. "Ave," I try again. This time Tex cuts me off.

"You mean brother? Lila has a little brother. Don't remember his name though." Tex frowns, then recognition dawns. "Miles. Lila and Miles. Oh shit, they did have an older sister, didn't they? A lot older? Different dad, yeah? Oh my god, is that your sister? No, wait, math. How old is your dad?" Her questions are rapid-fire and possibly rhetorical.

"Recognize her?" Avery asks, pointing to a dark-haired woman in the picture. "She's my half-sister's mom."

"Courtney," I say without thinking.

Sadie's mom, Courtney, who answered on the second ring when June, the school counselor, called less than an hour ago, and reassured us that Sadie was okay.

Tex's eyes fly to meet mine. "You knew?"

I wince. I can't deny it. I did know. Not for very long, but I did know. "Sadie is in my class. I just found out this morning."

"Sadie?" Tex asks.

"My sister," Avery replies quickly. "Half-sister."

"And she's in your class?" Tex turns to me.

I nod.

"Small fucking world," Tex mutters.

"Avery," I start, then pause as her stormy eyes settle on mine.

The rage I feel at Avery's father shifts aside. It's still there, still simmering, but now, with her gaze boring into me, all I feel is a desperate need to reassure myself that she's okay. Selfishly, I need reassurance that *we* are okay.

What should I say?

"I'm sorry your world keeps falling apart and now it looks like I added to the lies that surround you."

No. Not that.

Definitely not that.

Or maybe that?

Fuck. This silence is not helping. Both women stare at me.

"Are you okay?" I want to punch myself in the face. Does anything about this scene look okay? No.

Tex snorts, then turns it into a cough.

Avery *smiles*. She smiles at me before stepping forward and placing her palm lightly on my chest, right over my pounding heart. "Better now, seeing you."

I smile at her answer, at that little reassurance. "Yeah?"

"No, you know what? I'm not better," Avery says. The fire is back in her eyes; it's not just a quiet spark, it's an inferno. I brace myself. "I'm really fucking good."

I'm sure my jaw drops. "Oh," I say. Like an idiot.

Tex snorts again.

Avery lowers her voice. "Is your dad okay?"

"What?" My dad?

"This morning. I never asked. Is he okay?"

This morning. The phone call. The news I've pushed aside, thanks to the shit storm of a day I've ended up in.

I nod slowly, unwilling to add anything else to this day. "Just some routine bloodwork."

Avery's eyes narrow but she doesn't call me on the partial lie. "And is Sadie okay? Micah sounded really upset."

Micah. He'd do anything for Sadie. Of course that's how Avery found out. A rush of pride for the kid washes over me. He stood up for her, despite my suggestion of quiet support. I should have told him to trust his instincts. With Matthew Moore as her father, I think Sadie will need everyone she can get in her corner.

"She's okay. I can't tell you much, it's not my place, but I can tell you she's okay."

I want to tell her more. I want to tell her that they have the same smile and similar eyes. That they're both cautious, both smart as hell.

"Good." She smiles again, this one sweeter. "I meant what I said though, better now. When you walked in, it just…got quieter."

I drop my forehead to hers. "Yeah?"

Instead of answering, she slides her hand up my chest and winds it around my neck, tugging me down for a soft, slow kiss.

I'm confused as hell but I'm not an idiot, so I draw her closer with an arm around her back and she softens at my touch, melting into me. I'm supposed to be the one reassuring her, but I think it's the other way around right now.

"Gross," Tex says.

Avery smiles against my lips before pulling back. "Harper!"

"No, not y'all. This." She holds up the photo album.

"What do you mean?" Avery asks, frowning.

"Courtney," Tex says, the photo album shaking in her hands. "Your dad is staring directly at her in this picture. What a fucking sleaze." Tex pulls a different picture out of the album and holds it up to the light. "She's like early twenties here, right? Young."

"Really young," Avery confirms.

Avery shoots a glance at me and I can see Sadie in her eyes. There is no doubt in my mind that they are sisters. Not only am I following this jumbled conversation as much as anyone could, but the truth is right in front of me. The tilt of her head as she studies the photo, the way she drums her fingers against her thigh as she paces, I'd be more shocked at this point if they aren't siblings.

"Holy shit," Tex says, a smile slowly spreading across her face. "You have a sister. You lucky bitch."

"Holy shit," Avery repeats, nodding. "Sadie Hope Howell. My *sister*."

"Wait. Hope Howell. I recognize that name," Tex says with a frown. "How do I know that name?"

"Hope Howell-Evanston is Lila and Miles's mom," Avery replies.

"I need one of those conspiracy theory boards, with like, the red string and pictures, connecting clues," Tex mutters.

Avery laughs. "I nearly had one of those earlier," she replies. "But in this case, I think you mean a family tree."

"Or that." Tex shrugs. "Either way, I'm a visual learner. Let's get the sticky notes out."

She pushes past me out the closet door, Zero following.

I catch Avery's hand before she can leave. "Hey, I didn't know, I really didn't, until this morning."

She reaches up and cups my jaw. "I know."

I know? That's it?

That's it. She laces her fingers through mine, her hand warm and reassuring, and leads me to the kitchen.

***

"It's just something you picked up?" Tex asks incredulously an hour later. "Just some light computer hacking between gardening and kindergarten drop off?"

Jessie's cheeks pinken and she shifts in her chair. She glances across the table to Grant, who grins at her, and she just shrugs. "Everyone needs hobbies."

"Knitting is a hobby. Puzzling is a hobby. Yoga, bird watching, woodworking, pickleball, fishing, those are hobbies. This is…" Tex waves her arms like she can conjure the right words.

This is not what I expected when Avery's door swung open and Jessie stood there, laptop tucked under her arm. There's now an entire group of people pouring over laptops, papers are scattered all over the kitchen island, the chaos seemingly spilling into the dining room, and Lucas's elderly grandfather is making a pot of coffee and grumbling about cinnamon rolls. I think I hear another car coming up the driveway.

"Impressive?" Grant offers when Tex comes up empty.

"Badass?" Zoe suggests.

"Amazing? Incredible?" Grant adds as Jessie's cheeks turn bright red.

"Morally gray! Here I thought you were a rule-following law student," Tex replies, shaking her head at Grant.

I also thought the same thing about the law student Avery mentors; suddenly I have a newfound respect for the guy though.

"Sorry I'm late," a middle-aged man with total dad vibes says, walking in with a briefcase in hand. He looks around the room and pauses, mid-stride, when he sees how many people are in the house. "Hello, I'm Edward, Mr. Moore's assistant."

"And you," Tex points at the newcomer, who flinches at the shift in her tone. "I don't even know where to start with you. You've worked for him for ages! I'm supposed to trust you?"

"Edward!" Avery rounds the corner from her office, a coffee mug full of brightly colored pens and highlighters in one hand and a blanket tucked under her other arm.

Tex and I exchange glances as she shoves everything at Zoe and wraps Edward in a hug. Avery isn't a hugger.

"The spiral for the ages," Tex whispers.

She might be right, but I don't think she is.

Avery might not be a hugger and she's not the kind to invite a group of people into her home to help with morally gray research, but this isn't a spiral. This is the unrelenting determination that she possesses, the same determination that made her a best-selling author in high school, showing up in a new way. This is her seeing the problem and knowing exactly how to find the solution, perhaps partly thanks to law school.

This is just Avery.

"A job is just a job," Edward says, looking around the overcrowded kitchen at the rest of this odd assortment of people. "There're a lot of people I'd burn bridges for, Avery is one of them."

Avery's face flames as she smiles, still tucked under Edward's arm.

"May the bridges I burn light my way," a man that rivals my size says. Dane, if I remember correctly.

I think he's here with Zoe. Or possibly Henry, Lucas's grandfather, which begs questions, but there's no time for that.

"You literally just met her," Tex says in disbelief.

Zoe whacks Dane across the chest. "You sure talk big for a guy who-"

"There's something here," Jessie says suddenly, interrupting Zoe mid-sentence. "But where is..."

Everyone looks at her, but she doesn't finish her thought. She's been doing that often. She was the first to arrive, about ten minutes after Avery buried herself in her phone while Tex was trying to talk me through Sadie's complicated family tree. Thanks to the multi-colored sticky-note crime board buried under the papers and laptops on the island, I think I have it.

Hope and James Howell had a daughter, Courtney, just before James was killed in a car accident. Years later, Hope remarried, this time to a man named Dan Evanston. Hope and Dan had two children together, Lila and Miles, who are close in age to Avery.

Hope, Dan, Courtney, Lila, and Miles all lived at Evanston Orchards, which Dan took over after his own father, Dan Sr., could no longer run the operation.

Today, Lila and Miles help Dan run the farm. Courtney and Sadie live in Rock Beach.

In a whispered conversation, Tex and I agreed that it was likely that Courtney moved away shortly after getting pregnant, probably due to threats from Matthew Moore. He'd already done it once to Bethany, Alex's mom, why not do it again?

"Coffee's ready," Henry announces as Edward takes a seat at the table next to Dane.

Avery opens a cabinet and starts pulling down coffee mugs. There's definitely not going to be enough.

"Want me to run down to my place?" I ask. "Get a few extra?"

Avery bites the inside of her cheek and shakes her head. Her eyes dart around the room and she angles herself so I'm blocking her from view. I snag her waistband and tug her closer.

"Stay." She says it so quietly, I think I might have imagined it.

I might also be imagining the flicker of uncertainty as she looks up at me. "You okay?"

She lifts a single shoulder up in a small shrug and smiles. "Really fucking good, remember?"

I know that's what she wants me to think, wants everyone to think, maybe including herself. So I nod. "Really fucking good," I repeat.

I slide a mug next to hers and she pours me a cup as well. The voices behind us fade into the background as I study her profile. She's been the picture of strength, wearing a neutral expression like a shield as she quietly laid out the entire fucked up scenario to the first group that showed up, but now she's gripping her mug like it's a lifeline.

"I just need to know that he can't do anything else to hurt Sadie," Avery says quietly. "No threats, nothing like he did to Alex."

I tip my head toward the table. "It seems like they've got that covered."

There's anger burning in her eyes as she turns to face the room, leaning her hip back against the counter. "I wish we could blackmail him and call it good."

"Oh, well, we can," Jessie says, looking up from her laptop. "I thought you wanted something more....legitimate."

"Define 'legitimate,'" Avery says.

Jessie glances at Grant, who ducks his eyes. Her eyes move to Edward, who grimaces without moving his eyes from the laptop. Dane smirks, Zoe shimmies her shoulders, and Tex just looks wide-eyed at Avery, like she's never seen her before.

A throat clears. West stands by the door, glaring, as usual. "Blackmail?"

No one speaks. Then, everyone speaks.

"Well-"

"We're already hack-"

"Jessie-"

"Her father is a scumbag." Dane is the first to get a full sentence out.

West nods slowly. "And the blackmail?"

"It was a joke, right?" Tex asks in a high-pitched voice. "It can't be that easy."

"Bummer," West says.

Jessie purses her lips and Grant's eyes move back to the screen.

"Wait, is it that easy?" Tex asks the room at large.

Jessie grins, Edward shifts in his chair, and Dane points to something on one of the laptops, making Grant nod.

"They have something," I say, looking between them.

Avery pushes off the counter and slides into the empty chair next to Jessie. She looks at me, then around the table. "Show me."

Chapter Twenty-Nine
Avery

Relief floods my veins. She got him. She actually got him. Jessie did in an hour what I couldn't do in two weeks.

"I need a little more time and to get on Edward's computer, but honestly," Jessie says, barely pausing to glance over at me. "If the goal is to stop him in his tracks, freeze his life, then we've already got him." She looks back down to the multiple laptops in front of her.

"Yep, we've got him six ways til Sunday," Dane says.

"What does that even mean?" Zoe asks, sitting down across from Henry at the small table in the corner.

"It means that I'm going to have so much more than blackmail," Jessie says. "But I need you to walk me through it again."

"I also need to walk through it," Edward says, opening his laptop and pushing it toward Jessie.

I rub my forehead. How did I forget he wasn't here for my rushed explanation?

"What do you have now?" I ask.

"Right now I just have access to all of his accounts," Jessie says.

"Just?" Tex says from over my shoulder.

"Accounts?" Edward asks.

"Banking," she replies.

Tex laughs. "That's it? You 'just' control his finances?"

"Quickest way to compliance, right?" Dane says. "Easiest blackmail."

I should be elated. They have him. I am, but I'm also just so…numb.

Cooper's hand lands lightly on my shoulder. I look up.

"Want me to quarterback it?" he asks quietly.

For the second time in the last two minutes, I feel pure relief. I nod. I'm done with the noise, the chaos. I'm done allowing my father to take any part of me. I'm ready to move on. Move forward.

I know who deserves my time, my energy, and it's sure as hell not my father.

It's the people in my house, the ones that showed up, no questions asked, dubious morals in tow when I closet-spiraled myself into asking for help. The ones that have *been* showing up with dick plants and croissants, mochas and thank you notes.

It's my best friend, with her tiny, barely-there baby belly and her sometimes scary protective instincts. The one who always knows when I need to break out of my shell and just how to help me get there.

It's my brother, who tried to protect me all those years ago. Who showed up, all these years later, asking me to be in his life.

It's my nephew, who I haven't even met. Whose smile lights up my phone screen.

It's my sister-in-law, the blushing bride I should have watched walk down the aisle to my brother. The one who encouraged Alex to find me.

It's my sister, who I haven't even spoken to, who I just found out about mere hours ago.

And I hope it's my mom, who I still haven't had the courage to call.

It's definitely the man standing behind me. The one who quiets the noise, even as he hands me a lead pipe and tells me to take a swing. The one who helped me find my writing again, who has held me together every single night since my brother walked through the door, who has had a place in my heart since I was fifteen.

Cooper gives my shoulder a gentle squeeze before raising his voice and motioning to the kitchen. "Okay everyone, help yourself to the coffee and then let's all get on the same page."

"That teacher voice," Harper whispers to me as Grant and Dane stand and move toward the coffee pot and Cooper starts plucking the sticky notes from the island and moving them to the table. "So hot."

Zoe laughs. "Agree," she says, playfully wincing when Lucas overhears.

I just shake my head. Jessie gives me a small smile and then focuses back on her screen. Her eyes move rapidly back and forth before narrowing.

It only takes a couple minutes for coffee mugs to be filled and for Henry to start another pot. Instead of paying attention as Cooper explains the messy family tree, placing sticky note after sticky note in the middle of the table, I watch the coffee drip slowly into the carafe. It's oddly calming.

Was it only a few hours ago that Harper showed up, coffee in hand? No. Wait. Did she bring me coffee? Maybe. No? My brain feels like mush.

She didn't. Cooper did. Right before…right before my original epiphany.

"Timing," I blurt out, interrupting Cooper. I stare at the sticky note with my sister's name on it. "It's the timing. Sadie is why he went after Evanston Orchards to start and why he won't give it up now."

It clicks into place again. Timing. He made an offer on the farm *before* the accident. Is that when Sadie first found him? Does that mean…?

My hands shake, I grip my mug tighter. No. It can't.

"Because he did it." Jessie says, voicing the thoughts running through my mind. "It wasn't an accident. It was him."

Edward reels back. Harper's eyes find mine. Her thumb goes to her scar.

That feeling from the riverbank, the white-hot rage, burns bright.

Cooper sinks into the chair beside me, slides his hand onto my thigh. Still, my rage builds.

"I don't have proof," Jessie quickly adds. "Yet. But it's obvious."

It's so obvious I can't believe I didn't see it earlier.

"First, the timing, right?" She looks around the table, waiting for someone else to catch on.

She's met with dubious looks and a single nod from West.

"He approached them the same day he sent this," Jessie says, turning Edward's laptop around. "An email to Courtney, 8 a.m., warning her that the terms of their agreement had been broken."

"Sadie," I say. "She found him, contacted him. That must be his reaction."

"And his offer to buy the farm was…a threat?" Dane doesn't sound convinced.

"Courtney didn't fall into place and apologize like he thought she would. She stood up for Sadie," Jessie says. "So yes, it was a threat."

My admiration for Courtney grows. Whatever my father put her through and still, she stands up to him.

Edward nods. "Matthew isn't going to just buy a farm," he says. "I thought that the second it landed on my desk. What does he always say? 'Does it build my wealth?'"

"Dumbest thing I ever heard," Henry grumbles from his chair at the smaller table against the window. "A farm building wealth? That's not why you buy a farm." He looks up at Zoe, who is sitting across from him, and she nods in agreement, her lip twitching slightly.

"Matthew went out there later that day," Edward says. "Small town, make the offer in person."

Zoe shakes her head. "I don't get it."

"Your turn," Henry says, motioning to the checkerboard between them.

"Recon." West's single word reply just makes Zoe's frown deepen. Or maybe it's her game of checkers with Henry.

"Information," I add. "He always says the person with the most information comes out on top. It could have been an attempt to find out if they knew he was the father of their granddaughter. Or if they even have a relationship with Courtney and Sadie. Any number of things."

"He definitely likes information," Jessie says. "It's one thing to need to know the value of a piece of equipment if you're buying a working operation, it's another to deep dive into the machinery, how it works, like he did the week after he visited with his so-called offer."

"Proof?" Dane asks.

"Of the searches? Yes. And…wait…" Once again, Jessie trails off, lost in a thought, fingers flying.

"But *why*?" Zoe asks. She jumps her checkers across the board with force, making Henry shake his head, then turns in her chair, facing the rest of us. "Okay, he's trying to hide that he has a daughter. If it comes out, what's the big deal?" She turns to me. "Your parents divorced a long time ago, right?"

I nod. "Nearly a decade."

"So, again, why does it matter?" she repeats.

"She was nineteen," Harper says quietly. She holds up her phone, an Instagram account. "I thought Courtney was mid, maybe early twenties. She was *nineteen*. He was at least forty."

Saliva rushes to my mouth.

Nineteen.

I might throw up.

The conversation turns into a buzz.

I'm definitely going to throw up.

Cooper squeezes my thigh gently. "Ave."

I look over at him and he tilts his head toward the table. Harper's staring at me.

"Breathe," she mouths. She taps the table with the pad of her finger in a quiet, steady rhythm.

Tap. Tap. Tap. Tap.

I watch her shoulders rise and fall as she breathes slowly. I breathe with her. In for four taps, hold for four taps, out for four taps.

I focus on the warmth of Cooper's hand on my leg, the steady pressure, the way his thumb moves back and forth, back and forth.

Harper's shoulders rise and fall again. I follow, still focused on Cooper's hand on my thigh. On his slightly citrusy scent. On the sound of West's deep voice in the background.

I take another breath, eyes closed this time, and let the conversation around the table come back into focus.

"If we can find proof, does motive even matter?"

I open my eyes as Dane sits back in his chair and crosses his massive arms. I don't know who he's arguing with.

"How long between the day he was at the farm and the accident?" Grant asks.

"Two weeks," I reply automatically.

"I found reference to the security system on the property," Edward says. "There's cameras. It's all right here."

Jessie glances at his screen and gives a quick nod. "One sec."

"So you guys are really saying that Matthew Moore got mad at his preteen daughter for trying to out him as a pervy old man and so he tried to kill a guy by tampering with a fucking tractor?" Harper, usually my father's harshest critic, asks in disbelief.

I wonder what I missed while I was just trying to breathe, but that does sum up our assumptions nicely.

"The man hates getting his hands dirty!" she adds.

"Never trust a man with clean fingernails," Henry interjects.

Dane looks at his hands. "Well, shit. No more manicures for me."

"No, go back," Lucas says, looking over Grant's shoulder. "There."

I think I missed more of the conversation than I thought.

"That's exactly what we're saying," Jessie says, looking up at Harper when no one else answers her question. Instead of any explanation, she goes back to her laptop.

"Jake's family used to have a small orchard, that's a hell of a piece of machinery, notoriously hard to work on," Lucas says as he looks at Grant's screen. "Maybe it wasn't an attempt to kill a guy, just a botched attempt to break the most expensive thing on the farm. Those are more expensive than a house."

I nod slowly. This makes more sense. "His offer-"

"Holy. Shit." Jessie cuts me off.

The table goes silent. We all look at Jessie.

"Lucas just might be right," Jessie breathes. "Oh my god."

"My reaction, too, when he's right," Henry says loudly.

Zoe laughs. "Same!"

"That's why she sold…"

No one reacts when Jessie trails off again.

Well, I do. My leg starts shaking. Cooper's gentle squeeze stills it and he gives me a reassuring smile.

"So then…" Jessie trails off again.

My leg starts shaking again.

"If Dan told…"

"I'm losing my mind," Harper whispers when Jessie trails off for the third time.

"I don't think I'll stop getting manicures," Dane says, holding his fingers out toward Henry. "What do you think?"

"Why are you even here again?" Zoe asks him.

"You're the one that invited me," he retorts.

"You know who bought that tractor that's as expensive as a house?" Jessie asks loudly, her eyes *still* glued to the screen. She doesn't wait for anyone to answer. "Courtney Howell."

My leg stops shaking. My brain scrambles. I blink at least a dozen times. "Wait, what?"

"And you know who has the security footage that shows Matthew Moore in the barn tampering with the tractor?" Jessie finally looks up, a huge grin on her face. "We do."

Chaos. The table erupts in mass chaos.

***

Quiet. Finally, quiet.

I carefully set my coffee mug on the small table and sink into my favorite chair, pulling my blanket tight around my shoulders. The quiet is worth the cold and this Pendleton blanket was worth the price.

I tip my head back and take a deep breath. How many times have I sat here beneath these very trees, my heart aching like it is now? These trees have witnessed so much, they've *been* so much for me.

They've been shelter when my parents would argue, my tears of anger falling fast as I sat with my back against a tree trunk, glaring at the horizon.

They've hidden the memories I returned to time and time again, silent tears streaming for the boy that took my heart with him when he left.

And finally, they've turned into a piece of my home, where I cried tears of joy the second a maze of 2x4's went up, the start of my future that I worked so hard for.

I take another deep breath, the scent of pine, rain, and ocean air mixing into what I know as home. Then, reality beckons.

Sitting forward, I take a sip of my rapidly cooling coffee and take my phone out of my pocket. There might not be justice for Alex, there's not for Harper, but there can be for Dan Evanston. For Sadie. Courtney. But that justice comes with an unknown price. One that isn't ours to gamble.

For every answer we found, there's another question. Questions that only Courtney can answer.

It takes way longer than it should, but I finally have a short, to-the-point email written. I don't say anything other than who I am, that I hope Sadie shared my earlier email with her, and that I'd like to talk as soon as possible. It doesn't seem like enough.

I bite the inside of my cheek and hit 'send' on the email anyway. Is this how Alex felt, mailing that card? Like him, I'm going to have to show up on her doorstep with life-altering news if I don't get a reply. It really *must* be how he felt.

It feels terrible.

"Hi," Coop says, stopping in front of me with his coffee mug in hand. "Want company?" He nods to the empty space next to me.

I nod. "I didn't hear you come out."

"You seemed a bit preoccupied."

Instead of asking any further questions, he sinks down next to me and rests his hand on my thigh. We sit in comfortable silence beneath the trees that we made naive teenage promises under so long ago, the breeze rustling through the branches above. It's quiet. Peaceful. I lean my head on his shoulder and breathe in the salty sea air. The rain, the coffee, him.

I take another sip of my coffee, disappointed when it's already on the colder side of lukewarm, and ask, "So, how long until I need to go back in there?"

"Whenever you need a reheat," Cooper replies, mindlessly tracing the seam of my favorite, double-lined leggings.

"That means now," I say. Instead of getting up though, I set my mug on the small table in front of us. "But I mean to deal with everything. Everyone."

The longer I sit out here in the cold, the less I want to go back in. The less I want this quiet to turn back to chaos.

"You don't." Cooper takes a sip of his coffee before offering me his mug, which still has steam rising in slow swirls. "I made sure it was scalding before I came out."

I shake my head. "I called them all up here and asked them to sort out my life, I should probably go back in. I'll just reheat mine."

He gently grips my thigh when I move to stand. "No need. I quarterbacked it."

I sink back down into the chair and look over at him. "You quarterbacked it?"

"Yep." He grins and again offers me his coffee.

I accept, cupping my hands around the warmth of the mug and taking a sip. I try to push down my rising hope. "Meaning?"

"Well, honestly I just told them I was coming outside with you and Dane gave me a chin jut but I took that to mean they don't need me. Or you, for that matter. But like in a nice way."

I can't help but laugh. "They don't need me, but in a nice way?"

"Exactly. It's the Jessie and Dane show in there now. Remind me never to piss her off."

"So if I'm not needed, now what?" I ask. "I can't just sit here."

"You can, though, if that's what you want." He accepts his mug back, taking a sip and watching me over the rim. "Or I have another option."

"Which is?"

He gives me that easy smile, the one that I fell in love with eleven years ago. "Go meet your nephew."

I can't breathe. Again.

My leg shakes. Again.

"Hey, are you okay?" Cooper asks softly. He reaches up and gently wipes the stray tears I didn't know had fallen with the pad of his thumb.

I nod. I am okay.

No.

I'm more than okay.

"I'm really fucking good, remember?" I whisper through more tears.

***

"A sister?" Alex finally speaks. "Another sister?"

"Sadie," I say, my voice cracking. I clear my throat. "Her name is Sadie."

"Another sister," Alex repeats.

Maybe I should have led with this news, instead of the news that our father might have, to quote Harper, tried to kill a guy with a fucking tractor.

Ava, his strikingly beautiful wife who gives the best hugs, laughs at his dumbstruck expression.

"Better than you thought, right?" she asks. "Everything you wished for, for so many years."

He wished for the same thing as me. A sibling. It was a good wish because from the second Alex opened the door to his home, it's felt like he's my brother. Like we lived the childhood we could have had, *should* have had, not just spent one traumatic afternoon together where my world was turned upside down.

"Who knew I'd ever want to send Matthew Moore a thank you card?" he laughs.

I have a flash of that day at The Merc, opening the thank you cards. Alex walking in. My entire life changing.

Suddenly, I want to send our father a thank you card, too. Not for anything he's actually done, but for Alex. For Sadie. For this second chance we have.

"You'll come meet her with me?" I ask as I place another block on top of the tower in front of me and watch as it sways.

"More!" Jack claps.

Jack, the dark-haired, gray-eyed, miniature version of Alex. Also, my dad.

Harper's college professor would have a field day with whatever drunken presentation she'd come up with over my family tree these days.

Nature versus nurture: are you a real introvert or is your dad just a real asshole? The Jack Effect! Squealing, leg-hugging, laughing, miniature-football-throwing Jack. He might be the one that proves Harper's point. He is anything but introverted.

Ava smiles at her son, watching as he hands me another block.

"Of course I'd love to come," Alex answers my question with zero hesitation. No pause.

My breath hitches. A brother by my side. The spot usually occupied by Harper. Recently, by Cooper. *Today*, by Cooper, who's sitting next to me on the floor, his arm flung across the seat of the couch behind us, his warm thigh pressed against mine.

"Even with…" I trail off.

"Even with the fact that we might need to share devastating news?" Alex asks.

"Well, yeah," I say quietly.

Alex looks at me, his gray eyes that match our father's, that match mine, full of warmth. "I actually have experience in that."

"True," I say quietly, smiling at Alex. I place another block on the tower and sit back to admire my work.

The tower promptly falls, which makes Jack giggle. It's the most adorable, addictive sound in the world.

"Auntie." Two small hands reach up and cup my cheeks, squeezing surprisingly hard.

I look at his cute little worried face through my watery eyes and smile. It's so surreal to be sitting here, with my nephew, getting called that. Auntie. A name I never knew I'd be called, let alone would cause tears of joy.

"No cry, Auntie," Jack demands.

"I'm sorry," I tell him. "I'm just so happy! These are happy tears."

While obviously still not convinced, Jack releases my cheeks.

Alex laughs thickly. "It's a good cry. Daddy has good tears, too, bud," Alex quickly reassures him. "Auntie Avery just made today the best day."

Auntie Avery. It hits me all over again. I missed the first two years of his life. Two entire years. Gone. He had no idea who I was when I first walked in.

I swipe at stray tears. "Good tears," I agree. "The best."

Cooper's fingers trace along my shoulder, drawing my attention. "You okay?" he mouths.

I smile. I'm really fucking good. I don't think I should say that in front of my nephew though.

"Can y'all stay for dinner?" Ava asks.

Looking down into Jack's eyes, I almost say yes. But I know there's one more stop I need to make and it scares me even more than a two-year-old.

What if she knew?

Chapter Thirty
Cooper
(before)

"You're early," Avery greets me as I walk up the steps to the deck.

She's sitting in one of the adirondack chairs, notebook in her lap, and a soft smile aimed directly at me. Nerves tighten in my stomach and I have to push them aside before I can speak.

"Hi." I bring one hand out from behind my back and hold up the small bouquet of flowers.

Her eyes widen and she takes the flowers cautiously, like they might bite. "What are these for?"

"Well, this is a date," I say. "So I brought flowers."

"Neither of us can drive so we're not really going anywhere," Avery says, smiling at the flowers in her hand before looking back up. "So does it really count as a date?"

Maybe asking her on a date when we have a day and a half left together is ridiculous, even more so because she's right, I can't drive the rental car my family has and she's only fifteen, but I want to take her on a date. Even if it's just once.

"I brought flowers and planned a date activity, so it's a date," I tell her, bringing the hand holding the beat-up box out from behind my back.

"Scrabble?"

When her face lights up, I send a silent thank you to whoever owns the rental we're staying at. This was the only game in the cupboard that didn't seem to be missing half the pieces.

"Acceptable?"

"Acceptable date activity," she says, sending another smile my way.

Relief washes over me. I didn't realize just how nervous I really was.

I offer her my hand and she lets me pull her out of her chair. We move around to the side deck and Avery ducks inside while I set the game up at the table we had lunch at earlier. She returns with a mason jar of water and carefully arranges the flowers before setting them on the table between us.

After a short recap of the rules, we draw tiles. Within just a few turns, I know I'm going to lose. Not just lose, lose badly.

"Coyotes?" I groan a few turns later, watching as she places her tiles. "**And** the seven letter bonus?"

"And the 's' is at the end of 'zoo' so I get those points, too," she says, grinning. "Which means double word for both."

I lay my head down on the table in defeat. "I knew I didn't like coyotes."

"They're actually really smart and adaptable, it's how they survive in urban areas," Avery says mindlessly as she adds up her score. "They also mate for life, which not many people realize."

I lift my head and raise an eyebrow. "Random coyote facts?"

She gives a half-shrug and looks down at her tiles. "I had an idea for a character. Did a little research."

"A coyote?" I nudge her foot under the table.

She looks back up, right at me, a flush creeping up her neck. "A nickname. He shows up out of nowhere and tries to rescue the heroine, who obviously doesn't need to be rescued."

"Hmm," I hum, biting back a grin. "Sounds like a good guy."

She draws new tiles. "Guess you'll have to read my books to find out."

Wait.

"Books, plural?"

She doesn't reply, she just bites her lower lip.

"Ave?"

She tips a single shoulder up. "Guess you're a pretty good quarterback."

"What does that mean?"

"After last night, with your help," she starts then stops, considering her words. "I could see the rest of the story, and it's not just this book."

My heart beats a little faster as I pretend to look at my letters. Is she talking about more than her book? Is she talking about us?

I clear my throat. "There's more?"

Her eyes lock on mine. "I think there could be more to the story."

Best. Date. Ever.

Chapter Thirty-One
Cooper

"Confession," I say as I open the car door for Avery. "I'm a little in awe of your mom."

"Confession," she replies, glancing back at the house and giving one last wave to her mom. "I did not realize she was half-feral."

It's late and we have an hour or so drive ahead of us, but it's worth it to let Avery have that conversation behind her. The conversation that took a turn neither of us saw coming.

"At least she was half-feral in a good way," I say as Avery slides into the passenger seat.

"There were about three seconds when I was a little nervous," she admits, smiling up at me. "I'm not a trial lawyer. I'd have to call in some favors."

"You mean when she tried to demand Alex's address?" I ask.

Avery's shoulders shake with laughter in the dark as I close the door and round the hood.

Her mom, Jenn, did not take the news that her ex-husband had a son nearly the same age as Avery very well. Not because of what it meant for her former marriage, but what it meant for Alex. He never knew his sister, he was never welcomed into their home.

Her heartbreak turned to something closer to rage though, when Avery quietly explained Sadie's story. She listened carefully, nodding in the right places, and then stood.

Turning to me with a dangerous glint in her eye, she calmly asked, "Would you like a shovel or a tarp?"

It was at that exact moment that I realized what a good idea it had been to leave Tex in Three Rocks. West, too.

I slip into the driver's seat, push the button to start Avery's BMW, and, since this is not my hometown and I honestly have no idea where I am, pull up Apple Maps on CarPlay.

Avery gasps, startling me. She has her seatbelt pulled halfway across her body and is staring at her phone, which is shaking in her other hand. This entire day has been whiplash after whiplash.

"Oh my god," she whispers. "Courtney emailed me back."

"Is Sadie okay?" I ask.

She's been in the back of my mind all day, a miniature Avery that unknowingly set in motion a tragic chain of events with a single phone call.

Avery clicks her seatbelt and looks over at me, smiling softly at my concern. "Sadie's okay. And Courtney's better than okay."

"What does that mean?" I place my hand on the back of her seat, and look over my shoulder, carefully reversing out of the driveway.

"It means that Courtney and Jessie might run the world one day. Holy shit."

"Good?" My voice rises into a question.

I follow Siri's directions out of the neighborhood while Avery stares at her phone.

"Sorry, I think I'm in shock," Avery says, her phone turning dark before she sets it in one of the cup holders between us. "Based on how carefully she worded her email, I'm assuming she either signed an NDA when she was pregnant or doesn't quite trust me, possibly both, but she got across a few main points. One, she would like to meet me to talk. Two, we are correct in assuming her family does not know the identity of Sadie's father. No one does. Three, she's the absolute definition of a mama bear."

I don't know how to respond to any of that.

"Oh." That's it? Face. Palm.

Avery laughs. "This is the most fucked up, best day I *never* could have ever imagined."

"Yeah?" That's it? I'm on a fucking roll.

"I mean, I got a sister," she says. "Always wanted one of those. I had a closet epiphany, made a crime board. Edward showed up! I met my nephew and my sister-in-law. I hugged my mom. Maybe stopped a murder."

When she lists them like that, it definitely confirms that it was a good day. And also fucked up.

I flick the turn signal to take the ramp for I-5. "Closet epiphany? You mean the giant mess I walked in on?"

She sighs and leans her head back against the head rest. "I forgot you weren't there. But yes, it was a closet epiphany that started when my childhood crashed down around me, quite literally."

I reach my hand over and rest it on her thigh. "And the revelation was that you have a lot stored in your closet?"

"More like hidden. It took them almost hitting me in the face but I realized it was all the things my dad didn't approve of, hidden back there. I let him have such a hold over me for so long without even realizing it."

I nod slowly, trying to think of what all was in the mess of the closet. All I remember is the look in Avery's eyes when she turned to me. That stillness.

"But I decided at that moment that I was done allowing him a single piece of me, of my life. And it felt really fucking good."

"So that's where the really fucking good started?"

"Yep." She sighs again and drops her hand on top of mine. I flip mine over and she twines our fingers together. "It seems I need to wait a little longer to truly be done with him, but still. It feels good."

"Really fucking good?" I ask.

She squeezes my hand. "Exactly."

We fall into comfortable silence, the world passing by in darkness, occasional headlights flashing from across the median, and I think Avery is asleep until she turns toward me.

"Coop?" Her voice holds a trace of humor.

"Yeah?"

"We were idiots when we were teenagers, thinking it'd be so simple," she says. "Just show up. Leave it to fate. Meant to be. That's teenage idiocy at its finest. Like, look at all the life that happened since then. We had no idea."

All the life that happened. The days and weeks and years. Waiting rooms and weight rooms. Hushed hospital tones and wild locker room celebrations. The books and the law degree and the businesses. The ups and downs, the fears and regrets, the hopes and dreams.

She's right. We truly had no idea.

Siri interrupts my thoughts, telling me to take the next exit.

"Ave, I have to say, I think that's a huge understatement," I respond as I change lanes.

She huffs a small laugh. "Then you do just show up and…this."

This. What all the days and weeks and years could have very well been preparing me for, to be here, by her side, when her own life tipped sideways. I don't think my dad had to get sick for me to end up here, but living through that definitely changed me. It made me who I am today.

It also made me realize that sometimes those little silver linings that you catch glimpses of, that's what you need to focus on. Not just focus on, but seek out. Like right now.

"And…this? I take it you're not enjoying our third date?" I tease.

"Third date?" She shifts slightly, angling herself toward me. "Explain."

"Well, our first date was actually a double date," I say. I take the left as Siri directs and shoot Avery a quick smile. "You know, ease into dating with your best friend there."

"The rage room was our first date? Not the night I threw myself at you?" There's a teasing note in her voice that reassures me this is what she needs.

"*Very* memorable, but no, we didn't have a date activity." I squeeze her hand again and her thumb starts rubbing softly over my knuckle.

She laughs, obviously remembering our teenage date. "And smashing things is a date activity?" she asks.

"Absolutely. And our second date was pizza, just us, after you kneed Eli in the balls."

"Ah, very romantic, yes."

"Now, third date, I even met your mom. *And* big brother. Pretty serious."

"Moving fast, are we?" She suddenly tenses, her hand going still in mine. "Shit, we are, aren't we? You practically moved in the day after the *very* memorable non-date."

"Technically I moved into your house a week after I got to town," I joke.

She groans. "A rental! You know what I mean!"

"I think our pace feels just right," I say.

It does. I could have done without the eleven-year pause, but that's what life handed us. Now though? Now it feels natural. Like we're supposed to be here.

She sighs but her thumb resumes skimming my knuckle. "Third date then," she says. "But is driving really a date activity?"

"No, but Contexto is."

"I'm sorry, what?"

"It's a word association game the teachers play almost every morning," I explain.

"Is this your attempt at redemption from the last 'date activity' that included a word game?" she asks.

I groan. "Please don't remind me." She absolutely slaughtered me at Scrabble back then.

"How do you play?"

"We'll need a phone," I say, resetting my hand on her thigh when she pulls her hand away to unlock her phone. "And then it's just guessing random words, trying to get closer to *the* word."

"Found it," she says after a few taps on her phone. She looks up. "You're going to want to be in the far left lane to cross the river."

I change lanes and check my speed. "But, to make it date-ish, whoever guesses the final word gets to ask the other a date question."

"A date question?"

"Yep. We both get one question to start, then the winner of the game gets the next. So, Avery, what do you like to do in your free time?"

Avery laughs. "Well, Cooper, I've been a runner nearly my entire life and I enjoy hiking as well. I also like to cook."

"Wow, I'm learning so much about you. What'd you like to know about me?"

"I hear you're new in town. What's your favorite part of Three Rocks so far?"

You.

Probably not what I should admit on our pretend third date though.

"The community," I settle on. "It's honestly been full of surprises since day one."

"I have to say, I think that's a huge understatement," she deadpans, repeating my words from earlier.

I laugh, then spend the next hour laughing because it turns out, I'm not the only one terrible at this game. We need hint after hint and spend entirely too long asking each other ridiculous "date" questions. But with each question, the heavy parts of the day dissipate and our drive down a dark highway really does become a date. The best date I've had since I was sixteen.

I tell her about college football and she leans toward the center console. She tells me about law school and my hand slides up her thigh. I don't know if I want to drive slower to make this date last longer or if I want to get us home sooner, hoping to at least kiss her goodnight after walking her to her door. Tex already sent us a message letting us know Edward was settling into Avery's guest room. It might be the first night I sleep alone in weeks.

Either way, the miles fly by, Siri helpfully counting down the minutes until we reach Three Rocks, a playlist one of my students shared with me as our background music. It's a fairly terrible mix of songs and artists, but that just makes us laugh more.

"I should be better at this game!" she says in exasperation as her guess of 'tomato' only gets us further from the answer.

"Can't be good at everything I guess," I say, knowing she really is good at everything.

Our headlights flash across the sign for Three Rocks and I slow down, turning my blinker on to head up the hill to her cabin.

"Where are you going?" Avery asks.

"Taking you home?" I thought that's why Tex had let us know that Edward was still at her house.

"Oh." She sits back in her seat and crosses her legs.

"Is that not...with Edward there..." I'm a mumbling mess.

Just like this whole day, the moment has swung wildly from one end to the other.

"I don't think I can sleep without you," she says quietly. "I was hoping we were going to your house."

I change my turn signal to the left without a word and turn into town.

"Coop?"

I glance over at her. Under the glare of the single fire station light that lights the entrance to town, she looks nervous.

"Ave, just because we made it a date, nothing has-"

"No," she says, interrupting me. "I just wanted to make sure that you knew, even though I said we were idiots as teenagers earlier, I just meant we were so naive. Not idiots for feeling that."

I want to hear her say it again. Every day. Fake third date or not, I tell her the truth. "Ave, I've felt it for eleven years."

She inhales quickly but doesn't say a word. We cross the bridge over the creek and I pull into the driveway in front of my cottage. Avery quickly clambers out of the passenger seat and I follow her up the walkway.

As soon as I step up to unlock the door, which I'm unsure why I even bothered to lock, she's tugging me toward her. The key stays in the lock.

"Ave?" I cup her cheek, searching her eyes.

Her lips tip up in a smile and then they're on mine. It's the night in the rain all over again. But more. So much more.

We have the last two weeks between us. The moments that made us. The ones that felt broken, when she reached for me in the night, tears in her eyes and a hitch in her voice. The ones that felt whole, whispered words in the dark, laughter in the light.

I'm lost in her, in this moment, in the way she tastes, in the way she feels.

"Cooper," she breathes.

She tips her head back and I bring my hand up, tracing the column of her neck. At her shiver, I let my lips follow, eliciting a soft whimper. I want to spend all night finding new ways to make that sound fall from her lips.

The flicker of guilt I expect doesn't hit but I pause anyway.

"Avery, look at me," I demand. I have to know she's here with me.

Her eyes catch fire at my rough tone, one she's never heard. Still, she knows what I mean. What I need to hear.

"You've been here for some really low lows, please be here for the highs," she says quietly. Her eyes don't stray from mine, those little blue flecks dancing in the porchlight. We're in a standoff, a staring contest. One that could last forever.

It can't last forever. I need her now. "I want to be here for them all. Every single one."

The words are barely out before she yanks my mouth back to hers and climbs me like a tree. I forget whatever else it was I thought I needed to say. She locks her legs around my waist and I press her into the door as I fumble with the lock. And fumble again. And again. I wrench my mouth from hers.

"I'm never locking this again," I groan as she rolls her hips against mine.

With her lips on my neck, I finally manage to turn the deadbolt. Her thighs tighten around me, her heat pressing through the layers between us as I step inside. My vision tunnels. Avery. Only Avery. Every version of her, my teenage Dream Girl racing down the beach to the woman who took on the world today. Only her.

I kick the door closed, key left in the lock, and stalk across the room.

"In a hurry?" Avery laughs, her teeth scraping my earlobe.

"Eleven years," I bite out, gripping her ass tightly as I shoulder my bedroom door open. Somehow I manage to catch the lightswitch with my elbow, the one that controls the lamp in the corner. Soft light fills the room. "I've dreamed about this, about you, for eleven years."

I drop her gently on the bed and step back, toeing off my shoes as I stare at her. Fuck. How am I going to hold it together when she looks like *that*? Long legs, flushed cheeks, swollen lips, watchful gray eyes.

"You okay?" she asks, tilting her head as she studies me.

"No," I say. I scrub my hand down my face and tilt my head back, looking at the ceiling and taking a deep breath before bringing my gaze back to meet hers. "I'm really fucking good."

Avery laughs, scrambling back toward the center of the bed. I quickly shed my jacket and catch her foot, stopping her progress. I untie her boots, tossing them behind me, one at a time, not caring where they end up. Finally, I put my knee on the bed and push myself over her. Her legs fall, making room for me between them, and suddenly, nestled between her long, lean legs, I can't breathe.

I meant what I said. This moment isn't a month in the making. It's not since our eyes met across the bonfire. It's not weeks in the making. It's years.

Eleven years to this moment.

Eleven years of believing, doubting, hoping again. Of heartache and heartbreak, of everything she said, the highs and the lows.

This is an all-time high.

Really fucking good doesn't even begin to cover it.

Avery's legs squeeze my hips and I finally remember to breathe. It's a ragged inhale, the air as heavy as this moment.

Her.

More than air, I need her.

"You're so fucking beautiful," I tell her, brushing my thumb across her cheek, watching as her pupils dilate.

She feels this, too. This moment. This need.

I slant my mouth over hers, groaning the second her hands wind into my hair, pulling me closer.

"I have like seventeen layers on," she whispers against my lips. "What are you going to do when it's only, like, seven?"

I'm really not going to be able to breathe then.

"Die a happy man," I tell her truthfully.

Her tongue slides against mine, proving that even with seventeen layers, I will die a happy man. She arches and rolls under me, her breath catching when I finally find my way under all those layers to soft, warm skin.

I've had my hands on her for weeks now, every night, but this, this is different, this is… really fucking frustrating.

"You weren't kidding about the layers," I mutter when I fail to work her shirt up her ribs with one hand.

She laughs and pushes against my chest. I sit up, watching as she crosses her arms and pulls every single layer off in one movement, leaving her in a delicate, dark green lacy bra. My mouth instantly waters at this unexpected discovery. Avery and lace don't seem to go together, but fuck, yes they do.

My shirt and hoodie have barely followed hers to the floor when my mouth finds her neck. Collarbone. Lower.

"Didn't take you for the lace kind," I murmur. I kiss a path along the lacy edge of her bra, savoring every inch of exposed skin. Every whimper. Every moan. Every breath.

"Just wait, there's more." She gasps as I lick a straight line up between her breasts. I want to bury myself here, never come up for air. Except…

"More?" I lightly brush my thumb over one peaked nipple and lick the other through the lace as she shudders. I do it again, this time with teeth, and her hips jump.

"There's more," she whispers, rolling her hips. "Lower."

So I inch lower, kissing my way down her stomach, memorizing every freckle, every spot that makes her squirm, until finally, there's just a single button between me and *more*. I look up at her and she nods. I flick it open and slide the zipper down.

Matching dark green lace.

"I like pretty things sometimes," Avery whispers.

I practically tear her jeans from her body.

She's spread before me, hair fanned out on the pillow, matching lace barely covering the parts of her I want the most, and all I can do is stare.

I swallow hard.

"Fuck, Ave."

Chapter Thirty-Two
Avery

"Fuck, Ave," he whispers.

His eyes rake over me, his gaze so heated I can feel it burning along my skin. Tentatively, he reaches out and runs his hand up my calf. His touch is featherlight, like he thinks I might break beneath his fingertips. Desire pools low in my belly, so intense I gasp.

He pauses, one knee between my legs, one hand on my thigh.

"Please." One uttered word is all I have.

I roll my hips, needing friction. Needing the heat that's radiating from every soft touch to engulf me. Engulf both of us.

And it does. The instant his gentle touch finds the lace edge of my favorite emerald green panties, his already dark eyes turn darker. His deliciously broad shoulders rise and fall once, a single breath, a last chance at control that fails.

He's everywhere.

His mouth slants over mine, demanding entrance, licking inside, the opposite of gentle. His weight is between my legs, heavy and hard. His hand is searching for my bra clasp, steady but frantic.

Steady, how he always is. How he's always been.

Frantic like he can't wait another second.

I can't either.

"Front," I pant, arching into him.

He finds the clasp and groans as my breasts spill out. Like a man starved, he buries himself between them, licking, sucking, tasting. Each flick of his tongue over my pebbled nipples radiates straight to my core, the pressure building until I'm a writhing, whimpering mess.

I dive my hands into his hair and he looks up at me, the intensity in his eyes making it hard to breathe. There are still layers between us, I haven't even managed to push his jeans over his hips, but already I'm so fucking close to the edge I can see into the abyss.

With a smirk that tells me he knows just how close I am, he slides down my body, letting his day-old scruff rub across my skin, and hooks my panties with his thumbs, his eyes still locked on mine. He kisses me through the lace, just once, a gentle open-mouthed kiss, and a shudder racks my body. One more drag of his tongue and I'll be too far gone. A single breath could get me there.

"Coop," I grit out. "Wait."

He stops, his shoulder muscles tense between my thighs and his eyes never leave mine.

"I want all of you," I whisper.

His eyes flash in understanding and he sits up, dragging my panties off in one swift motion. His abs flex as he kicks off his jeans, pulling his briefs down with them. Now it's my turn to let my eyes roam. And hands.

Still chiseled like the college athlete he was, his hard lines and taunt muscles jump and quiver under my touch. I trace his abs down to the V that makes my mouth water.

But all too quickly, he's out of reach.

"Condom," he says, fishing his pants off the floor.

"I have an IUD," I tell him.

I meant what I said. I want all of him. Need all of him.

He freezes, pants in one hand, wallet in the other, and looks at me.

"I've never, I mean never without," I add when he doesn't move.

His mouth is back on mine before I know what's happening, a biting, urgent kiss that I never want to end. I wrap my legs around his waist, feeling him slide and settle at my entrance.

"Never?" he asks, pulling back and staring into my eyes. Searching.

I shake my head slowly. That teenage idiocy ran strong, that hope that one day he'd be back here, that we'd be here, with nothing left between us.

"Me either. I've never even considered not using one." He brings his hand up, rubs his thumb across my cheek. "I waited."

I close my eyes. I can't hope. But I do anyway. "Waited?"

"Open your eyes." Even in a whisper, it's rough. A demand.

I open my eyes.

"This, Ave. You."

I shudder, nearly drowning in the intensity of his words, his gaze, this moment. He kisses me again, slower, softer. He slides his hand down my jaw, my neck, my collarbone, pausing with it over my pounding, wildly erratic heart.

His dark eyes settle on mine.

My breath hitches.

In one push of his hips, he sinks into me.

I *am* drowning.

In the way he feels, in the roll of his hips, in the bruising way he grips my waist, the gentle bite on my lower lip before he pulls back.

There's no finding our rhythm, it's already there. We move together like we've spent the last eleven years in this bed, wrapped up in each other.

"You feel so fucking good," he groans, lifting himself and easily pulling my hips up with him.

My back arches off the bed with a gasp, the new angle bringing me right back to the edge. All it takes is his thumb between us and I'm shattering, falling, his name lost in a cry.

He follows me over, a final grip on my hips and a groan of my name before he falls forward, burying his face in my neck, more words of adoration whispered against my skin that make me melt into the mattress.

I shiver as he pulls away, not ready to let go. He shifts sideways, settling next to me, his head resting heavily between my shoulder and chest.

"Hey Ave?" His hand splays over my heart, thumb rubbing gently.

"Hmm?" I hum.

"That was really fucking good."

***

I wake up slowly, the room dark and quiet, and reach for Cooper. He's not there. I roll over only to find the other side of the bed empty.

This must be what Cooper feels like most mornings. I have a pretty good idea that I won't find him in an office, staring at a computer screen though. But after yesterday, nothing should surprise me.

I stumble into the small bathroom and blink against the bright light, staring at my reflection in the mirror. Disheveled. That's the only adjective that properly describes me right now. Hair a mess, mascara smudges, and a few telltale red marks on my skin. Also a slightly smug, completely satisfied smile.

By the time I'm done in the bathroom, I've realized it's much later than I thought. The light streaming in through the etched glass window makes me think it's nearly ten o'clock. But that can't be right. The blackout curtains in the bedroom can't be that effective, can they?

I pull Cooper's discarded hoodie on to go in search of my phone. And maybe coffee.

"Please be decent!" Harper's voice calls the second I open the bedroom door.

I look down. Definitely not decent. I shut the door, rolling my eyes at my breaking-and-entering friend. Glancing around the room, I see my jeans, but no underwear. That's not ideal.

I do find a note left on the bedside table, though. And it's perfect.

"This morning, waking up with you naked in my bed, also really fucking good." -Coop

After tugging on a pair of stolen joggers, I open the door again. This time I'm greeted not by Harper's voice, but her knowing grin. And, thankfully, my custom coffee mug.

"You break in everywhere?" I ask in greeting, accepting her offering.

"Yep," she replies, still grinning. She looks me up and down. "You always look like you've been fu-"

"No, I don't always look like this," I cut her off before she can finish her question, shaking my head. I step around her to join Zero on the couch. "Just this morning."

"Gasp!" Harper says with an actual gasp behind me. "Avery Anne!"

She flops down on the couch next to me and watches as I take a tentative sip from my mug. I keep my attention on her dog, stroking Zero's soft ears when she lays her head in my lap. I still have no idea what time it is, where my phone is, or how I slept so long.

Well, I have a pretty good idea why I slept so long. I just wish I had woken up earlier, while the reason for my sleep was still in bed. Instead, reality awaits. Or, Harper awaits.

"No details?" she asks.

"Nope."

"Unsurprising. But I'll take this look as my answer," she replies, waving her hand at me. "Quite the outfit."

"I'd think you of all people would understand the allure of not putting jeans on first thing in the morning," I reply, taking another sip of my mocha.

"Fair."

I glance at her out of the corner of my eye. "Especially when I can't find my underwear."

"Avery Anne!" Harper laughs. "Who are you this morning?"

"I really don't know," I answer honestly. "I just know that it feels like I'm getting another chance at so many things, and that feels really fucking good."

"Would me telling you that you have an alarming amount of missed calls and texts on your phone, which, by the way, I found in the driveway just now, change this mood you're in?" She pulls my phone from her pocket and waves it at me. It must have dropped out of my pocket when I got out of the car last night.

"Probably not." I'm sure there *is* an alarming amount, but they can wait another fifteen minutes until the caffeine hits my bloodstream.

When I don't take my phone, she sets it on the coffee table in front of us.

"What if I told you that Courtney Howell is sitting at The Merc, having coffee with Henry and Zoe while she waits for you?"

I'm off the couch in an instant. "Harper Freaking Sage!" I exclaim. "Maybe you could have led with that? Woken me up? Something!"

"I got here like three minutes ago!" she replies.

"I don't even have underwear!" I hiss. I lean down and snatch my phone. She wasn't kidding, notifications light up the screen. "I haven't washed my face! Or brushed my teeth!"

"But you have your fancy-ass car here, so you can drive yourself home, which is literally less than a mile away, and get ready."

"Where are my keys?" I groan. I hate this feeling, being completely unprepared.

Harper points to the counter. "Oh! One last thing!" she calls.

I turn back, not liking the tone of her voice.

"Edward and Jessie are in your dining room." She doesn't even try to hide her delighted smirk.

I close my eyes. Edward, the steady father-figure in my life, is going to witness me walking in like…this.

"Okay, okay. Fine. The real plan: Get your ass in the shower here," Harper says, standing up and holding out her hand. "Give me your keys, I'll go get your clothes."

It takes me one-and-a-half seconds to realize this is my best option. "Thank you."

Harper's already halfway out the door. "Don't worry! I won't forget your underwear!"

I groan. She is never going to let me live this down.

***

"I realized what kind of man he was in that instant, so I took what he offered and left town," Courtney says matter-of-factly. "I chose her over everything. And I'd make the same choice again and again." She raises her chin, ready for me to challenge her.

I don't know what happened since her email last night, but it seems that Courtney has suddenly lumped me with my father, or at least placed me firmly in enemy territory. I can't say I blame her. I wouldn't trust anyone connected to my father either if I were her.

"It's the best choice you could have made for both of you," I tell her. I brace myself for everything I need to tell her. This must be how

Alex felt, walking into The Merc. But maybe the full truth will help her see that I'm not the enemy. "My father is not a good man."

Courtney stares at me over the rim of her coffee mug. Hazelnut latte. She said it always reminds her of home. Evanston Orchards, one of the nearly one thousand farms in Oregon that grow acres and acres, rows upon rows, of hazelnuts. The home she had to leave, thanks to Matthew Moore.

"I gathered as much," she deadpans.

"Well I didn't," I reply, fighting to keep my voice as neutral as her expression. "Until a few weeks ago when my older brother, the one I had *no fucking idea* existed, walked through those doors."

Courtney's eyes show a flicker of surprise, either at my words or the fact I've failed to keep my voice steady, perhaps both, but she remains motionless in her chair. Watching. Waiting.

"He had a story very similar to Sadie's," I continue. "And it felt like my entire life was a lie. It was. Nearly twenty-seven years, a lie. All of it. I never knew my own brother. Never knew he even *existed*. But now it feels like my life is starting over. Thanks to him. Thanks to Sadie. Because, like you, I choose her. I choose him. Both of them."

"And that's it?" Courtney asks. She taps her fingernails along the side of her coffee cup and glances at her phone. "You'll push aside your father, your business partner, your *wealth*, for a twelve-year-old girl that you've never met?"

She still doesn't believe me. Not in the slightest. But that glance at her phone, that *wealth* comment, tells me exactly why.

This is my fault. We froze everything he has and he looked to the last person he pissed off. A mama bear that might have already pieced together what he did.

"He called you," I say. It's not a question. It's a statement.

Courtney doesn't react. She should be a damn poker player.

"I don't know what he said, but to answer your question, *yes*." I fish around in my pocket and pull out the flash drive that Harper handed me along with my clothes. I hold it up. "This is all of it. Me, pushing aside everything, for Sadie." I set the drive next to her coffee.

She stares at it without touching it. "What's on there?"

"The proof you need. I can't tell you how or where I got it though."

"Proof? Of?" There's a tiny break in her voice and I can't tell if it's hope because she knows, or confusion because she doesn't. I gamble on hope.

"Proof that my father is the reason your stepdad is currently in a rehab hospital."

Courtney inhales quickly and her eyes fly to mine. She's no longer a poker player, no longer an angry mama bear. She's a grief-stricken daughter.

"Dad," she says quietly. "Dan is my dad. Maybe not by blood, but since I didn't get the chance to know my father, Dan is my dad."

"I'm sorry he was hurt so badly."

"We talk once a week," Courtney says, moving her eyes to the small parking lot. "So when he mentioned Matthew Moore wanting to buy…"

"You put it together," I finish for her.

She nods. "I thought his offer to buy was the threat, but then…"

"I'm sorry," I repeat. I don't think there's anything else I can say.

"Sadie didn't know. She's just a kid, wanting a dad."

I was that kid, wanting the same dad. Only I lived with him. My resolve settles. I push the drive closer to her. "This is all you need. It won't get Sadie the father she thought she'd find, it won't hold up in court, but it's damn good blackmail."

Courtney reels back. "Aren't you an attorney? Isn't court your thing?"

"I've recently come to the conclusion that there are a few instances in life when it's best to say fuck it. This is one of them. I choose Sadie." I can see my words finally getting through. I am not the bad guy. I'm just the one that shares his last name.

Courtney tips her head back and forth, her eyes back on the flash drive. "And if I want more? If I want real justice for my dad?"

"Lila has everything you need, too, she just doesn't know it," I say. "She needs to access the security footage two days before the accident and she'll have it all."

Courtney's brow furrows as she looks back at me across the table. "Then why would you give this to me?"

"We," I start then stop. "I mean, *I* chose not to look into your family so I wasn't sure your relationship with them. I wanted to give you the choice, let you decide how to handle this. What's best for you and Sadie."

Courtney takes a slow sip of her latte, her eyes on mine. I can see the wheels turning. "You really do choose her, don't you?"

I nod. "He hurt a lot of people in a lot of ways," I say. I can see Harper through the window, sitting with Zoe, just like she was when I sat here with Alex. Courtney follows my gaze. "They've all come out stronger. I'll do everything I can to make sure the same is true for Sadie. For you."

She pushes the flash drive back across the table. "I don't think I need this."

I raise an eyebrow in question. Is she saying…

"Fuck it," she nods. "I'm going to need some legal advice on papers I signed a very long time ago, but then I'm going to call Lila. He doesn't want to be in Sadie's life? Good. He doesn't deserve to be. But he's not getting away with what he did to my dad. I'm getting the proof myself."

A shaky breath that I didn't know I was holding rushes from my lungs.

Justice.

Finally.

Chapter Thirty-Three
Avery
(before)

"Cooper! Wait!" *I call, jogging down the street after him.*

He turns. "I thought that was our last goodbye."

"Just, read this." *I shove my notebook at him before I can change my mind.*

He takes my notebook slowly. "Really?"

I nod. "It's not even close to finished, but I want you to read it."

He suddenly smiles, that very same smile he gave me that very first day. The one that made me do the stupidest thing in the world. Fall for him.

"I'll read it."

***

I find the notebook tucked under the doormat the next morning.

"My compass is pointed true north. See you in five years. -Cooper"

There's a compass drawn on the last page, north pointing directly toward a crescent moon. He read the whole thing.

Chapter Thirty-Four
Cooper

There's no hesitation in her swing. Even from our table across the room I can see the glass shards fly.

Next to me, Ava laughs. "She's definitely related."

On my other side, Courtney shakes her head. "I've never seen this side of her."

"Auntie!" Jack adds.

When Avery suggested the rage room as a fun, low-stress activity for their first time meeting Sadie, I wasn't sure how it would go. But now, watching Alex line up bottles for my quietest student, I'd say it's going just fine.

"I think they all needed this," Courtney says, smiling as Sadie smashes a bright red vase that Avery tosses in the air.

Courtney probably needs it, too. She's probably needed it for thirteen years now. Although, after sitting with her for half an hour, it's clear that while she might have once been a scared teenager who was easily bullied by Matthew Moore, she's well past that.

Raising a baby alone at twenty years old must not have been easy, but she found her way. Online classes, a real estate license, and the work ethic you learn growing up on a farm were the winning combination. Today, she and Sadie live in a small house tucked away along the river that runs through Rock Beach and she's been able to help her parents financially as well, which unfortunately might have led to Dan's so-called accident. I don't know if anyone will ever know Matthew's true intentions, but according to Courtney, Lila sent the footage to the detective this morning. A relief for everyone.

Like she can read my mind, Avery looks through the window that runs along the side of the enclosed space they're in and smiles at me. Relief. That's her smile. Relief that she, Alex, and Sadie are finding their way, one swing of a baseball bat at a time.

"Hi, Ms. Howell!" Micah steps up behind us. "Mr. Miller!"

Jack laughs in delight when Micah makes a face at him.

"Hi, Micah," Courtney says. "Pretty fun place you guys have here."

"Micah, this is Ava and her son Jack." I introduce them as Jack tries to launch himself at Micah.

"Can I take him?" Micah asks Ava. "I have little brothers, not like this little, but, little kids are fun. And we're setting up the bounce house."

"He's responsible," Courtney tells Ava. "A great friend of Sadie's."

Micah's cheeks turn bright red. "We'd just be right over there." He nods toward the opposite corner of the warehouse where a boy that looks a few years younger than him is watching the bounce house inflate. "Then you could go smash stuff with Sadie."

Ava looks between Micah, the bounce house, and the window to the rage room then nods. "Just wave if he cries, okay?"

"Come on little dude," Micah says, swinging Jack off my lap.

"Are you sure we should interrupt?" Courtney asks, standing slowly from her chair. "I mean, you guys are the significant others, I'm the lame mom."

Ava hooks her arm through Courtney's. "I'll be the lame mom in less than a decade, show me how it's done."

It only takes a few minutes to pull coveralls and hard hats on, then Avery opens the door for us. I let Courtney and Ava walk through first so I can linger in the hallway with Avery.

"You okay?" I ask, already knowing the answer.

"Better now," she says, smiling back at me.

"Yeah?"

"Actually, I'm really fucking good," she whispers, looking over her shoulder to make sure Sadie can't hear.

I laugh and follow her into the room.

"Batter up, Mr. Miller!" Sadie says, holding out a baseball bat.

"Nah, I think your mom gets to go first."

Courtney grins from behind her face shield and takes the bat from her daughter. Like Sadie, there's no hesitation. Glass shards fly.

***

Laughter is not what I expect to greet me when I push open Avery's door, but that's what I hear. The last handful of days have been like the last few weeks, an emotional roller coaster. At least now it seems like there's an end in sight. An emotional end, most likely, but an end.

I turn the corner and find Tex, Zoe, Jessie, and Avery sitting at the dining room table, which is now free of sticky note family trees, with an iPad propped in front of them. I pause.

"No, I'm telling you guys, *obsessed*," a very familiar voice says from far away.

"Told you!" Tex crows as Zoe shimmies her shoulders.

Avery buries her face in her hands.

"Uh, hi?" I say, hesitantly announcing my presence.

Four heads whip around, matching guilty expressions on their faces. Behind them, I can see the iPad screen, which confirms where the voice was coming from.

"Hi, Meg," I say loudly.

"Hi, Cooper!" the other girl on the split screen calls.

I look closer. I think it's Kelsey, the bouncy college student. "Hi?"

Megan laughs from her square on the screen and my eyes narrow. She mimes zipping her lips and throwing a key so I swing my gaze to the women in front of me.

There's a beat of silence as I look between Jessie, Zoe, and Tex before letting my eyes settle on Avery. The guiltiest of the bunch. The one I was hoping I'd find alone because she was once again sleeping when I left this morning. She must know exactly where my thoughts are because her cheeks flush.

"Well, this was fun, but I think it's time for us to go," Tex says, looking between Avery and I.

There's a quick chorus of goodbyes, and then it's just Avery and I, the black iPad screen, and a hell of a lot of questions. I don't have to ask any of them.

"I-invited-your-family-to-visit!" She says in such a rush the words bleed together. "I'm sorry!"

"You invited my family?" Maybe I should be shocked, but I'm not. Not at all. She sat next to me the other night as I talked to Dad, Mom, and Meg about Dad's bloodwork. There was a look in her eye that I didn't recognize, but now I know what it was.

"I know that it's been hard for you, so I just thought..." She shrugs helplessly and looks up at me hesitantly as I move toward her. I hate that she's questioning herself. I hate the man that taught her to doubt her decisions.

"That you'd invite my family to visit?" I shift my voice into a teasing tone, watching as she visibly relaxes.

She lets out a breath. "Yeah?"

When I reach out and lay my hand on her hip, she smiles, and the last bit of weight, that remaining piece that I've carried on my shoulders for years, seems to lift. I might never get over the initial jolt of panic when I see my dad's name flash on my phone, but now I have someone beside me. Someone who knows, even if I don't, what I need.

"Ave," I huff a laugh and shake my head, tightening my grip on her hip, "that's amazing. I can't believe you'd do that with everything else going on."

"I wanted a way to say thank you for everything you've done," she whispers. Her eyes search mine and she shifts closer, leaving barely a sliver of space between us.

"No thanks necessary, but I do have one question."

She tilts her head to the side, waiting.

"Do I want to know what Megan was talking about when I walked in?"

She shakes her head slowly, a playful gleam in her eyes. "Probably not."

I dip my chin down and ghost my lips over hers. "Tell me anyway." I slide my hand up her side, tucking it under her shirt.

Her breath hitches. "She might have mentioned that you were obsessed with me."

Obsessed doesn't even begin to cover it, especially now, after the last few nights, getting lost in her, learning every inch of her.

"She's right, except it's more like really fucking obsessed."

Her eyes flash, those little blue flecks sparking as I slant my lips over hers, taking her mouth in a searing kiss, the kind I know makes her melt. Pulsing, demanding, heated. Just before I lose control, I force myself to pull back.

"I mean it Ave," I whisper, pressing my forehead to hers. I swallow hard, the emotions of the past eleven long years finally getting the better of me. It seems impossible that I haven't told her. "But I'm not just obsessed with you, I'm in love with you. I love you."

She tenses under my fingertips, her ribcage stilling. "Coop?" She sucks in a shaky breath and my heart hammers in my chest.

I know she feels it. I *know* she does. But still, a trickle of fear creeps in. "Ave?"

She brings her palm to my cheek, cupping my jaw gently. "I love you, too."

The words I've wanted from her since I was sixteen.

I love you.

They hit just as hard as I knew they would. Harder. I feel them in my chest. In the air they steal from my lungs.

"Say it again," I request.

"I love you, Coop, I think I have since I was fifteen."

Without a word, I duck down and press my shoulder into her hip then stand.

"Cooper!" she shrieks as my hand lands directly on her ass, balancing her over my shoulder.

I stalk through the house and drop her on the bed, watching as she sinks into the comforter. Then I show her exactly how obsessed with her I am.

After, I lead her into the shower and gently wash her hair. As the scent of strawberries fills the room, I tell her again just how madly in love with her I am.

***

"Since we aren't committing computer fraud or breaking potentially devastating news to family members, what do you want to do tonight?" I ask, running my hand up Avery's bare calf.

She burrows her feet further under my thigh. "I'm pretty content with this."

We're back in our spots on the couch, the fire crackling in front of us, and content is a damn good description of how I feel, too.

"Me, too, Ave."

When we finally ventured back out of the bedroom, I built a fire while Avery made perfectly toasted triple decker grilled cheese sandwiches for dinner. Our plates and empty wine glasses sit on the coffee table and I'm getting more and more distracted by Avery's bare legs.

It's the first night that the house is quiet. *We* are quiet. There's not anyone else here, our phones aren't buzzing with texts and calls, we're not being pulled in different directions, we've stepped off the emotional roller coast for the night. It's just us.

When Avery reaches behind her, stretching to find the corner of her green notebook, I stand and stack our plates. There's no scratch of her pen on paper though as I clean up the kitchen.

"Stuck?" I ask when I return to the couch, holding out her refilled glass of wine.

She accepts the glass and takes a sip, her eyes on the notebook on her lap instead of me.

"You okay?" The worst question, every time, yet still I ask.

She huffs a small laugh. "Better now."

I sink back down next to her and loop my hand around her ankles as she tucks her toes under my leg. She leans sideways, setting her glass back on the table.

"I wrote a book," she says, bringing her gray eyes to meet mine. "Two, actually."

"Yeah?" I try not to react, but I want to celebrate, not that my seventh-grade writing plan worked, but because of that small smile playing on her strawberry lips and the happiness in her eyes. The happiness that only writing brings her.

She nods. "The first is on my laptop, it's a novel, I think, about the magic of this town, but this…"

She bites her lip, looking nervous. She holds it toward me. I don't take it.

"Just," she takes a breath, "read this."

That night. The last night. Those same words.

I take the notebook slowly. "Really?"

"I want you to read it." She smiles, silently telling me she also remembers chasing me down the street.

"I'll read it."

One memory at a time, I read our story. What was. What's meant to be. And with every word, I fall a little more in love with her.

Epilogue
Avery

"She looks just like you," Mom gasps, peering out the window of our family's beach house.

"Mom!" I say, nudging her toward the kitchen. "Don't-"

She does anyway, swinging the door open and smiling brightly, like this isn't the most awkward family reunion ever. "Hi! Welcome! You must be Sadie! I'm Jenn, Avery's mom."

Sadie freezes, hand held up like she was about to knock. "Hi," she says quietly, giving my mom a small smile. "Nice to meet you."

Sadie steps inside and Jack leans toward her from Cooper's arms. She takes him and tickles his side, making him squeal with laughter.

"I just wanted to make sure Sadie was comfortable," Courtney says, still standing on the worn welcome mat.

"Nonsense," Mom replies. When Courtney doesn't move, she steps forward and pulls her into a hug.

"Mom, you can't just…" I trail off. There's no stopping her.

"Half-feral," Cooper whispers in my ear.

She really is. She basically demanded that we host this weird reunion/party at the family house instead of mine as soon as she knew when Cooper's parents would be in town. After everything she's been through in the last few weeks, I couldn't say no.

"Sorry," I mouth to Courtney, who is looking wide-eyed at me over my mom's shoulder.

Mom whispers something in Courtney's ear and she closes her eyes, finally surrendering to my mom's hug. When they pull apart, both quickly wipe their eyes.

Luckily Colt chooses that moment to fling open the door, plowing directly into Courtney as he rushes in. She catches him before he trips.

"Sorry!" Jessie exclaims from the steps. "I stopped to grab this, which was sticking out of the planter by the steps." She holds up a white envelope with 'Team Merc' written in block letters on the front.

"Brian!" Zoe hollers from her spot between Lucas and Henry on the couch.

As my gaze swings to Brian, who has a grin a mile wide, I remember what Alex said.

"Who knew I'd ever want to send Matthew Moore a thank you card?"

"Dad!" Colt exclaims, spotting Liam. "Are you making a fire? Can we have s'mores?"

My heart pounds.

"You okay?" Cooper asks quietly.

I blink and look around the room. I'm surrounded by my future, all the people I choose to have in my life. The ones that showed up when I needed them. The ones that will continue to show up, whether they live here in Three Rocks or if they'll be using the guest cabin we're having Rick build on Cooper's lot.

My eyes find Harper, curled into West, the two of them sharing a chair that looks out toward the ocean. She catches my eye, her hand going to her barely-there belly.

"I'm really fucking good."

***

"Hey, I'm going to walk my parents back to my cottage," Cooper says as he pulls me in for a kiss.

Nearly everyone has gone home, it's just his parents, my mom, West and Harper, Jessie, Colt, Liam, Megan, and Zoe left gathered in the living room, watching Colt lick the last of the melted marshmallow off his fingers.

"Will they get lost if you don't?" Colt asks worriedly, peering into the kitchen where Cooper's parents are saying goodbye to my mom.

"It's the polite thing to do, just like I'm going to walk you and your mom home," Liam says.

Colt looks around the room, taking stock of who's left. "What about Miss Zoe and Miss Megan?"

"I'm going with Cooper and my parents," Megan reassures him.

"I think that means you need to walk me home," Zoe says.

"Can I?" Colt's eyes light up. "Please, Mom?"

Jessie smiles. Zoe's house is just across the beach path, clearly visible through the living room window. "How about this, you walk Zoe home and your dad and I will wait on the porch for you?"

"Yes!" Colt fist pumps and runs to Zoe, pulling on her hand with what I'm sure are sticky fingers.

After yet another round of goodbyes, West ducks into the kitchen with my mom, leaving just Harper and I by the fireplace.

"What was that look you gave me earlier?" she asks immediately.

"I want to write my dad a thank you card," I say.

"Pass." She shakes her head. "Hard no from me."

I laugh. "No, like a 'thank you for my future that doesn't include you' sort of card."

Her expression turns thoughtful as she considers the idea.

"Then I'm going to throw it in the fire," I add. "Because that man deserves nothing from me, or anyone."

Harper smiles. "I want to write one, too."

"I'll be right back," I tell her, standing and trying to remember where I last saw the basket of pens.

"Wait. Look." She tilts her head toward the side deck.

Jessie and Liam are standing side by side, heads bent together. I can see her faint smile as he leans closer, whispering in her ear.

I hear Jessie's words again.

"Sometimes things are just a lot."

Yes, yes they are.

They feel like a lot when I toss my card into the fire next to Harper's, hers with "Eli" on the front, and we watch them turn to ash, silent tears streaming down both our faces.

They feel like a lot less though, when I give West and Harper a wave before slipping into my quiet house.

I find Cooper sitting in his spot on the couch, the stack of papers I printed and bound earlier in his lap.

"You okay?" he asks the second he sees the dried tears on my cheeks, his tone laced with worry.

"Better now." I sink down into my spot and tuck my toes under his thigh.

He holds up the pages. "It needs a title."

I shake my head. "It's always had one, since before it was even written."

Meant to Be.

Afterword

Wow. We did it! I wrote it, you read it.

I hope you enjoyed Avery's story. I could see so many pieces of it while writing the first book but, confession, this isn't how it was supposed to be. Cooper and Avery, yes. The story, no.

As you probably assumed if you read Harper's story, it was going to be Liam. Right? It *had* to be him. I thought I had set it up pretty well.

Well, when it came down to it, I couldn't do that to Colt. He's a special character to me, he'd been through enough.

I. Could. Not. Do. It. So I pivoted and wrote myself into a corner.

Once again: oops.

But also, it was always *their* love story, right? Harper and Avery's? I wanted that piece of the story to end with the two of them.

I really hope you have a "anything and everything, always" friend in your life. I really do.

So, that's the story of the story.

I mean, Kelsey and Jessie are in the works, but that gives you a little insight into Harper and Avery.

Love it? Hate it? Find me on Instagram, where things are a little chaotic.

Acknowledgements

To say I struggled while finding my way with writing and authoring and all that goes with it, with this character, this story, the whole dang thing...understatement of the year. The following people deserve Brian-level thank you cards. But they wouldn't be able to read my awful handwriting, so this is what they get.

First, to my roommates, for not saying no when I brought home a car full of puppies, thank you. Thank you for letting me avoid the failure of my writing and instead be covered in dog hair and surrounded by chaos. Also, thanks for always delivering coffee. And, you know, believing in me.

To each one of the Averys in my life, I can picture your half-smile right now as you say "I told you so." Thank you for believing in Avery. Also, thanks for always being the one that has their shit together.

SWAG, the group I never knew I needed, thank you for attempting to understand the chaos that is my thought process. For helping me see things from a different perspective and not judging how many pastries I eat in one sitting and for helping me stumble upon ROMEOs, book placement already determined.

To my alpha and beta readers, well, this was a doozy, huh? Your comments kept me going at times, reeled me in at others, and I couldn't have done it without you. Thank you.

Lauren, specifically, is owed a Liam of her own for preventing multiple Avery spirals. I owe you about three hundred pages, I believe. But really- thank you.

Chris, not of the husband variety, MVP of last-minute edits, I am so thankful for your attention to detail, reading speed, and general book-ish knowledge.

And to you, reader, for once again giving me a chance. Thank you.

About the Author

Wesley Harper is an amateur author, semi-professional coffee drinker, and advanced overthinker.

After thirty-nine-and-three-quarters years not writing books, she decided to write a book before her fortieth birthday.

And then another. And another.

When not making random goals and accidentally writing books, she enjoys working out in her garage gym, fostering puppies, and embarrassing her nearly adult offspring. And maybe sometimes running away to the Oregon Coast.

www.ingramcontent.com/pod-product-compliance
Lightning Source LLC
LaVergne TN
LVHW030318070526
838199LV00069B/6490